I0768347

THE REAPING

MATT AYNES

DANCING ROBOT
PRESS

Published in Duncanville, Texas, by Dancing Robot
Press LLC (*https://dancingrobotpress.com*).

Publishers Note: This novel is a work of fiction. The story, all names, characters, and incidents portrayed in this production are either products of the author's imagination or used fictitiously. No identification with actual persons (living or deceased), places, buildings, and products is intended or should be inferred.

Library of Congress Control Number: 2024909988

ISBN (paperback): 979-8-9906950-0-9
ISBN (ebook): 979-8-9906950-1-6
ISBN (hardback): 979-8-9906950-2-3

Book Cover and Typesetting by Damonza (*https://damonza.com*)

God became human so that humans could become divine.

Athanasius of Alexandria

They are in you and in me; they created us, body
and mind; and their preservation is the ultimate
rationale for our existence. They have come a long
way, those replicators. Now they go by the name
of genes, and we are their survival machines.

Richard Dawkins, The Selfish Gene

Prologue

Twenty-two years ago

"Is this where we're camping?" Charlie asked.

Mark Ferguson looked away from his seven-year-old son's calm, hazel eyes and watched a pale sun sink into an endless field of verdant winter wheat. No way to avoid the truth much longer.

"Not here," he said. "I just needed to stretch my legs. We'll be there soon."

They walked to the pickup truck and climbed in. He shifted into drive and pulled back onto the road. "Listen, Charlie, we're not going camping. Not yet."

Silence.

"Where are we going?" Charlie asked.

"A hospital." Another lie, but it was easier this way.

Charlie lowered his eyes. The boy hated anything involving white coats and needles.

"I'm going to tell you a secret," Mark said. "You can't tell anyone else, not even Mom. Can you keep a secret?"

Charlie nodded but didn't look up.

"Your doctor thinks you might be a little sick. It's nothing to be afraid of, but that's why we're going to the hospital. They can make you better."

"Why can't we tell Mom?"

"If we did, she'd get scared. We don't want her to be scared, do we?"

"No." Charlie's voice was just audible over the road noise.

"That's my boy. As soon as we're done at the hospital, we'll go camping for a couple nights."

"Promise?"

"I promise."

When the headlights swept around a bend in the road, they illuminated a man in a camouflage uniform who stood beneath a towering blue spruce. He had a walkie-talkie near his mouth and a sniper rifle slung over his shoulder. He nodded to Mark as they drove past.

"Who's that?" Charlie asked.

Mark turned onto a one-lane dirt road. "Must be a hunter."

The lies kept getting easier by the minute.

Charlie's forehead wrinkled into an anxious look that belonged on a much older face. "Am I going to die?" he asked. "I don't feel sick, but that doesn't mean anything, does it?"

"You'll be fine." Mark reached over and squeezed his son's shoulder. "Don't worry."

The dirt road ended at a sprawling array of dark gray buildings surrounded by a twelve-foot-tall perimeter fence. He pulled up to the front gate and lowered his window as a security team emerged from a guardhouse, assault rifles clasped over their chests.

"Mark Ferguson?" one of the guards asked in a rumbling baritone voice.

"That's me. This is my son, Charlie."

The guard peered through the window. "Hey there, Charlie. Glad you made it here safe and sound. There's a spot for you by the front door, Mr. Ferguson, just over there."

The gate slid open. Mark drove through and parked in front of one of the frowning, opaque windows that lined the complex's central building.

"Is this the hospital?" Charlie asked in a quiet voice.

"This is it."

"I don't want to go in there."

"Try to be brave. Mom would want that. She'd want you to get better, and this is the only way."

Charlie held his gaze for a long moment. "Okay, Dad."

Mark got out of the truck, crossed to the other side, and opened Charlie's door for him. As his son climbed down from the passenger seat, the steel doors of the main building swung outward. A thin-framed man with silvery hair and a dated, jet-black suit emerged. In the faint glow of the parking lot lights there was something wraithlike about him, the way his skin clung to the bones of his face and the hollow, purplish caverns from which a pair of hungry gray eyes gleamed.

"This is the child?" The man walked up and snatched Charlie's chin between bony, tapered fingers. He turned the boy's head from side to side, examining him.

"Leave him alone." Mark's hands clenched into fists. "He's frightened enough already."

The man smiled and let go. He tousled Charlie's hair. "You're not afraid of an old scarecrow like me, are you?"

Charlie remained silent.

"You'll be my friend soon enough." The man's smile abruptly vanished. "If you know what's good for you. Did your daddy tell you that you were sick?"

Charlie nodded.

"He lied to you, Charles. You're as healthy as a horse. Your father has told you a great many lies. He's not a good man, and he certainly isn't a brave one. Here's the truth. We gave him lots of money, so he gave us you in exchange. Isn't that right, Mr. Ferguson?"

The words were like a knife to the heart. He could feel Charlie's gaze, feel his son waiting for him to fight back, to deny the accusation.

"Stop it," he said. "You've already won."

The old man's laughter was cold and mirthless, like a breeze rattling dead leaves. "So we have. We looked all over the world for you, Charles. A prodigy, a genius without parallel. We're going to enhance you, turn you into something we call a Paragon. We'll go right through here"—he tapped the side of Charlie's skull with the tip of his forefinger—"and do a little procedure. When we're done, your mind will be unlike any the world has ever known. The initial quality of the material determines how much we can accomplish. With you, the possibilities are endless. Now come along. Your procedure begins at once." He grasped Charlie's arm and pulled him toward the building.

"Daddy!" Charlie shrieked and tried to writhe out of the man's grasp. "Daddy, help!"

Mark watched, powerless, as the old man dragged his son away.

"This way, Mr. Ferguson," said a deep voice behind him. He turned and saw the guard who'd let them in at the gate. "We've set up a room for you in the barracks. You can stay there until it's over."

"And that's it?" Mark put his hand on the guard's shoulder. "You'll cancel the debt, and we can go home?"

"Sorry." The guard pried off Mark's hand. "That's above my pay grade."

"But the other kids, these Paragons—they did well, right? All the enhancements, no side effects?"

The guard's eyes narrowed. He shook his head slightly, then turned and walked off toward one of the side buildings. "Follow me, Mr. Ferguson."

The old man was trying to haul Charlie through the doors to the facility.

"Daddy, help me!"

Mark stood rooted to the spot. He glanced at the retreating figure of the guard, then looked at his terrified son.

This time, they'd gone too far.

He lunged forward and sprinted toward the old man. His mind screamed that it was an act of suicide. So be it. At least one of them would pay for what they'd done.

He was halfway to Charlie when something dull and heavy crashed into the back of his skull. His field of vision exploded into a thousand shards of light. He tumbled to the pavement. Dazed and disoriented, he raised himself up on his elbows.

"Listen to me, you idiot," the guard hissed in his ear. "You're no good to him dead. Some of the kids survived, but their parents disappeared. Now do exactly what I tell you, and you might be an exception."

Mark wiped his eyes and knelt on the pavement.

"My boy." The father's quavering voice rose to the silent heavens. "My beautiful boy. Forgive me."

Chapter One

The Contract

CHARLES FERGUSON HUFFED up the galvanized stairs to the second floor of the old-town apartment complex. He hustled down a concrete walkway to number 209 and rang the doorbell. The air boiled with the sultry summer heat that had crept over Virginia like a blanket and smothered everything. He peeled off his suit jacket and wiped a layer of sweat from his forehead.

He raised his hand to knock when a slender, dark-haired woman flung the door open. She wore a fluffy orange bathrobe with palm trees on it. A matching towel was wrapped around her head. She clutched the bathrobe together in a white-knuckled grip.

"I'm running late, I'm sorry." Her eyes narrowed. "Hey, are you laughing at me? I couldn't find the stupid belt. Buried somewhere in the heap."

He clamped his mouth shut. He'd developed an unfortunate habit in the three weeks he'd been dating Nadia Petrova. He'd stare at her, grin like an idiot, and mumble semi-coherent nonsense with all the eloquence of a Paleolithic halfwit.

Who could blame him?

He still couldn't wrap his mind around the fact that this woman was his girlfriend. Out of his league? She was out of his solar system. To him, Nadia Petrova in a billowy orange bathrobe was Venus rising from the sea with damp, raven locks and diamond-drops glistening on her eyelashes.

She gave him a peck on the cheek, bolted back inside, and disappeared down the hallway to her bedroom. "Don't stand out there sweating," she called. "Come in, make yourself at home."

His favorite chair, an old rattan rocker, was covered in a chaotic pile of sheet music, some of which had tumbled to the floor. Another pile, larger in magnitude, was strewn across the sofa.

"Do you want something to drink?" Nadia shouted from her bedroom.

"No thanks."

"Good, because I forgot to do the dishes. No cups."

Imagine that. He smiled and shook his head.

"Black or red?" she called.

"What?"

"The dress! Black or red?"

"You're asking me? You'd get better fashion advice from an Amish farmhand."

"Black it is, then."

He knelt in front of the rattan chair and began organizing the music. As far as he could tell, this was his sole contribution to the relationship. She provided the beauty, artistry, conversation, intelligence, and confidence. His job was to fumble around, grin like an idiot, and pick stuff up.

This time it was Rachmaninoff's preludes. Twenty-four of them, one for each major and minor key. He arranged them numerically in a neat stack and placed it on the center of the coffee table next to a worn copy of the Orthodox prayer book.

He went to work on the sofa next, sorting through scores from a variety of pianists. The Russians and Ukrainians were well-represented as always. Prokofiev, Lyatoshynsky, Rubinstein, Lysenko, Rimsky-Korsakov.

The sheet music from her apartment sometimes came to him when he drifted off to sleep. His mind would summon up entire scores, recalling every line and note as it recalled all things, in perfect, crystalline detail. Not that he could play any of it. He could barely clap without embarrassing himself.

He'd nearly finished clearing off the sofa when she burst into the room.

"How bad is it?" she asked. "Are we really late?"

A few wayward tresses hung in careless splendor on either side of her forehead. She wore a simple black dress, powerful as an army with banners.

He swallowed. "We're, um…we're doing great."

"How do I look?"

"You look…"

Word. He needed a word. Any word that wasn't blisteringly stupid.

"Good. I mean great. Um, captivating."

Paleolithic man strikes again. Amazing how eloquent he could be with a doctorate and two master's degrees under his belt.

"Shouldn't we be going?" she hinted.

"Hmm?" The lights gently flickered on somewhere in his gray matter. "The meeting!"

They scurried down the steps and raced across the parking lot to his aging sedan. It took him a minute to find his keys, which were inexplicably hiding in the same pants pocket he'd kept them in for the last thirteen years.

They jumped in and buckled up. He hit the accelerator and pulled out of the parking lot.

"You keep looking in the rearview mirror," she said after they'd been driving a few minutes. She craned her neck to peer out the back window. "Is somebody following us?"

"If they are, it's the police. I'm burning rubber over here."

She leaned over and examined the speedometer. "I'm glad you're not like my father." She patted him on the knee.

"He likes to speed?" he asked.

"He says it's not real driving until you hit triple digits."

"Are you serious?"

He'd never driven a hundred in his life. Come to think of it, he'd never driven eighty.

The Tolleson Hotel loomed into view as they rounded the corner. It was a plush, five-star affair known for lavish fountains, maroon-coated bellboys, and room service caviar. The street entrance had been sealed off by the police, who were busy blowing whistles and waving rubber-neckers and would-be lodgers along. Makeshift signs by the curbside announced in a bold, silky script that the hotel would be closed from six to ten for a special event.

"What on earth?" Nadia said. "Is all this for your meeting?"

"I have no idea." They slowed to a crawl in the traffic. "Maybe they moved the location. Nothing from Thompson, though."

He edged the car toward the curb as they neared the checkpoint. One of the policemen approached the driver's side window as Charles lowered it.

"Hotel's closed unless you're on the guest list," the officer said. "Short one, too."

"I'm Dr. Charles Ferguson. I'm supposed to be at a meeting here at seven."

"All right, let me check."

The officer took a clipboard from one of his companions and examined it.

"Yeah, you're on here. Ha! Wonder who wrote this up?" He began reading. *"Mild-mannered biology professor. Bringing Nadia Petrova as guest. Guest way too hot for professor. Will arrive in dung-colored grandma car."* The officer peered at Nadia, stepped back and took in the sedan, and barked a laugh. "Looks about right to me."

Eugene Thompson, no doubt about it. Charles could always count on his best friend and colleague at the university for the important things in life.

Public humiliation, for instance.

"Guess we'd better be safe, though," the officer went on. "I'll need to see some ID for you and Ms. Petrova."

"Dr. Petrova," Charles corrected him. "Just a minute."

He handed over his and Nadia's driver's licenses.

"All right, looks good," the officer said. "You can park in front of the main doors. Might want to keep your ID handy. Their security team is doing some kind of check over there."

He and the other policeman stepped aside to let Charles into the lot. Parked near the entrance were a handful of identical black SUVs, a silver Mercedes-Benz with opaque windows, and Thompson's cherry-red coupe. Three chic security guards—charcoal-gray suits, navy ties, black sunglasses, earpieces—blocked the front entrance to the hotel.

"Who are you meeting with?" Nadia asked. "The President?"

"According to Thompson, they're Alpha Financial, some investment group from California. Globalist zillionaires, apparently. I don't know where he finds these people."

"You think they're interested?"

"Thompson promised me we'd both be raking in seven figures by the end of the night. Of course, he said that last time, and all I ended up with was a bottle of water and a nine-hour layover in Chicago."

He pulled in next to Thompson's coupe and killed the engine.

"Look," he said, "are you sure about this? It's just a glorified sales pitch. It could go on for hours, so I'd completely understand if—"

"Listen to me." She reached over and cupped his face in her hands. He relished the warm caress of her palms against his skin. "Your scanner is going to change the world, and I want to be with you every step of the journey. I'm your cheerleader, your co-captain, your wing girl. I've got your back."

He exhaled and felt some of the tension slip away. "You really think we can pull this off?"

She straightened his tie for a few moments and gave him a shy glance. Then she curled her fingers around the lapels of his suit coat, drew him toward her, and kissed him full on the lips.

He'd never kissed a woman like that. It left him stunned and speechless. As in mute. It was even worse than Paleolithic man.

"You're the man of the hour, Dr. Ferguson," she said, her voice soft and a little self-conscious.

"I, um—wow." He ran a hand through his unruly hair. "Okay, that was awesome, just so you know. We're going to have to do that again sometime. Soon. Really soon."

Caveman like kiss. Caveman want more kiss.

"Ready for the meeting now?" she asked.

"I'll get your door."

When they walked out of the hotel two hours later, he had a signed contract from Alpha Financial tucked beneath his arm.

⥻

Thompson tossed down another shot of Irish whiskey. "Poor girl." He waved vaguely toward Nadia, who slept with her head resting on the table between her arms. "Mind if I finish off her margarita? Looks like she barely touched it."

"I think you've had enough."

"Nonsense! The night is young, and the pub's still open."

Wilford's had it all. The pendant lamps with their dim bulbs, the English oak bar polished to a shine, the flags of the UK countries dangling from the ceiling. King Charles III hung in a gilded frame next to a neon welcome sign behind the bar, smiling his royal approval of this tiny outpost of the Kingdom.

Charles and Thompson had breezed through countless evenings here over the last five years. Chatting about nothing after long days of research, sipping English ale from tumblers so large they made you feel like a child.

But tonight was different.

He speared a slice of treacle tart with his fork. "My car's not dung-colored," he said in a voice that brooked no argument. "It's sepia."

Thompson laughed. "Whatever it is, you'd better buy a new one when the cash rolls in."

"I still can't fathom it." Charles pressed his fingertips against his temples. "They jumped all over it. It's like we didn't even have to try. We've been turned down so many times that I was planning on failure. Where did you say you met them?"

"Oh, I don't know." Thompson popped the last bit of a Scotch egg into his mouth. "Friend of a friend."

"They were odd, weren't they?" Charles added. "Especially that woman with the black veil. She just sat there and stared at us without saying a word. You think she works for Alpha Financial?"

"For all I care," Thompson replied, "she could be the Queen of Denmark. You know how it is. The richer they are, the weirder they get."

Their waiter, Sanderson, shuffled toward them, his aquiline nose tilted upward. He'd only worked at Wilford's a few months, but people were already dropping by to see the genuine Brit in his natural habitat as if he were a zoo exhibit. He did have that dinner-theater butler look about him.

"A thousand apologies, gentlemen." Sanderson offered them a stiff bow and took their plates. "We'll be closing the pub in a few minutes. I've taken the liberty of bringing you the bills."

"Give me those." Thompson snatched both bills and pulled out his wallet. "Don't worry, Charles, you can pay me back after the money rolls in. With compound interest, mind you. If you can't think of anything, I'm partial to Maseratis."

Charles nudged Nadia. "Better wake up. They're closing on us."

She sat up and stretched. "I fell asleep?"

"Trust me, you didn't miss anything. Well, other than Thompson here downing more than he should have."

Thompson turned his empty shot glass upside down. "I've drained the sea, my friends. Now point me toward my chariot."

"Not happening." Charles stood and handed Nadia her purse. "You're riding with us."

"I'm quite well, mother, and it's only five minutes away."

"You drank too much. Now come on."

"Yes sir, Mr. Boy Scout." Thompson tossed a pair of hundred-dollar bills on the table. "I'm amazed you could sleep at all, Nadia. Dreaming of caviar and fine wine, I bet. Or fine tea since you don't seem to have any Bacchanalian propensities. What do you think? Twenty million for me and ol' Charlie boy here, fifty-fifty down the middle. Woohoo!" He grabbed a handful of paper napkins and threw them in the air.

They strolled out of the pub and into a clear summer night. Thompson hummed the theme song from a popular sitcom as he climbed into the back seat of the grandma car. He was sound asleep by the time they got to his house and only half-woke when Charles shook him. After hauling him through his front door and into his bedroom, they left him fully clothed on the bed with a blanket thrown over him.

Charles and Nadia got back into the car. "It's really true, isn't it?" she said as he started the ignition. "You two are going to be millionaires."

He rested his hands on the steering wheel. "We shouldn't get too excited yet. I'm sure they'll have an easy out if they change their minds."

"I don't think that'll happen. They sounded serious."

"Yeah, they did, didn't they? Oh, what the heck." He threw his hands up. "Woohoo!" He leaned over, cupped her face in his hands, and kissed her on the lips.

Happy caveman.

"Hm. You should sign contracts more often." She gave him a playful shove. "I hope being rich doesn't change you too much."

He cleared his throat. "It is a lot of money."

"There's the fame, too."

"You think I'll be famous?"

"Didn't you hear them?" She took his hand in hers. "The World

Health Organization, UN resolutions, global production lines. Can you imagine?"

His car suddenly felt small and stifling. He shifted in his seat. "Actually, no. I can't."

"Once it starts saving lives, they'll follow you around with cameras and call you up for interviews every time you blink."

"But I don't want that. I've never wanted that." He pressed the palms of his hands against his forehead. "I should never have let Thompson talk me into all this. I just wanted to create the scanner. He's the one who said we had to go out and market it and turn ourselves into gazillionaires. It never seemed real until tonight. And you know what? I don't want to be a gazillionaire. I want to keep teaching my courses at the university. I want things to stay exactly the way they are."

"I know." She pressed his hand to her lips. "It's one of the things I love about you. But this was bound to happen someday. You're brilliant, Charles."

"I shouldn't have signed. I should have walked away."

"No." Her smile was bittersweet. "You did the right thing. I'm just processing. Which, by the way, will go a lot better after some more shuteye. How about breakfast tomorrow morning? I'm thinking raspberry pancakes for my conquering hero."

He grinned. "Can't say no to that. Better make it brunch, though. Elevenish?"

"More sleep? Deal."

They held each other for a few moments at the doorway to her apartment. The kiss she gave him before she slipped through the door left him giddy as a teenager. Or a triumphant caveman. He drove home and parked his car in the driveway. He started to unlock the front door but changed his mind. No way he could sleep after everything that had happened. He needed a good, brisk jaunt. He strolled back toward his car and turned down the sidewalk.

What would he do with that kind of money? Bigger box to live in, bigger box to drive?

"What a mad world." He took a deep breath of crisp night air. "I should just buy her a diamond ring and bury the rest in the backyard."

The wind picked up, rustling through the branches as it bore down from the north with unseasonable coolness. It carried with it the sound of footsteps. Charles froze, his senses suddenly at full alert.

He glanced behind him. A man in a dark polo was walking in the same direction, head down, hands tucked into the pockets of his jeans.

Charles upped his pace. The footsteps quickened as the stranger followed suit. He looked back again. No doubt now. The man was coming for him.

Two-thirty in the morning. Could be a robber.

Or a murderer.

His pursuer broke into a run. Charles hesitated for one moment and then took off as fast as his legs would carry him.

He darted down a side street. Kensington Road. He had to get somewhere where there would be people, but it was so late at night.

Downtown. That was his only hope.

He swung right on Pearl Avenue. He felt sweat trickling down his brow. He looked back and saw the stranger, closer now than he would have thought possible. Twenty yards at the most and running at a dead sprint.

God help me.

The muscles in his legs burned like fire, his chest heaved with every gasp. He couldn't keep this up for long.

A patrol car made a leisurely turn onto the road ahead, its warning lights off. It was going the wrong direction, moving away from him.

"Hey!" he screamed with all the air in his lungs. He waved his arms in the air. "Help!"

The police couldn't hear him.

He looked back one last time. He could see the man clearly now— pale, blond-haired, face hard as steel. Fast as the wind. The man reached behind his back to grab something tucked into his belt. Charles looked away. Gun or knife, he didn't want to know.

It was now or never.

He ducked down, snatched a decorative rock from a curbside flower garden, and hurled it at the police car with all his might. The rock clattered to the ground yards behind its target. The car turned down a side street and vanished.

He missed a step on a sloped driveway and tumbled to the ground. The man closed the gap in seconds.

It was over. He was going to die.

Chapter Two
Night Stalker

THE MAN STOOD over him, panting and leering at him with bared teeth. In his hands he held something small, white, rectangular. An envelope. He tossed it on top of Charles's prostrate body.

"Open it."

Charles wiped the blood away from a scrape on the side of his hand. He'd hit the pavement hard, but nothing seemed to be broken.

"Are you going to rob me?"

"Shut up. Open it."

Charles tore the seal on the envelope. A typewritten note and a photograph. He held the photo up against the dim orange glow from a nearby streetlight. It was Nadia. The picture had been taken through the front window of her apartment. She was at her piano, eyes closed, lost in the music. And there was his rattan chair, still covered with Rachmaninoff's preludes.

"Where'd you get this?" he asked.

"Read the note."

He picked up the piece of paper with a trembling hand. There were two lines written on it.

Do not keep her from us. Tell her nothing of the past.

"I don't understand."

The man snatched the letter out of Charles's hand and set it on fire with a lighter. He tossed the burning remains on the ground, then reached for the photo. Charles scrambled to his feet.

"What's this about?" he said, clutching the picture behind him. "Why'd you chase me like that?"

The man reached into his pocket and swapped the lighter for a switchblade. He clicked it open. "The picture. Now."

Charles gave him the photograph. The man knelt on the pavement and slowly, methodically sliced Nadia's body out of the picture with the tip of his knife. He burned the tiny image of her with the lighter and handed the rest of the photograph to Charles.

"Do what you're told." He pocketed the knife and strolled off into the darkness.

Charles stood under the glow of the streetlamp, shivering, the tattered photograph clasped in his fingers. He was alive, he wasn't injured, he wasn't even robbed.

All the same, something terrible had happened. He couldn't understand it, but he knew that it could slip between his ribs like that switchblade and murder the heart of his world, the woman he loved more than anything.

Do not keep her from us.

Should he call the police? No. Who knew how closely she was being watched, how close they were to her at this very moment?

He went home, cleaned up his cuts, and lay in his bed, where he stared at the ceiling until the sun crept over the horizon.

"Did you get a hold of Alpha Financial?" Charles asked.

"No." Thompson glowered at his reflection in the windowpane. The first waves of freshmen were milling about on the grounds outside.

"Look at the poor guppies. Mindless slaves of all those juvenile hormones. Why are there so many of them?"

"You were a guppy once, you know."

"I was never that age." Thompson strode over to Charles's bookcase and absently fingered the bindings of a row of microbiology books. "Everston told me that they'd wrangled you into one of those intro sessions. Can't believe you let them."

"I promised Nadia I'd help her out. Didn't you hear? They made her the course head since Bailey's on sabbatical."

Thompson snorted. "Freshman bio should be one of the nine levels of Hell. The questions those infants ask! *Why do you sciency people, like, use stupid words like mitochondria when you could use, you know, a real word like guts or powerhouse or something?* Blithering twits."

"You sure sound chipper today, Thompson." Charles rose from his desk and walked to the window. When he looked out at the sea of youthful faces, he saw an endless tide of potentiality, an inexhaustible supply of human quirks and passions and dreams. "What's bothering you?"

"It's been nine weeks, and not a word."

"I'm sure they're just testing out the scanner like they said they would."

"I'm not." Thompson plopped down on the faded wingback chair by the window. "They won't even answer the phone now. I think the whole thing's dead in the water."

Good.

Charles didn't say it out loud. That would make Thompson furious. But the truth was that he wanted to forget that day in its entirety. The black-veiled woman at the meeting, the secretive old lawyer, the marathon-running psychopath—he could never really forget. But it was all moving out of focus, and that was fine with him.

"Are you going to teach that research course?" he asked. "Might be fun with the right students."

"Might be fun? Dear God, Charles. Twenty million dollars,

gone—poof—just like that, and you're talking about some stupid research course?"

"I was already happy before the money came into the picture. You were, too, weren't you?"

Thompson gave him a look that could freeze a desert. "It's easy for you to be happy. You've got her. What have I got?"

"I don't know. Great career. Decent salary. Better car than mine. Extremely brilliant and charming best friend."

"Well, you're right about the car, anyway." The corner of Thompson's mouth curved into a lopsided grin. "Fine, you cheerful idiot, I'm teaching the research course. I think we'll dive into epigenetics. All the rage these days."

"I've been diving into that one myself lately."

The bells outside rang in the five o'clock hour. The throng of freshmen swarmed toward the dining halls under the direction of their dorm leaders.

"I'd better get out of here," Charles said. "Nadia wants to prep me for this weekend."

"Finally caving in, are you?"

Charles raised an eyebrow. "Finally visiting her church, if that's what you mean."

"Oh, I understand." Thompson shot him a knowing wink. "Believe me, Charles, I understand. By the gods! For a woman like that I'd turn myself into a raging Creationist. I'd write books—whole shelves of them—to promulgate the faith and eviscerate the infidels. I'd fill them up with pictures of our hairy progenitors, clothed in the skins of saber-toothed cats, riding around on pterodactyls and hurling spears into the quivering flanks of a triceratops. I'd storm the gates of biology, tear down the soaring ramparts of Reason itself!"

"How noble of you," Charles said drily. "To be honest, I have no idea what to expect. I haven't been to church since my mother died. I imagine it'll be very Russian. If you'd like, I'll give you a full report on Monday."

Thompson nodded. "I look forward to it. By the way, pay special attention to the hair."

"The hair?"

"I'm writing a paper on televangelists for that online psychology course I'm taking. Did you know you can learn absolutely everything about a televangelist by examining their hairstyle?"

"What if they're bald?"

"They're not. But if they were, I suppose you'd have to move on to secondary features—suits, cars, private jets…women, perhaps."

"See you, Thompson."

Charles cranked up the air conditioner on the way to Nadia's apartment building. It was the beginning of September, but the Virginia summer wasn't letting go without a fight. He yearned for the coming days of overcast skies, brisk autumnal breezes, and the multihued splendor of the maples and black gums.

A few of Thompson's freshman guppies had arrived at the apartment building, though most of the students moving into the apartments were upperclassmen. He parked next to an iconic Volkswagen van coated with graffiti drawings of peace signs, rainbows, and an infamous five-leaved plant. He could hear a dull, steady thumping from a speaker in the distance.

He ducked to one side as he went up the steps to allow a couple of students hauling a mattress to pass by. Nadia flung the door open as soon as he punched the doorbell.

"How's it going?" he asked, sagely avoiding any mention of the rings around her eyes and her unusually disheveled appearance.

"It was so quiet when I moved in this summer." She stepped aside to let him pass and shut the door after him.

"The perils of a college town."

He claimed his favorite chair while Nadia tossed a load of clothes off the couch so she could stretch out on it.

"There's a band of neo-hippies downstairs," she said. "A real band, I mean. Moved in last night and proceeded to serenade everyone with

African drums and out-of-tune guitars. Smoking their peace pipes, too. I could smell it even with the windows closed. Reminded me of Peter."

"Your brother? Does he, ah, partake?"

"What? Oh, no, I didn't mean that. It's just that his favorite music group is this old hippie band. I think he's even got Dad listening to them." She groaned and sat up again. "I don't know if I can survive here."

The rhythm from the booming speakers outside accelerated as a new song began.

"How much would it cost you to bail on the lease?" he asked.

"Probably more than I can afford."

"Why don't—" He hesitated. He didn't want to be too forward. On the other hand, her mental health was at stake. "Why don't you let me cover that? I bet we can find you a good rental home around here if we move fast."

"Oh, Charles." She got up from the couch, perched on his lap, and started messing with his hair, which, for some inexplicable reason, made his heart gallop like a racehorse. "I'm sorry for whining. We'll figure it out. But come on, I've got something I want to show you."

She took his hand and led him down the hallway to her guest room. He'd glanced through the doorway to the room once or twice and had noticed the expected twin bed and dresser, but he'd never had any reason to set foot inside.

"Close your eyes."

She guided him to the front of the bed, turned him a little, and let go of his hand. "Okay, now open up. What do you think?"

Nine pieces of ancient, stylized artwork hung in three rows on the interior wall. They were religious paintings. Most had red wooden frames just visible around the borders of the image. A few of the subjects he recognized, but the rest were a mystery—silent, attentive figures with slender fingers and luminous oval eyes that gazed back at him. In one image, a miniature king bore a scroll on a platter as he emerged from a pitch-black hallway. In another, three majestic figures were seated on thrones around a golden table with a small rectangle carved into it.

"I've never seen anything like them." He took a step closer.

"They're icons," she said. "They try to capture two things at once, the outward form and the inner, spiritual dimension. We don't like to divide the two. We think of them as aspects of a single reality."

He cleared his throat. "I don't know much about that sort of thing. When it comes to religion, the only things that stand out to me are stained glass windows and a fuzzy cut-out Jesus from Sunday school. He had a white robe, a red sash, and an endless smile, like he'd never had a hard day in his life."

"A smile can be an act of courage," she said. "All the same, that doesn't sound like the Jesus I know."

"What about that one?" He pointed at an icon on the top row, a portrait of Christ with glaring chunks ripped from the top and bottom. "Where's it from?"

"Russia. They found the original buried in a shed in Zvenigorod in 1919, right in the middle of a brutal civil war. It's one of Rublev's, maybe five hundred years old. It's like us, you know. Battered and bruised, but the face remains. The image of God…if we have eyes to see it."

She rested a hand on his shoulder.

"Listen, you don't have to go with me this weekend if you don't want to. It's okay."

"I'll go." His eyes were still fixed on the watchful face in the icon. "It's important to you, so it's important to me."

She kissed him on the cheek. "Thank you."

They went back to the living room. Nadia began practicing Chopin's *Fantasie-Impromptu*. It started off like a wild dervish, the complex layers of rhythm brimming with irrepressible energy.

"Would you mind opening the blinds?" she asked. "I could use the sunlight."

He walked over to the window and turned the plastic rod. The blinds angled upward. He froze.

A stranger stood inches away from him on the other side of the glass. Pale, short-cropped blond hair, gray eyes flat and soulless. The night stalker. The man pressed a forefinger against the center of his lips.

Charles stumbled back from the window and tripped over an end table. The lamp that had been on top of the table shattered when it struck the hardwood floor.

"Charles!" Nadia darted across the room to help him. "What happened? Are you okay?"

"I'm fine." He sat up and began collecting ceramic shards with shaking hands. "There was a man out there watching us."

They glanced at the window, but the stranger had slipped away. "I'll see if I can still spot him." She ran to the front door.

"Don't!"

Her hand clutched the doorknob but didn't turn it. "You think we should call the police?"

"No," he said. "It's probably just a student who heard the music and was curious. Startled me, that's all."

She came up and knelt in front of him. "Did you see his face? What did he look like?"

"I, um…no, I didn't get a very good look. Too busy making a fool of myself. Let's just clean this up."

"If you say so." She went to the kitchen and got a broom and a trash can. "Here, let me get that. You'll cut your fingers."

He tossed the pieces he'd gathered into the trash. "Listen, this whole thing just proves my point. We need to get you out of here, and the sooner the better. Can you talk to them Monday, see about getting out of your lease?"

"I guess so. It would be nice to get some sleep."

He went over to the window and closed the blinds. "Right, so we'll get you a hotel room until Monday."

"A hotel room?" Her eyes widened.

Where else could she go that the stalker couldn't find her?

"I don't like the idea of you being here by yourself," he said. "So yes, a hotel room. Just a couple of nights. We'll start looking for another place and hopefully get you moved out of here early next week."

She took his hand in hers. "There's something you aren't telling me, isn't there?"

He pressed his lips together and nodded. "Let's just get you somewhere safe, okay?"

"Okay." She leaned up, kissed his cheek, then hurried to her bedroom. Charles took the broom and swept up the rest of the broken ceramic.

He needed a plan, and he needed one fast.

Chapter Three
The Invitation

"So what did you think?" Nadia all but shouted to be heard over the roar of the car's air conditioner. They were on their way back from his first service at Saints Cosmas and Damian Orthodox Church. The world outside broiled under the last oppressive gasp of summer.

"It was…different."

Fantastic description, professor. Caveman make good talk.

"You're trying so hard." She turned down the air conditioner. "Listen, I appreciate you coming with me. I know it must have been tough. It's very Russian. You don't have to do it again. I just wanted you to know what it's like."

"Thanks for the out," he said, "but I'd like to keep coming. I know I don't fit in there, but it wasn't as bad—I mean, it wasn't as *difficult* as I thought it would be. It was even in English."

She stopped at a red light and dropped the air down another notch. "I've always liked Father Maximov." The local Orthodox priest was a plump, native Russian who had grown up in Canada, married a plump, French-speaking Quebecer and had four bright-eyed children who rendered their father's sermons inaudible with their chattering and squeals. "He seems so level-headed."

"Now there's a virtue I can admire," he replied. "I liked those old guys we had lunch with. They could be in a National Geographic article."

"Sorry about the joke," she said. "I just couldn't translate it right. It's really funny in Russian, the fat sheep and the Communists and all."

"I'll take your word for it."

"Hey, did I tell you about the letter I got?"

He caught his breath. "What letter?"

"It came to the apartment yesterday. I dropped by there to grab the mail after I'd checked into the hotel. From some group I'd never heard of. The Magnus Foundation, I think? They want to fly me out to New York for a meeting, said they might be interested in funding some research."

His fingers dug into the seat belt. This was it. It had finally happened.

"Will you go?" His voice sounded tinny in his ears, hollow and unnatural.

"I'm thinking about it. It's only one day. I'll leave Friday morning and be back here that night."

"Ah."

"What do you think?" She glanced over at him. "Charles, are you okay?"

"What?" He let go of the seat belt and breathed. "Sorry, my mind was wandering. Friday, you said?"

"Could you take me to the airport?"

"Of course."

"Great, I'll let the Foundation know so they can get the flights taken care of."

"Right."

The light turned and she hit the gas. A line of trees raced by outside his window. The grass was a blur, the evenly spaced telephone poles rhythmic blips in his awareness.

They pulled into his driveway. He went to the front door, put the key in the lock, and felt the rush of conditioned air as the door opened. The springs creaked beneath them as they sat on his mother's old floral print couch. Nadia pulled out her cell phone.

"Guess I'll go ahead and call them," she said. "Up for a movie after that?"

"Sure." Still that monotone voice. He felt distant from it, as if some stranger was manipulating his throat and tongue to make the sounds come out. "Do you have the letter with you?"

"It's here in my purse. It has their number on it."

She pulled the letter out and began tapping her cell phone. He heard ringing on the other side of the line.

"Mind if I look at it?" he asked.

She handed him the letter, got up, and walked into the kitchen.

He read it, which was unnecessary since he'd read it before. He still had his own letter from the Foundation tucked away in his security box at the bank, and it was a near facsimile. Had it really been six years?

He listened to Nadia's voice from the kitchen. High-pitched, nervous.

"Well, that's that." She plopped down on the couch next to him and laid her head against his shoulder. "Wild, isn't it? I've heard of things like this, research money dropping out of the sky, but I never thought it would happen to me. They read my dissertation and liked what they saw. Said they were planning some kind of genetics project. I'll find out more Friday."

"Okay."

"Charles, are you all right with this?" She leaned back and looked him in the eye. "You're hiding something. Again. Do you think I shouldn't go? I can just call them back and cancel."

Do not keep her from us.

Did the Foundation really send the night stalker? It was the logical conclusion, but he couldn't imagine a research foundation doing such a thing. Either way, he had no choice. If the Foundation was behind the stalker, warning her now would put her life in danger.

"I'm fine with it," he said. "If you want to meet with them, you should."

"Then what's going on?"

He swallowed. "I don't know. Maybe I got a little wound up going to church after all these years. Let's rent that movie you were talking about yesterday. *Persuasion*, wasn't it?"

"Might help you relax," she said.

"Might put me to sleep."

She picked up a remote, browsed through an entertainment app and clicked on the movie. It was a Jane Austen film, a new version from the BBC. She curled her feet up on the couch and leaned against him. Within moments her attention was lost in the slow-paced romance of Anne Elliot and Captain Wentworth.

ॐ

She had no name, and she wasn't human. She was a voice, crisp and clear with a British accent. She was a disembodied intelligence built on a cloud of single-atom transistors.

She was incredible.

He'd met her six years before when he was twenty-three years old and on the brink of finishing his doctoral degree. A letter showed up in his mailbox, and a few days later he was flying first class and dining at a 3-star restaurant in New York City. He was introduced to two Magnus researchers, Tom Murrow and Raj Bhandari. He'd never heard of either of them.

He agreed over dinner to visit their facility outside the city. They said it was only a small branch location, but the Victorian furniture in Raj's office could have been stolen from Buckingham Palace. Charles sat in a leather Windsor chair and listened as Raj laid out the details of the Phoenix Project.

"It's a biotech organism." Raj's English, spoken with a distinctive Indian British accent, was flawless. "It's similar in many ways to bacteria. We'll inject a Phoenix into a human host and it'll replicate into a networked swarm. It will sustain itself by harvesting energy from its host."

"You sound pretty confident about this," Charles said.

"Oh, we are." Raj flashed his Hollywood smile. "The Phoenix will lay dormant until the host faces a life-threatening event—a gunshot wound, a heart attack, maybe a deadly virus. When the threat is recognized, the organism will expend itself to save its host. Hence the name."

"Ah."

"Sound like something you'd be interested in?"

Charles shook his head. "What it sounds like is something I should be watching on the big screen. Are you serious? Nobody's ever done anything remotely like this. It's decades away."

"We're very serious," Tom Murrow piped in. "See for yourself."

Tom slid a tablet across the mahogany desk. Charles scanned through the document, which was a summary of the progress they'd made on the Phoenix so far. If what he was reading was accurate, they already had a working prototype. Not one that could raise the dead, but something that could, for a brief amount of time, survive and replicate within its host.

"I don't understand," he said. "How on earth did you get this far?"

"Independence." Tom jabbed the tip of his forefinger into the desk. His voice quivered with enthusiasm. "With all this globalization, the odds of any of us developing technology that is not only inaccessible to the rest of the world but even incomprehensible to them are infinitesimal. We're used to minor differences of degree or quantity when it comes to advances, not qualitative leaps."

"I'm not following you," Charles said.

"Think of the Magnus Foundation as an entirely different country," Tom said. "One with walls so high that the rest of the world knows next to nothing about us. It's like the old days, when one nation had cannons and battleships and another had rocks and slings. For the Magnus Foundation, everything started in the forties, back at the dawn of computing. A scientist in a Magnus-owned company drew up a blueprint for a neural processor that mimicked the human brain. Alexander Magnus's grandfather leapt on the idea, hired a team of scientists to support the work, and flew them out of the country. They worked in secret, and after twelve years they had a prototype. We've been blazing our own trail ever since, and we've left everyone far behind us. Welcome to the future, Dr. Ferguson."

Charles agreed to stay on and was promptly subjected to a whole ream of legal contracts and non-disclosure agreements.

The next morning, he went to work.

They were testing their device on apes, and on his first day Charles injected one of the Phoenixes into a chimpanzee named Tanis. They had placed a microchip under the chimp's skin that could relay data about the host. As expected, the Phoenix began to replicate throughout Tanis's bloodstream. This was the latest model, and unlike the last one, it could communicate. It sent detailed reports on Tanis. His oxygen levels, the levels of various neurotransmitters, the presence of toxins or known bacteria, his liver function—the list went on and on. Charles was astounded. And terrified.

"So what language did you use to program this thing?" he asked.

Raj and Tom exchanged glances. "English. Computer?"

"Yes?" a soothing voice replied from a wall speaker.

"There, you see? She's always listening. Just talk to her."

"Right now?"

Raj nodded. "Right now."

Charles cleared his throat. "Okay. Ah, Computer, let's try something basic. Can we have the Phoenix run a constant analysis of Tanis's heart rate?"

"I see," the Computer said after a pause. "Are you looking for heart rate irregularities, then?"

Charles looked at his new colleagues in disbelief. "Yeah, that's it. I want to trigger an alarm if the heart rate reaches a critical level either above or below the standard. It's basic, I know, but it could help the Phoenix recognize something like a heart attack."

"Excellent, Dr. Ferguson. I've added alarms to the Phoenix using levels calculated from medical research databases and taking the host's age, size, and species into consideration. For the current host, Tanis, those levels would be one-seventy-three beats per minute for the upper heart rate and forty-eight for the lower heart rate. We will also analyze the rhythm to account for palpitations. Is that acceptable?"

It wasn't acceptable. It was miraculous.

With the Computer's help, Charles developed an idea he called mimicry. One of the project's major limitations was the host's immune response. Inevitably, the body would reject the Phoenix, targeting it with immune cells.

To get around this, they took a blood sample from Tanis, analyzed the epitope structure of various cells, then modified the Phoenix cells so that they mirrored that same structure. Theoretically, this would give the Phoenix the camouflage it needed to trick the immune system. Since these structures were unique to each individual, it also meant that each Phoenix could only work in one specific host.

Raj and Tom helped him bring the concept to fruition, and within a few months the Phoenix cells and Tanis's immune system were humming along together without a hitch.

Charles began to believe that they might actually achieve the ultimate goal, a Phoenix that could bring its host back from the brink of death. Maybe even back from death itself.

And then, suddenly, the project was terminated. There were no explanations, no apologies about dried-up funding or political pressure, nothing but a short letter informing them that the Phoenix Project had been suspended indefinitely along with a firm reminder that they were bound to strict confidentiality.

The three of them were reassigned to a second project, Alpha. It started off as standard genetics, trying to determine positive and negative traits from a DNA sample, but the more he worked on it, the more the possibilities frightened him.

Every trait they identified was directly related to longevity, intelligence, physical strength, beauty, and reproductive capability. These were characteristics that could give someone an edge from a biological perspective. The data could be used for all sorts of purposes, but he couldn't shake the feeling that some kind of human profiling would be involved.

Alpha ended as abruptly as Phoenix. Raj and Tom were assigned to Magnus Foundation Headquarters, wherever that was, while Charles was released from the Foundation without any explanation.

Struggling to nail down research grants, pretending he had no knowledge of all that he had experienced at the Foundation—it had been a painful transition for a research scientist.

Phoenix and Alpha had flickered in and out of his thoughts through the years. Phoenix, in particular. His mind circled around the obstacles that remained when the project was terminated, inventing and exploring potential avenues of advance. New questions arose, questions that could never be answered back in the real world.

The Outside, as they called it in the Foundation.

✦

The movie credits rolled up against a black background. Charles's thoughts returned to the present.

"Now for the hard part." Nadia sighed and picked up her phone.

"What do you mean?"

"I have to call Dad."

"I thought you weren't talking to him."

"I'm not." She folded her arms over her chest. "It's so frustrating. What could I do? It was a department store, Charles, and he was stone-cold drunk, roaring about who knows what, and there were at least a hundred people staring at us."

"Yeah, you've mentioned it once or twice."

"I shouldn't talk to him until he apologizes, until he can prove that he's been sober for more than twenty-four hours."

"Sounds like a plan." Charles switched the TV to a music app. Her father once had a decent job with the CIA, but alcohol had ruined his career. Sooner or later, he'd have to meet Boris Petrov, but as far as he was concerned, the later the better.

Nadia bit her lip. "I have to call him."

"Why?" He muted the volume on the app.

"When I went to college, he made me swear that I'd never jump on an airplane or drive out of state without telling him first. He's funny about that kind of thing, always has been since Mom left. He must think I'll disappear on him someday like she did."

"Guess that makes sense. Have you heard anything from home lately?"

"Nothing new. Julia Pearson said that Dad's still job-hunting, heading to out-of-town interviews all the time. And drinking, of course. He wants something in sales again. I keep telling him he can do better, but he says he's already lost the best job in the world, so why bother? But he'll never get another job like that unless he cleans himself up."

"He's got a tough disease."

"You're telling me. Vodka. How many empty bottles of *that* did I see growing up? Russian water, he calls it." She let out a deep breath. "All right, here goes."

She dialed the number and started pacing.

"Hey Dad, it's me. No, I'm still not talking to you, I'm just letting you know that I'm flying out to New York City this Friday."

A pause.

"Yeah, that's right. I got a letter from a group called the Magnus Foundation. They said they might want me to do some research for them, so I'm going over there for a meeting."

Another pause.

"You're *what?*"

She clamped her hand over the microphone, shot Charles a look brimful of terror, and mouthed three words.

He's coming. Tomorrow.

"Um, all right, Dad. Dinner? How about we take you out to—oh, okay. Bamboo Dragon Palace at five-thirty. See you there."

She tapped on the screen to end the call. "Charles, listen to me. I love you. You know I'll always love you, but you should run away. Now. Run while you can and don't look back."

"Oh, come on, Nadia. He can't be that bad."

She crouched in front of him and cupped his face between her hands.

"Yes, he can."

Chapter Four
Boris

THE BAMBOO DRAGON Palace was the only restaurant in town that Charles had avoided since landing a job at the university. He'd looked up reviews online a few years back and found a detailed description of an inch-long cockroach climbing out of a cream cheese wonton and skittering across the dining table.

But that was the past. A new outfit had gobbled up the Palace at the beginning of the summer and renovated everything. New dragons on the windows, new green corrugated roof, new menu with higher prices.

He and Nadia arrived a few minutes early so she could prepare herself for the encounter. A slender waitress in a crimson cheongsam brought them ice water in enormous plastic cups. Charles tapped the side of his shoe against a table leg, stopped for a few moments, then started tapping again.

"Dad's full name is Boris Ivanovich Petrov." Nadia sat bolt upright on the edge of her chair, her facial muscles taut. "He might talk with an accent. Or not. I'm sure I've told you before, but he can be blunt. And aggressive. And he'll be slightly intoxicated. Or flat-out drunk."

No pressure, Charles.

Boris Petrov was also six foot four, apparently, and looked like he could wrestle down a Siberian tiger. Charles stood and shook one of Boris's enormous hands, getting his own crushed in return. The faint but unmistakable odor on the man's breath betrayed his addiction to the infamous *Russian water*. Boris pulled his chair up close to Charles and squinted at him.

"Mr. Charles." He laughed and slapped Charles on the back. "Mr. Charles Ferguson!"

It was an accent day, thick and Russian. Charles smiled weakly and tried not to grimace.

The Bamboo Dragon Palace offered the mandatory buffet, but they ordered from the menu. As soon as the waitress left, Boris pulled a small silver flask out of the pocket of his bomber jacket.

"In the name of the Father and the Son," he mumbled with his head lowered. He crossed himself Orthodox style and took a swig.

"You promised!" Nadia hissed the words across the table, her eyes flashing. Charles had never seen her like that before. Not just angry, she was red-hot.

"Okay, okay." Boris slipped the flask back into his jacket. "I'm nervous, you know! It's not every day that a man gets to meet the future husband of his one and only beloved daughter. You *will* marry my one and only beloved daughter, won't you, Mr. Charles Ferguson?"

Was that a joke? Boris certainly didn't act like it. Was it some Russian thing Nadia forgot to tell him about?

"We, um, we haven't really—"

"Ugh!" Nadia said. "Stop being ridiculous, Father. You aren't going to scare him off."

"I hope not!" Boris's booming voice brought them all sorts of benevolent glances from the other restaurant-goers. "He'd be a coward, a little boy. You aren't a little boy, are you, Mr. Charles Ferguson?"

"That's it." Nadia stood and grabbed her purse. "We're leaving."

"Nadia, Nadia!" Boris moaned theatrically. He leapt out of his chair. "Forgive me, my angel. I'm ridiculous, you're right. I'm a clown, a buffoon. Forgive me, Mr. Charles Ferguson. I won't be a clown any longer. I'll be somber, I'll be sober, I'll be a noble Russian patriarch!"

He plopped back into his chair and gazed fixedly at a teenage girl at the next table who had been staring at him. She blushed and turned the other way. Nadia stood a moment longer, glaring at her father, then sat down again.

"Do you like Samuel Finley Breese Morse, Mr. Charles Ferguson?" Boris asked suddenly, as if this were a question of paramount importance.

"I, um…I suppose he was a decent sort."

"A decent sort?" Boris burst into laughter and clapped Charles on the back again. "You're my kind of chap, Mr. Charles Ferguson. Prunes and prisms. Ha! Well, let me tell you, other than the misfortune of being a rabid Calvinist and a stalwart defender of that horrifically useful enterprise called human slavery, Samuel Finley Breese Morse was, as you said, a decent sort. A genius, Mr. Charles Ferguson.

"One day Samuel Finley Breese Morse battles the Catholics and shields the slaveholders. The next day he paints Grecian gods with fiery visages. He goes to sleep and wakes up to build the first telegraph machine. He takes a nap and arises with Morse code streaming from his cerebral cortex. It's wonderful, isn't it, Mr. Charles Ferguson?"

"Maybe not for the slaves," Charles murmured.

"Not for the slaves? No, no, not for them. But that was their eternal destiny, decreed with dread solemnity before the foundation of the cosmos by the merciful benevolence of the Divine Wisdom, world without end. Amen. Poor Samuel Finley Breese Morse! He would have been a much happier man if he had been Russian. Everyone's happy in Russia, Mr. Charles Ferguson. Tragically happy."

The teenager was gawking again. Doubtless she had never seen anything like Boris Petrov in her life. Charles hadn't either, come to think of it.

"Now tell me, Mr. Charles Ferguson, do you know Morse code? If I tapped the table like this…"

Boris grabbed a metal chopstick and began rapping the table in measured beats. It went on for a minute or two.

"There! Do you know what I've said to you?"

"I'm afraid I don't. I've never studied Morse code."

"Really?" Boris looked crestfallen. "Never studied it? Not even once? Not even a little?"

"Normal people don't learn Morse code unless they have to," Nadia said, though without a trace of her earlier anger. Boris was apparently on his best behavior.

"Ah, and you're normal people, are you, Mr. Charles Ferguson? A decent chap, prunes and prisms. Ha! Well, I thank the Blessed and all-holy Mother that you're not normal people. No, no, no. Normal people don't get nominated for Nobel Prizes, do they, Nadia, my angel, my own?

"Let me encourage you to learn Morse code, Mr. Charles Ferguson. It won't take you long. I've heard about that memory of yours. Ah, what a gift. Sweet Saint Barbara Yakovleva! If I'd only had a memory like yours, Mr. Charles Ferguson…" He broke into a complacent smile. "That would have been the life for old Boris, eh? Learn Morse Code. Will you do that for me, Mr. Charles Ferguson? Will you do that for the one and only father of the glorious heaven-tinged creature that you love and adore?"

This was Nadia's father? Would he really have to befriend this man and spend every holiday with him for the rest of his life? He looked over at Nadia and took a deep breath.

"Sure, Boris." His voice sounded a lot calmer than he felt. "I'll learn Morse code if you'd like."

"Mr. Charles Ferguson, you're a living saint. Now, my angel, what was I saying with this chopstick? Tell him, tell your beloved Charles!"

"You're so ridiculous." Nadia tried, and failed, to keep a straight face. "*Prūna et prismata*. You said *prunes and prisms*. In Latin."

Boris smacked the table with the palm of his hand. "Sharp as a saber! You're a lucky man, Mr. Charles Ferguson. Do you know something? My Nadyezhda has never been in love until now."

"Father!" Nadia exclaimed breathlessly.

"What?" Boris shrugged. "It's true, Mr. Charles Ferguson. There were some rascals who pursued her, of course. There are always rascals. But they were children, they were boys, they were as enjoyable as a colonoscopy. Have you ever had a colonoscopy, Mr. Charles Ferguson? I met a few of the rascals, but I never met the same one twice. Funny, isn't it? I wonder why? Ha!

"But with you it's different. I heard it in her voice, I knew it from the first moment. *He's wonderful, Daddy! He's kind, Daddy! He's brilliant, Daddy!* Well, let me add something to that. *He's faithful, Daddy.* Because you are faithful, aren't you, Mr. Charles Ferguson? You wouldn't trifle with my one and only beloved daughter, now would you?"

"Father, that's enough!"

"No, no, my darling, this time I'm completely serious. Answer me, Mr. Charles Ferguson."

Boris's eyes gleamed. The accent had vanished. In that moment, Charles remembered the man's history with the CIA. He wondered what Boris was capable of doing. What he had already done.

"I, um…" He swallowed. "Of course not, Boris. Nadia's everything to me. Everything."

Boris stared at him in silence for a few gut-wrenching moments, then broke into a warm grin.

"Good, good!" He slapped the table again with a broad palm.

So there were two Borises. Terrifying Boris—former CIA assassin, perhaps?—crept out for a question and then quickly shuffled back into the shadows. Now Boris the Clown returned, accent and all.

"Ah, finally they bring the vittles. Look at those crayfish, Mr. Charles Ferguson. Red as Communists!"

They enjoyed a few brief moments of blessed silence while Boris inhaled a plate of stir fry topped by the proletariat-hued crustaceans.

The fare was decent, though Charles excavated his soup to see if there were any roaches lurking beneath the surface.

Boris pulled out his phone, sent a few texts, then pocketed it again. The accent now became so faint that it was almost undetectable. "So, Mr. Charles Ferguson, is it true what Nadia told me last night about this scanner of yours? You press it against your arm and five minutes later all the hidden mysteries of your genome come fizzling into the light?"

"I don't know about all the mysteries, but that's the general idea."

"How do you analyze blood samples when they never leave the device?"

"Well, that's the beauty of it." Charles leaned forward. "Have you heard of the Bergmann camera? It's really more of a tiny microscope. Bergmann got a Nobel for it last year."

"You're taking photographs of the blood?"

"Exactly. You see, Thompson knows Bergmann somehow or other. Bergmann owed him a favor, so he let us use one of his prototypes for the scanner. It takes hundreds of pictures of the blood cells at different magnification levels. Once the scanner gets Internet access, it uploads the images to our cloud servers. It's amazing, Boris. With Bergmann's camera, you can even see individual DNA strands."

Boris scratched his chin. "And you keep all the data from these blood samples on your servers?"

"Well, yes. We've been keeping the trial runs at the university. I imagine whatever company ends up producing the scanner will store the data, but everything's anonymous. There's no way you could link a sample back to the person doing the test. I mean, I guess you could find out the general location the results were sent from, but that doesn't give you a name or anything."

"How reassuring." Boris took a sip of his iced tea. "Okay, you have their blood in your servers. What happens next?"

"That's when the real magic begins. Thompson and I came up with a program that does all the testing and genetic analysis. And it's accurate. Not laboratory standards, but we're getting close. Once it has the results, it sends them back to the scanner, which can connect to our app on mobile devices or computers. People will still need to go in for normal blood tests to verify everything, but the scanner's going to point them in the right direction. This thing could be the end of the silent killers. Right now, it's testing for hundreds of real and potential health issues, and we're adding to that number all the time."

"So," Boris said, "you might discover that you have hepatitis, or you might learn that you're going to end up like the neurotic uncle who hangs kittens from his tree limbs?"

"Um, yeah, I guess. Something like that."

Boris regarded him in silence for a moment. "I'm impressed, Mr. Charles Ferguson."

Nadia reached over and squeezed Charles's hand beneath the table. He might just survive dinner with Dad after all.

When he'd ordered, he'd noticed that his meal included something called century eggs. He'd already finished a bowl of watercress soup and a bed of noodles with beef strips and vegetables. On one side of the plate remained two eggs that were a strikingly translucent brownish orange with deep gray yolks.

He cut one in two and popped one of the halves in his mouth. The taste was potent, and the egg had a strangely familiar smell, though he couldn't place it.

"Century eggs!" Boris exclaimed, the accent suddenly reemerging. "Do you know how they make those, Mr. Charles Ferguson? They soak them in urine. Horse urine. That's what they call them in Thailand. Horse urine eggs!"

A half-dozen chunks of century egg tumbled from Charles's mouth to his plate. *That* was the strangely familiar smell. Boris roared with laughter.

"Well, that's what an old comrade of mine told me, but I'm sure it's all nonsense." Boris wiped his mouth and pushed away a plate littered with the broken remains of the crayfish. He leaned back against his chair, which creaked ominously under the weight.

"Nadyezhda tells me that you went with her to the Church. You should be careful, Mr. Charles Ferguson, or she'll turn you into a red-blooded Orthodox! So, then, when are you going to get baptized?"

"Baptized? I, um, I don't—"

"Ha!" Boris clapped him soundly on the back again. He would need to find a chiropractor if this kept up. "Yes, you'll get baptized, Chuck. All in good time. Can I call you Chuck? It's such a plain and uninspiring name."

"I prefer Charles."

"So, Chuck, you should know that the Russian Orthodox Church is doing quite well these days. They had a little problem with the Communists. Maybe you heard about it? The problem was that the Communists liked to kill them. Maybe ten million, maybe twenty million. There were thirty thousand churches when the Revolution started. There were less than five hundred by 1940. Can you imagine?

"But that's over. Now they're sublime. They open churches all over Russia. And they have quite a leader over there. You see, Chuck, they're the only church in the world that has the distinction of being led by a KGB informant. Isn't that something? At least, they say he was an informant. What a career he's had! He led the sheep into the labor camps, and now he leads them into the cathedral. What do you think of that, Nadia, darling?"

"I think…" She paused. "I think the Church usually forgets her bureaucrats but remembers her saints. I think the least of us really are the greatest. People like our Peter, they're the heart of the Church."

Boris lowered his gaze. "Peter? Yes, my dear boy. Well, if he and his kind are the stars of the show, then maybe it will all work out in the end. Anyway…" He cleared his throat. "Now that we're talking about religion, let me tell you a joke."

It was a fateful coincidence that their part of the restaurant grew quiet at that precise moment. Boris's voice was loud enough to be heard all the way back in the kitchen.

"How do we know that Adam and Eve weren't Chinese?"

Charles couldn't breathe. Was this man really going to tell a Chinese ethnic joke in the middle of a Chinese restaurant?

"Because if they were Chinese, they would have eaten the snake. Ha!"

"Father!" Nadia hissed. "That isn't—"

"I know, I know." Boris held out his hands in protest. "You can't tell jokes like that anymore. Everything is off-limits these days. But I heard it from a Chinese person, Nadia. And he was authentic Chinese, too, not one of those cheap knockoffs."

Charles had never felt more awkward in his life. The waitress, who was almost certainly Chinese herself, had approached their table in graceful silence as Boris told the joke and now stood right behind him, her hair tied up in a long, narrow hairpin. Charles wondered if she was going to stab Boris with it.

Boris noticed her and leapt to his feet.

"Ah, there you are, you little ninja. Sneaking around like that. Why, you could hunt squirrels barehanded, eh? And people, too, I'd wager. Brought the bill? And the cookies. Yes, yes, we won't leave without fortune cookies!"

He pulled his wallet out of his back pocket, and then, to Charles's astonishment, began a conversation with the waitress in Chinese. His voice was transformed, like he had become a different person. The waitress burst into laughter at one point and covered her mouth with a delicate hand. Boris pulled out a hundred-dollar bill, handed it over, said something else to her and sat down again.

"It's a strange world, isn't it, Chuck?" Boris cracked open a fortune cookie, read the message, grunted, and stuffed it in his jacket pocket with the Russian water.

"It's sure strange when you're around, Boris."

Boris broke into a rumbling laugh that earned him one last stare from the young girl at the opposite table. "Good, Chuck, good for you. You've found your voice. You know, I think I might actually like you, Mr. Charles Ferguson. Just Charles, you said? Well, well, I'll call you Charles, then."

"Thanks, I guess."

"Nadia, darling, it's been wonderful as always." Boris stood again. "You shouldn't worry so much about me. I drink too much, it's my weakness. But before I go, I'd like to take a little walk with Mr. Charles. You wouldn't mind if I borrowed him for a few minutes, would you, Nadia, my dear? He can drop you off, then I'll meet him at that park by the campus. There are woods there, right? What do you say, Mr. Charles, can you be there in twenty minutes?"

This was unexpected. Charles glanced at Nadia, who nodded eagerly.

"All right Boris, I'll see you there."

"Excellent. Goodbye, Nadia." Boris leaned down, kissed her on both cheeks, and lumbered out of the restaurant.

"You survived!" Nadia wrapped her arms around Charles. "You were wonderful."

Not one to pass up a chance for caveman bliss, he gave her a quick kiss on the lips. "What was all that about prunes and prisms, anyway?"

She snickered. "I keep forgetting you've never read Dickens."

"But what is it? Does it mean I'm boring?"

She patted him on the knee. "It doesn't matter what it means. I love that you're sane and stable, unlike some men in my family."

Translation? Mild-mannered professor driving a dung-colored grandma car. But hey, if Nadia was happy, life was good. He cleared his throat. "Anyway, I haven't survived yet. Your dad and I still have that little walk in the park, remember?"

"Don't be ridiculous. I can't believe he likes you! I know he must seem crazy, and he drives me crazy most of the time, but underneath it all he's a good man. You'll see."

Charles leaned over and kissed her again. "If you say so. But what about that business with the waitress? Does he really speak Chinese?"

"Hokkien. He asked if her uncle was still in the kitchen. She said yes, and he told her to tell her uncle that the food was delicious but that the poor foreign devils didn't like the joke."

"Wait, *you* speak Hokkien?"

"I'm afraid so." She sighed. "And Mandarin Chinese. And Arabic. And Greek. And Russian and Ukrainian, of course, but you already knew about those. There are a few others. I guess I don't think about it much."

"But how did you learn all those? *When* did you learn them?"

"I'm the daughter of Boris Petrov." Her lips curved into a grin as she straightened his collar. "I didn't exactly have a normal upbringing."

Chapter Five
Disaster

AFTER A LONG and scorching weekend, the departing summer had exited the stage with grace. Billowing cumulous clouds drifted languidly across a cerulean sky, a gang of children gamboled with shrieks and squeals in a soccer field under the lengthening shadows of sycamores while their parents lay scattered about on blankets, basking in the waning sunlight.

Boris leaned up against the hood of a dark gray SUV, waiting for Charles. A few yards off, an unmarked trail wound its way into the woods. It was one of Charles's favorite haunts, a quiet escape when the lectures and research grew wearisome. The nicest spot was a glade a few miles down the trail that was carpeted with wildflowers in the spring. The locals took their kids there every year for family pictures.

He pulled up next to Boris's SUV. He was about to open his door when Boris tapped on the window and then pressed a piece of paper against the glass. Scrawled on it, in spidery handwriting, were the following words.

Leave all electronics in the car. No cell phone.

"What on earth?" Charles pushed the door open a little, though actually moving Boris out of the way was far more than his limited upper body strength could accomplish. "What's this about? Why—"

Boris touched a thick forefinger to his lips. Then he zipped open a camouflage backpack that was slung over his shoulder, took out a pen, and scribbled four more words on the paper.

Humor me, Mr. Charles.

"He's insane," Charles muttered to himself. He tossed his cell phone into the passenger seat. "He's going to murder me out there. I can hear it already. *Hey, Nadyezhda, good news, my little angel! Mr. Charles Ferguson broke up with you. Isn't that wonderful? You'll never see him again, my darling!*"

He raised his voice. "All right, Boris. This is nuts, but I'll humor you if you want. Tell you what, can you at least let me write out a will so Nadia gets my stuff when I'm gone?"

"That's funny, Mr. Charles," Boris replied. "Don't worry, I took care of it on the flight here. All you'll have to do is sign. Now hurry, we're going ghost hunting."

He had to jog to keep up with Boris as they hustled down the meandering trail. About a quarter mile in, Boris broke away from the path and headed straight into the woods. Charles followed as best as he could, dodging branches, tripping over roots and rocks, and trying to avoid the brambles.

Boris stopped after a few minutes and removed a silver cylindrical device, about ten inches in length, from his backpack. He placed it on the ground, pushed a small button on one end of the device, and buried it under some leaves.

"What is that?"

"Watchdog. Barks at ghosts."

After another fifteen minutes of nonstop trudging through dense forest, Boris halted under a towering white oak whose stout branches were laden with acorns. Motioning for silence, he looked around in all directions, including up.

"Yes, yes, this will do nicely. Let me just get Little Boris. He always likes to be in on the action."

Boris pulled a roll of duct tape from his bag along with a two-foot-tall stuffed doll that did look eerily like him. It was carrying a plastic machine gun in each hand and wore a black T-shirt with a camouflage jacket and pants. *Got Napalm?* was written in bold white letters on the front of the shirt. Boris taped the doll to the back of a maple tree about ten yards away and came back with a big grin on his face.

By that point, Charles was confident of two things. The first was that Boris was insane. The second was that Boris was about to subject him to a notably unconventional death.

"Don't you love the forest, Mr. Charles?" Boris said. "It's filled with possibilities. Just imagine, this very moment, hidden from our sight, some illiterate inbred—a Cletus or a Jim Bob—has his shotgun levelled on us. His uneven breath reeks with corn-laden moonshine as he fumbles with the trigger, ready to blast us into oblivion so he can rob us of our meager possessions."

Why hadn't he called Thompson on the way over to tell him where they were going? At least it would have saved the police dogs some time when they went hunting for his body.

Boris continued his monologue. "A half-starved copperhead might be curled up under that pile of brush right there at your feet, ready to sink its fangs into your ankle." Charles took a few hasty steps away from the brush pile. "The smallest, most harmless-looking tick in these woods could send you to the hospital with a pounding head and a racing pulse. Life is an adventure, Mr. Charles. That's why I brought you here."

"To get shot by hillbillies?" His breath was still a little ragged from the journey. Boris, despite the graying hairs and twenty-plus years on him, had barely broken a sweat. It was pitiful.

"I'm glad it wasn't you who informed them, Mr. Charles. It would have broken her heart. She loves you. Did you know that?"

"Well, yeah, but I'm not following you, Boris. Why did you want me to leave my phone in the car? And why did you just tape a doll to that tree?"

"What, Little Boris? Don't worry about him. He's good at diversions. Comes in handy when you're catching ghosts. As for what this is all about, why, it's about your old boss. That kind benefactor of the human race, Mr. Alexander Magnus."

Charles was stunned. "You mean the Magnus Foundation? How did you know I worked for them?"

Boris grunted. "I'm a very simple man, Mr. Charles. When it comes to my children, life is black and white for me. You treat them well, and Boris is your friend. You treat them badly, and Boris is your enemy. You put their lives in danger, and Boris will become your executioner." He said the words in a matter-of-fact way, as if executions were just another part of the daily grind. "So I have to ask myself, who was it that told Magnus about my Nadia? I wasn't always a salesman. Maybe you've heard?"

"On our first date, Nadia mentioned that you worked for the CIA when she was a kid. That is, until—"

"Until I got plastered and spilled all my intel to a blonde dishrag they'd planted at the bar? Yes, yes, that was the end for poor Boris. Still, I've kept up with some of my friends from those days. You've met one of them before, Dr. Raj Bhandari. You remember him, yes?"

"Raj Bhandari?" Charles pressed a hand against his forehead. This was surreal. "Raj is with the CIA?"

"*Was* with the CIA. Raj used to go sailing out in the ocean blue. I'm sure he told you about his hobby. A few days after that last project you two were working on ended—Alpha, right, or was it Phoenix?— his boat was caught in a tropical storm. They found the boat, but they never found Raj. It's very peculiar. Raj used to check the weather all the time to see if it was good for sailing, and that day he sailed straight into one of the fiercest storms of the year. He was as close as we'd ever been to Magnus. They have fingers in every pie, but they never leave any fingerprints."

"So you're still with the CIA?"

"And yesterday, out of the blue," Boris went on, ignoring his question, "my own Nadia tells me that Magnus wants to fly her out for a meeting. I call her later that night and learn that she's dating a Dr. Charles Ferguson, and I say to myself, *Boris, Boris, you've heard that name before, haven't you?* And then I remembered. Charles Ferguson worked with Raj and with Tom Murrow, the same Tom Murrow who disappeared after a conference in Southeast Asia. Gone without a trace, just like good old Raj. So I begin to wonder, did this Charles Ferguson tell them about my daughter? Did *he* get her tangled up with an organization that could put her life in danger?"

At this, something in Boris's backpack emitted a soft, mechanical bark. Boris pulled a black handgun out of his bomber jacket. He popped in a clip of bullets and then began attaching a silencer to the barrel.

"Oh my god!" Charles blurted out, his heart pounding. This was it. Should he run? Would Boris shoot him in the back if he tried? "Are you...are you going to—"

"Relax, Mr. Charles. Hold this for me, will you? I've got something else for the ghost."

Boris handed him the pistol. It was surprisingly heavy. He held it at arm's length as if it were a poisonous reptile while Boris began assembling an odd-looking rifle. The weapon seemed familiar, and then he realized he had seen something like it on nature shows. It was a tranquilizer gun. Boris finished mounting its scope and then loaded it with darts that were filled with a dark green substance.

"What is that stuff?"

"It's a fast-acting paralytic agent mixed with a sedative. The details are classified. If I get a decent shot, the ghost will drop before he realizes what's happened. Sit down here behind the tree. I'll stand next to you. If things don't go well for me—that is, if I *don't* get a clear shot and the ghost makes a ghost of me—point that pistol at him and pull the trigger. He'll kill you first, of course, but at least you'll have a fighting chance. You're really living now, aren't you, Mr. Charles? Like a cowboy in the good old days."

"I don't really think those were—"

"What was I saying earlier?" Boris lowered his voice. "Oh yes. Who told Magnus about my daughter? Is her life in danger? These are very important questions to a doting father, so I caught the next plane to look for answers. And I've found one. Like I said, I'm glad it wasn't you. I'm a very good judge of character. It's crucial when you work in sales. You would make a lousy poker player, Mr. Charles. Take that as a compliment."

"Thanks, I guess."

Boris practiced lifting the tranquilizer gun to his shoulder and aiming a few times. He could do it in the space of a breath. "I hate to tell you this, Mr. Charles, but you'll be living in Boris's world from now on. And Boris's world is a little bit like these woods, only instead of venomous snakes, you have to deal with their human counterparts. I came here to protect Nadia. Someday, assuming we survive this little adventure and you don't do something remarkably foolish afterwards, you two will be married, and I'll be your father-in-law. Lucky you, eh, Mr. Charles? So from now on, as far as I'm able, I'll protect you as well."

Charles leaned back against the tree. In that moment, he felt rooted to the ground as firmly as the oak was. He couldn't keep his eyes off the pistol, which he held barrel downward with both hands. This ghost Boris was talking about had to be the pale-faced stalker. And what about Raj Bhandari and Tom Murrow? Had they really died?

"If you think Nadia's in danger," he said, his voice cracking from nervousness, "then we need to stop her, right? We get her out of here, somewhere where they can't find her."

"Quieter, Mr. Charles. I had that same thought at first. When we talked on the phone, I nearly told her everything—about Raj, about you, about a few other things I've learned. But you have to remember that Boris's world is different than the one you're used to. You have to think everything through carefully, move by move. So I asked myself, could this be a coincidence? Could it be that they are interested in my Nadia only because she is good at what she does, because she earned a doctorate from a decent university? It's possible but unlikely. Has she ever shown you her unpublished papers?"

"She never mentioned them," he said.

"Good. If you haven't read them, maybe Magnus hasn't either. So then I wondered, what if this is really all about you, the renowned Dr. Charles Ferguson? It's looking more and more likely. Ah, the ghost is coming. Silence, Mr. Charles, or we'll both be killed."

Boris crouched next to him behind the tree, the tranquilizer gun held at the ready. For a minute or two they didn't hear anything, but Charles somehow knew that they were no longer alone. He bit his lower lip and tried to control his panicked breathing. A breeze picked up, rattled the tree branches, and then died down again. He heard dry leaves crackle under a footstep.

Boris touched the screen on a device at his waist, and immediately Charles heard Boris's voice, not next to him where it should have been, but somewhere in the near distance. It said, quietly but clearly enough, "Do you see him? Where is he? Wait, there he is!"

The voice was coming from Little Boris.

In the same moment, the real Boris leaned over to one side of the oak tree. Charles heard a muted popping sound, a sudden scattering of leaves, and then all became silent.

Boris stood and began disassembling the tranquilizer gun. He tucked the pieces away in his backpack and put on a pair of black leather gloves. He then pulled a syringe filled with bluish liquid from his bag.

"Antidote," he said. "Just in case."

He walked out of view. Charles was too terrified to move. A few moments later, Boris came back and stood over him. He took the pistol from Charles's hands and tucked it away in his jacket, then grabbed Charles by the elbow and lifted him to his feet.

"Come and see the ghost."

He stumbled after Boris. Their pursuer lay face upward on the ground.

"It's not him!" Charles exclaimed.

Boris glanced at him sharply but said nothing. The prostrate figure had a swarthy complexion, dark gray, close-shaven hair, and was dressed in a long-sleeved black shirt and black pants. A handgun with a silencer lay a few feet from him next to a lone, stubborn wildflower.

"Who is he?"

"Ali Hamid." Boris said the words with pride, as if Ali Hamid was a species of wild game. "Former terrorist. I noticed him lurking in the shadows outside the restaurant. He was a member of the Hand of God over in the Middle East. You've heard of them, yes? Ali was one of their hired guns. Not really a terrorist by ideology, but he had talents they desired. And here's the real mystery. Ali was proclaimed dead after a drone attack about a week ago. So, you see, he really is a ghost."

"But why did he come after us?" Charles asked. "Was he coming for you? For me?"

"For both of us. He would have killed me and kidnapped you. After I talked to Nadia on the phone, my friends and I decided to play a little game. There's a company called Tessara. They make weapons, very dangerous ones, and they sell them to anyone who will pay. We let word get out last night that I had heard about Magnus's letter to Nadia and that I was coming here in person to keep her from accepting their offer. I would also secretly try to convince you, Mr. Charles, to work for Tessara instead of Magnus. A generous sum of money fell into my bank account at one o'clock this morning, which was presumably my cut from Tessara. Magnus took the bait and sent his newest ghost."

"Wait, so this…this Ali Hamid is working for Magnus? I thought you said he was a terrorist."

"Former terrorist. You must always remember that things are rarely what they seem in Boris's world. The official story was that Ali's comrades in the Hand of God buried him after the drone attack. They didn't do a very good job of it, did they? My guess is Magnus offered Ali far more than the terrorists could afford. He accepted, and Magnus framed the bombing to get him off the radar. The Hand of God found some dead bodies all right, but Ali wasn't one of them. Ghosts always make the best assassins. Unfortunately for this particular phantom, I knew him by sight, so we were ready for him."

This was a lot to process. The black-veiled woman, the pale-faced stalker—now Charles found himself out in the woods with a known terrorist and a deep-cover agent. And if an assassin was hunting for them…

"Nadia!" he cried. "If they sent Ali Hamid after us, what about her?"

"That's right, Mr. Charles, that's how the game is played. When I heard about the letter yesterday, I contacted some of my local friends. Angels, we'll call them, only the human type. They are watching over her now. But enough talk. I'll get Little Boris. Here, put these gloves on and start taking off the ghost's clothes, everything but his underwear. Mr. Ali is going to have some explaining to do when he wakes up."

Charles did what he was told. Boris retrieved the doll and threw it in his bag. Then he emptied the bullets out of Ali's gun, leaving one in the chamber, and put them in his bag along with Ali's clothes, wallet, and keys. He then slung the boxer-clad Ali over his shoulder and carried him back toward the trail. He had Charles pick up the "guard dog" along the way.

When they got back to the trail, Boris dumped Ali on the ground. He fired a muffled shot into the air with Ali's gun, then put it in the assassin's limp hand. After checking Ali's pulse for about a minute, he took a syringe from his backpack and injected it into the ghost's forearm.

"Our friend here has a penchant for opiates." Boris placed the needle in Ali's other hand. "A nasty habit he picked up while he was in Afghanistan. Magnus will hear about it soon enough."

Boris took a can of black spray paint from his bag and sprayed something in an Arabic-looking script on several nearby trees. He scattered the remaining bullets from Ali's gun on the ground along with the terrorist's clothes and wallet. Finally, he pulled a cell phone out of his pocket.

"Hey, 911, right?" Boris now sounded like he had just crawled out of a Brooklyn subway. "Look, there's this nutcase wandering around in his underwear here at the park on East Delving over by the college. I saw him on that trail, the one on the far side of the parking lot. Yeah, and listen, I think he maybe had a gun or something. I was scared so I got out of there, you know what I mean? Yeah, yeah, short guy, silver hair, little tan or something. And he was yelling like crazy, maybe strung out. You better get somebody down here. There were little kids playing out on that soccer field, you know what I'm saying? What, *my* name? Listen, lady, I don't want to get tied up in nothing. I'm just trying to do the right thing, you hear me?"

Boris hung up and tucked the phone away in his pocket. "All right, we need a place to talk." He was back in what Charles began to call *standard Boris*, which was evening-news-American with the faint hint of a Russian accent. "I'll meet you at your house, we'll debrief, and then you can get back to your life. For now."

"Right, okay." Charles felt like he was about to hyperventilate. "Do you need my address?"

Boris chuckled as he climbed into his SUV. "See you in ten minutes, Mr. Charles. And leave your phone in the car when you get there."

Charles's hands trembled so violently that he dropped his car key as he tried to get it into the ignition. He finally crammed it home, shifted into reverse, and slammed the accelerator. Tires squealed as the old sedan lurched out of the parking spot. Boris's SUV was already out of sight.

He took a deep breath. He needed to stay calm and avoid drawing attention to himself.

He would have killed me and kidnapped you.

Killed. Kidnapped. If Ali Hamid worked for the Magnus Foundation, his fears about them only scratched the surface. Most research outfits kept their work secret, especially when it could have military applications. But who could set up a drone strike on the other side of the world to fake the death of a terrorist? What scientific foundation would hire trained assassins?

A few miles from the park, a police car whizzed by in the opposite lane, its siren blazing. Charles panicked. Had he committed a crime out there in the woods? Boris had just injected narcotics into an unconscious man. Would they pull him over and arrest him for being an accomplice?

He kept his eyes peeled, but the police didn't slow down.

Boris's SUV was parked in his driveway. Boris himself was rocking in a chair on the front porch and smoking a thick cigar.

"Nice place, Mr. Charles," he said as Charles unlocked the front door.

"Are you sure my house is safe?" Charles whispered. "Couldn't they have bugs planted in it or something?"

"Any modern device with a microphone is a bug." Boris pushed past him into the house. "But yes, someone was monitoring you through your television. Camera under the screen and an extra mic. It's a good thing you swapped your TV out this morning for a new one."

Charles frowned. "I didn't swap out my TV."

"The screen was flickering, remember? It's all on record down at the electronics store. Your phone's bugged, too, of course. You left it in the car like I asked?"

Charles nodded. "Should I get rid of it?"

"Keep it for now. We don't want them getting too suspicious. Just watch what you say when you're near it. Do you have anything to drink?"

"If you're looking for vodka, no. How about a glass of wine?"

"Even better." Boris sat on the couch. "You should have some yourself. You need to relax before you go back to Nadia. Like I said, you're an awful liar, and I don't want her knowing about our little adventure with the ghost."

Charles poured two glasses of Pinot Noir and handed one to Boris.

Boris took a long sip and exhaled appreciatively. "You have excellent taste in wine and women, Mr. Charles. Now back to business. We didn't expect Magnus to move that quickly, but it does make it clear that the real target isn't Nadia. It's you, and Nadia is only bait. You're the key to the riddle, and we need to find out why."

"I'm more concerned about Nadia." Charles sat in an old-fashioned burgundy recliner across from Boris. "Are you saying we should let her walk right into a trap? They could kill her."

Boris took a deep pull on his cigar and blew out a cloud of gray-white smoke. "You think I'm being reckless with my daughter's life? That I care more about spying on the Magnus Foundation than my own daughter? Let me tell you something, Mr. Charles. If I had to kill you to save Nadia, I would do it in a heartbeat."

He crushed the cigar against the glass coffee table. "We're too far in to back out safely. If Nadia ran away now, they'd just hunt her down. I can't keep her safe, not forever. And even if you were dead, they would come back for her someday. She's the sort of person they're looking for even if they don't realize it yet. We have to play their game, and we have to win. We've already passed the first test."

"You mean Ali Hamid, right?" Charles drank some of the wine, hoping it would calm his nerves. "I have to tell you, Boris, I'm glad you didn't kill him."

"Who says I didn't?" Boris's voice was grim. "Put yourself in his shoes, Mr. Charles. Even as we speak, Ali's old terrorist friends have discovered that he didn't die in that drone attack. No, he betrayed them and joined a Western corporation for the money. On the other hand, Magnus will soon learn that their newest employee got drugged up in the park and sprayed terroristic threats on trees instead of doing his job. I'd be very surprised if Ali Hamid doesn't become a permanent ghost within the next few days. But who knows? Maybe he will slip through their nets. The important point is that I kept my cover and protected you at the same time."

"Do you always keep opiates around for this sort of thing?"

Boris shook his head. "The drugs were a last-minute plan. I texted my friends from the restaurant. They did some quick intel on Ali, found out about his troubled Afghanistan days, and had the backpack ready for me by the time we left. We've done a lot of ghost hunting together through the years. Sometimes you avoid them, sometimes you kill them, and every now and then you frame them. Speaking of my friends…"

Boris took out his phone and dialed a number. He was apparently checking in with someone about his son, Peter. It was an odd conversation. From what Charles could gather, Peter had spent the entire day picking vegetables with a monk.

"What do I tell Nadia?" he asked as soon as Boris hung up.

"You tell her nothing. You and I took a walk in the woods. It was stressful. I was being absurd. I threatened you in one minute and hugged you the next. She'll feel sorry for you and try to calm you down. As far as she knows, I'm just a salesman. I want to keep it that way. Now I have a question for you. Who were you expecting?"

"I'm sorry?"

"In the woods. You were expecting someone other than Mr. Hamid. Who was it?"

"I don't know his name, but I think he's with the Foundation." Charles told him about his encounter with the night stalker after the Alpha Financial meeting.

"And you never saw him afterward?" Boris asked. He was typing away on his phone as they talked.

"Once. He was looking through Nadia's window last week."

Boris's face clouded over. "He was, was he? This was before she got the invitation from Magnus?"

"The day before."

"And that's why she's staying in a hotel?"

"Yes. Well, that and the noise. Those apartments get a little crazy once classes are in session."

"It was a good move on your part, Mr. Charles." Boris set his phone down and took a sip of wine. "Anything else I should know?"

Charles shifted uncomfortably in his chair. "There was this woman at our meeting with Alpha Financial. They're the ones buying our scanner. She was dressed all in black with a veil over her face. She just sat there and watched us, didn't say a thing. Kind of creeped me out. I can't explain it, but something about her seemed familiar."

Boris drummed his fingers on the tabletop. "Was anyone with her?"

"The guy running the meeting was named Rius. I think he's maybe Eastern European or something."

"Rius?" Boris picked up his phone again and started typing. "Yes, yes, he's well known. That may point us in the right direction. Now, before I leave, there's one more thing to discuss. This memory of yours, is it really like Nadia told me? Do you remember everything?"

"Maybe. I don't know if it's really *everything* or not, but it seems that way. If I really focus, I can recall things in detail—events, conversations, books I've read."

"And you took a few courses in linguistics when you were at MIT, yes?"

Charles's eyes widened. "You seem to know everything about me."

"Can you remember English phonology?" Boris asked. "Do you know how many vowels there *really* are in the English language?"

"Hm, give me a moment." As often happened when he tried to remember something remote, he began with images. A picture of the classroom where they'd met for his second linguistics course, the one that focused on phonological analysis. In his mind, he saw the professor, Dr. Mallory, a humorous septuagenarian who managed to fill all three whiteboards with phonological charts and problem sets in the space of a one-hour lecture.

He focused his memory on the boards, recalling the day Dr. Mallory began teaching on English phonology. At last, he found them, the charts of vowels and consonants all written in the International Phonetic Alphabet.

"Fourteen on the lower end." He opened his eyes. "There were fourteen in the chart I remember, but he said the number can be higher depending on the dialect."

"Very impressive, Mr. Charles. An incredible gift."

Boris reached into his jacket pocket and handed him a piece of plain copy paper folded into a small rectangle. "Look it over, memorize it, and when you're done, burn it. I mean that. Don't leave a trace. It's a little variation on the code that the magnificent Mr. Morse created. My father created it back in his KGB days when he started leaking intel to the Americans. It's phonologically based, and, of course, the patterns he used are different. Quaternary instead of binary. Simple alternations, but enough for a basic cypher. Hopefully you'll never need it, but it's good to be prepared."

Boris rose and shook his hand.

"It was a pleasure to meet you, Mr. Charles Ferguson. I'm glad I didn't have to kill you."

−ʃ

Charles and Nadia lay side by side on a blanket in his backyard, looking up at the stars that were visible through the city lights. He pointed out his favorite constellations—Orion, Pegasus, Gemini. Nadia made up one of her own, Glousermorg the Great, a sprawling dragon that stretched across the entire sky. Try as he might, he couldn't see her ferocious invention and gave up the attempt with a laugh and a bite of homemade *pryaniki*. It was a recipe from her mother's Ukrainian side of the family, and he had quickly become addicted to the little glazed bursts of sugary, spice-laden bliss.

"Are you sure you're okay?" she asked. "This whole Magnus business and then my father—it's been a rough couple of days. I was terrified that dinner would be a disaster. He can be intimidating, especially if you don't know who he really is. But it turned out all right, didn't it?"

"Um, yeah. I guess you could say that." It was bad enough hiding the truth about Magnus from her. She didn't even know who her own father was. Or did she? "Boris was a tough one for me, but I'll get used to him. Maybe. I thought he was going to murder me out there on that trail, but when he left, he shook my hand like I was his best friend in the world. I don't know what to make of him."

"If you ever figure him out, let me know."

⁂

He spent the next few days casting furtive glances over his shoulder, but no pale stalkers lurked in the bushes, no terrorist assassins ducked behind newspapers.

On Friday, he drove her to the airport at six in the morning for her flight. He waved to her after she'd made it through security, then returned to the drudgery of a rainy day at the university.

Thompson dropped by his office around three that afternoon.

"How's it going?" Thompson asked.

"Nadia's out of town, so I had to teach two rounds of freshman bio."

"Ouch. Still think she's worth it?"

"Funny, Thompson. You know, I don't think anybody in the classroom listened to a single word I said. I need a career change, maybe a door greeter at a superstore."

"Don't throw in the towel just yet." Thompson pulled a chair up close to the desk. "You can't share this with anyone yet, not even Nadia. The fact is, you might be able to buy that superstore in a few weeks."

Charles leaned forward. "You heard something from Alpha Financial?"

"Just got off the phone with them. It sailed through all the tests. They've been pulling strings, working their contacts. It's going to be huge, Charles. Global. Rius said you and I could both make a hundred million by the end of the year."

"A hundred million! Wasn't it going to be ten million each?"

"That was the deposit, remember? We're on the gravy train now.

He said they've lined up massive government funding from all around the globe. They've even set up a nonprofit so the blue bloods can dump their tax deductions into it. And you and I will get our little percentage on every transaction."

Charles stood and put his hands on the desk to steady himself. In the last week, he'd had to deal with Nadia and the Magnus Foundation, Boris Petrov and his terrorist ghost, and now this.

"Is there anything else we need to do for them?" he asked.

"Not a thing, it was all taken care of when we signed that contract. Rius said they'll transfer the twenty million in a few days."

"What are we supposed to do with that kind of money?"

Thompson barked out a laugh. "You do what you want, Charles. I'm starting with the Cayman Islands. Open a little offshore bank account and then do a tour of Europe—Paris, Lucerne, Rome. All in a brand-new Maserati, of course." He struck a palm against the top of the desk. "My god, Charles, we finally did it!"

"Yes." Charles tugged on his shirt collar. The room suddenly felt too hot, the air stifling. "I need some water. Back in a minute."

He stumbled out of his office in a daze, closed the door behind him, and took a few deep breaths. He wandered toward the nearest water fountain, mumbling acknowledgements to the students who greeted him in the hallway.

Could that kind of money keep the Foundation away? Surely, he could just pay them to leave him and Nadia alone. Or maybe he could pay Boris to help them disappear. There had to be somewhere safe out there where he and Nadia could rough it on their meager millions.

His phone rang while he was walking back to the office. Nadia.

"How did it go?" he asked.

"It was—I can't say, not now, not on the phone." Her words were clipped, her voice taut. "You'll be there, won't you? 8:15?"

"I'll be there."

"I love you, Charles."

She hung up before he could reply.

❧

The moment he set foot in the terminal, he knew something was wrong. The well-modulated voice of a famous news reporter echoed from a half-dozen televisions. Everyone was huddled together in groups, gazing up at the screens, including many of the airline workers and security guards.

A young father hunched over on the ground near one of the luggage returns. Face buried in his hands, he was rocking back and forth and sobbing quietly. His daughter, a little wisp of a girl with braided black hair and a forest green dress, patted him on the back. "It's okay, Daddy, it's okay."

Loved ones clinging to one another with terrified desperation. Trembling, weeping, moaning, shocked silence.

"God, don't let it be Nadia's flight," Charles whispered.

"This story is still developing," the news anchor said. "What we know at this point is that Flight 109 from La Guardia exploded in midair shortly after takeoff. According to our sources, there was no communication from the pilots or other aircraft personnel before the explosion. Authorities say they are not expecting there to be any survivors."

Flight 109 from La Guardia. Nadia's flight.

"We have just received footage from—where was this taken? Okay, Metuchen Township in New Jersey."

The video was from someone's backyard. A family event, the father grilling hamburgers, kids throwing a baseball around while a black Labrador barked and ran between them. A glimmer in the sky, light from the setting sun reflecting off a plane overhead.

The plane abruptly turned into a ball of fire. The mother behind the camera shrieked and the video began trembling. The father yelled at his kids to go inside, then grabbed a phone and called 911. They cut back to the news studio, and the reporter continued her grim work.

Charles couldn't pull his gaze from the screen. He had no idea how long he stood there. Maybe an hour, maybe two. His face was damp with tears. He hadn't wept since his mother's funeral.

A middle-aged lady from the airline began talking to him. Latrice Jones, according to her silver nametag. Her deep brown eyes looked at him with a mixture of pity and concern.

"Sir, can you hear me? Did you know someone on the flight?"

"I…did." Past tense. He trembled and couldn't stop. Was it a seizure? "Or do you think…do you think maybe she…"

He hurriedly pulled out his cell phone and called her number. Why hadn't he done that earlier? Of course, she must have missed the flight!

It went straight to voicemail, and he listened to the recording of her bright, cheerful voice.

"Sir, can you tell me her name?" Latrice asked him. "Sir?"

"Nadia. Nadyezhda Petrova."

She flipped through a list she was carrying. An ice-cold emptiness settled over Charles.

"Are you Nadyezhda's spouse or a relative?"

"We've been together for a few months. I wanted to marry her." His words were calm, their tone perfectly level.

Latrice looked away and wiped her eyes with her hand.

"Sir, can I ask you to write your name and number here? We'll want to contact her family, and we may need your help if we can't locate them."

"Sure." He took the pen she offered. He remembered Boris's number, so he wrote it in as well.

"Boris Petrov is her father." He handed the clipboard back to her.

"Thank you, sir. I'm so sorry for your loss."

"Thank you, Latrice." As he walked out of the terminal, his footsteps were measured and precise, as if he were a machine.

When he got home, he sat behind his desk in the office and stared at a picture of Nadia. It had been taken a month ago when they visited a zoo downtown. She had looked so beautiful with her dark hair tied back in a ponytail, loose strands hanging down over her temples. She had felt sorry for the capuchins. They'd all been lying motionless in their cage that day.

A glass of wine sat untouched beside the picture. The clock on the wall chimed twice.

Eyes forever closed, lips forever silenced, heart forever stilled. The shroud and the casket. Dust, decay, worms. Annihilation.

He was missing something. A gun. And a bullet. Could he purchase a gun somewhere in the middle of the night? Would they let him buy just one bullet, or would he have to buy a whole pack of them? He only needed one, any more would be a waste.

He turned on his computer to look up pawn shops.

The doorbell rang.

He didn't bother checking to see who it was. He unlocked the bolt and threw the door open. It was Boris, soaking wet from the rain.

"Hello, Boris." He had an idea. "Do you still have that handgun? The one you let me carry in the woods last Monday? I'd like to borrow it for a few minutes. You'll get it back."

Boris didn't give him the gun. He took Charles in his arms as if Charles were already Nadia's husband, already his own son through marriage. Perhaps, in Boris's mind, he was.

Chapter Six

Anatoly

Boris walked over to the counter and grabbed Charles's cell phone. He filled the kitchen sink with hot water and dropped the phone into it.

"Hey!" Charles raced over to the sink. "What are you—"

Boris clamped a hand over Charles's mouth. After a few moments, the screen flickered on the phone a few times and went dark.

"We're leaving." Boris placed his hands on Charles's shoulders. "I need you to be strong now, Mr. Charles. Pack your suitcase. You'll be gone a week at least, maybe two."

"Where are we going?"

"I'll tell you on the way. Hurry, your life could be in danger."

"I don't care about my life. If someone wants it, they can have it."

"That's not what Nadia would have wanted."

He lowered his head. "Fine."

He went to his bedroom and tucked some clothes and toiletries into a duffel bag.

There was a black BMW sedan with tinted windows in the driveway. Boris took Charles's bag and tossed it into the trunk. A few minutes later, they were flying down the interstate at a hundred miles per hour.

"Why are you driving so fast?"

"Because I'm in a hurry. What, are you worried? I thought you didn't care about your life."

Charles grabbed the leather handle above the passenger door. He'd always wondered why those handles were there. This probably wasn't the reason, but it seemed to help.

"We're going home." Boris said. "Beecher, Illinois, where Nadia grew up. There's a tablet at your feet. Take a look."

Charles picked up the tablet and tapped on it. The screen came to life and displayed a news website.

Terror in the Skies. The words were emblazoned in large black text at the top of the page. Below were two pictures side-by-side. The first was from the home video the news had played the night before, Flight 109 at the moment it was converted into fire, shrapnel, bone, and ash. The second picture was a young man with scraggly black hair and shadowy hints of a beard. *Fazal al-Najjar* read the caption.

"They're trying to pin it on him," Boris said. "As most people would see it, the kid was guilty before he set foot on that plane. A Middle Easterner, a Muslim. Worst of all, his cousin is Fakhir al-Kadar. You've heard of him, perhaps? The Butcher of Beirut. It should be an open and shut case, but there's a problem."

Charles kept looking at the picture. He felt an overpowering desire to hate this young foreign man with his dark hair and his juvenile peach fuzz. "What's the problem?"

"Fazal was innocent."

He pursed his lips. "How do you know that?"

Boris glanced at him. "It would be easier if it was him, wouldn't it? We could move on, perhaps, and channel our hatred in a clear direction. But I want the truth, Mr. Charles, and the truth is rarely easy. Fazal and his family never contacted their infamous relatives in Lebanon after they immigrated to the States. Not once. The Hand of God claimed responsibility for the attack, but it was hours later, and they don't seem to know who the bomber was. The poor kid was just a passenger on the wrong plane, and the only reason he was on that plane was because he had been invited to a conference in New York."

"I don't know," Charles pulled his eyes away from Fazal's photograph. "It seems like it often is these people when this kind of thing happens."

Guilt pierced him even as the words left his mouth. Some of his best students had been from the Middle East, and they were no more likely to blow up a plane than he was.

"Let me see that." Boris reached over with his right hand and snatched the tablet. The car jerked to one side and made Charles's heart do a somersault. "Hold this, will you?"

"The steering wheel?"

"Yes, the steering wheel. There's a video you need to watch."

Charles reached over and kept the wheel steady. At least it was the middle of the night and the road was clear. After tapping around for a moment, Boris gave him the tablet again.

"Play that. It's footage from a security camera near one of the tarmacs at La Guardia. They installed the camera and others like it after that airplane bombing in Pakistan."

"I heard about that. It was some of the airline workers, right?"

"Exactly. They conspired with terrorists to get the bomb on the plane. TSA just added these cameras to keep a closer eye on the airline employees, and they were quiet about it. One of our contacts sent us this a few minutes after the bombing. She contacted us again a half hour later to tell us that the original footage had been deleted from the TSA servers and their backup systems. The attackers apparently didn't have knowledge of these cameras at first or we would never have seen this. We may be the only ones who still have a copy."

Charles tapped the play button. A stout, square-shouldered young man with a bright orange safety vest was pacing up and down an empty hallway.

"That's Michael Donovan. He's a baggage handler at La Guardia. Ran drugs when he was younger, but he got out of it with a mistrial."

Another man entered the screen, tall and lanky with blond hair and a dark black suit and tie. Charles recognized him at once. The night stalker set a small tote bag against the wall, nodded to Donovan, and left the same way he had come.

Donovan waited a few moments, looked up and down the hallway, then grabbed the bag and walked out of view.

"The second person you saw was a tough one for my friends to trace. He's the one you told me about earlier, right?"

"Yeah, that's him."

"His name's Franz Heimler now. Used to be Otto Dressler."

"He changed his name?"

Boris nodded. "Strangely enough, my friends found his info in the CIA's human resources database. He worked there for a year after college. He was a gifted recruit, but they did some digging and found out that he was secretly a member of a neo-Nazi group. He changed his name and moved on to private security for a large tech firm. Three years ago, he resigned and, as far as we can tell, became the head of security for the Magnus Foundation."

"Magnus?" Charles stared at Boris, bewildered. "You're saying the Magnus Foundation bombed her plane?"

"It looks that way. They now know the explosion originated in the cargo deck. Donovan was assigned to loading Flight 109 yesterday. The flight left about an hour after the footage. As for Fazal, he was a nineteen-year-old college student majoring in mathematics. Disabled, too. He was injured by a drone airstrike when he was a kid, which, of course, would give him a motive for hating America."

"Wow." Charles looked at Fazal's picture again, this time with a feeling that verged on compassion. How could he understand what someone like that had gone through? How would he feel about a country that was dropping bombs on his hometown, no matter how lofty their alleged motives?

"They're saying the Hand of God took advantage of his disability," Boris went on, "and that Fazal trusted the more relaxed protocols to sneak the bomb past security. It's nonsense, but, perhaps, believable nonsense.

"We've also heard that Fazal was a math prodigy. I don't understand the details, something about finding probabilities from data sets. He was invited to a STEM conference in New York hosted by NovaCorp, which just happens to be controlled by Alexander Magnus. They even paid for his airline tickets to make sure he was on that flight. Nice of them, wasn't it?"

"But why did they bomb the plane at all?" Charles cried. "Was it only to get to Nadia?" He wiped his eyes with an angry swipe of his hand. "I did what they asked, I told her nothing. She couldn't possibly have been a threat to them."

Boris wove the car through a line of truckers, one of whom gave a long and angry blast of his horn as the sable BMW slipped in front of it. "There are lots of mysteries here, Mr. Charles. A plane is destroyed on U.S. soil with all the passengers on board. Video footage is deleted from the TSA system. A government agency immediately leaks the name of the alleged bomber to the press, but it's the wrong person. The Foundation is behind all of this, but they aren't acting alone. We've heard a rumor that Magnus is handling a classified military contract. We haven't figured out the details. We still need more information."

"Oh, you need more information, do you?" Charles replied with sarcasm. "Isn't that why you let her meet with the Foundation in the first place?"

Boris glared at him but didn't take the bait. "I have more bad news for you, Mr. Charles. They're coming for you next. My friends and I need a week or two to check out a theory of ours. If we find what we're expecting, the next step is for you to join the Magnus Foundation."

"What?" he cried. "Are you insane? Don't answer that, you are insane. I thought you didn't want me to kill myself."

Boris whipped the car around a battered pick-up that was cruising at the minimum speed limit. "They won't kill you. Trust me."

"How do you know that? They weren't going to kill her either, were they? If we'd just told her the truth, Nadia would never have been on that plane in the first place. I trusted you because you acted like you knew everything, like you had them all figured out. But you didn't, did you? You tried to use her to spy on them and you got her killed."

Boris exhaled. "I might as well tell you. The fact is, I haven't abandoned hope."

"Hope?" He was stunned. "Hope for what?"

"Hope that Nadia is still alive."

Charles put his hand over his eyes. "Look, Boris, I want to believe that. Of course I do. But she was on that plane."

"Was she?" Boris glanced at him. "At first, yes, I blamed myself for sending her to those wolves. But the more I considered it, the less it added up. You're right, why blow up the plane just to kill Nadia? They could have killed her while she was with them in New York without risking anything. Whatever this bombing was about, it wasn't about her. And then there's you. Without Nadia, they would lose their control over you. We know you're the reason they were recruiting her."

Charles clenched his hands together. "I'm telling you, Boris, she was on that plane. They had a list of everyone who had checked in and was on board. She was on the list. She hasn't contacted either of us. If she was alive, she would let us know, wouldn't she?"

"Lists can be changed, Mr. Charles. As for contacting us, she would if she had any way of doing so. We should assume that she can't. But she's a clever girl, my Nadia. She'll find a way."

"I don't know." He shook his head. "I think you're in denial."

"Have it your way." Boris cleared his throat. "By the way, someone called you after the bombing, didn't they?"

"What? Oh, yeah, Thompson called when I was on my way home from the airport. How did you—no, never mind. You always know, don't you?"

"If only that were true. Anyway, we have a new phone for you. It's in the glove compartment there. A new number, one that only my friends and I know about."

Charles opened the glove box. The phone was the same model and color as the one Boris had drowned in the kitchen sink.

"Thanks."

"Don't mention it. So what did Thompson say to you?"

Charles tucked the phone into his pocket. "I let it go to voicemail. He said he heard about Nadia's plane and offered his condolences. He even offered to take over freshman bio, which, for him, is quite a sacrifice. He's my best friend, I guess."

"It's good to know who your friends are. Here's to hope, Mr. Charles." Boris reached into his jacket pocket and pulled out the infamous silver flask. "Care for a drink?"

"No thanks, I don't think we should—"

"I insist!" Boris shouted abruptly. "Drink!"

Vodka on the interstate at a hundred miles per hour. What could possibly go wrong?

He took the flask from Boris's hand. If nothing else, it might help him get some sleep. As he unscrewed the lid, he considered all the harm the contents of this little piece of metal had caused Nadia over the years.

He took a hesitant sip. His brow furrowed. He drank some more.

"It's—Boris, is this *water*?"

"Guilty!" Boris slapped the steering wheel. "Now you know all my secrets, Mr. Charles."

"Wait, does this mean you're not an alcoholic?"

Boris shrugged. "I came close after Elena left us, close enough to frighten myself. Liquid anesthesia, but it never fixes anything, does it? One night I poured a half-empty bottle of vodka down the drain, and I never looked back. It was the children, Nadia and Peter. I saw how they looked at me, how they feared what I was becoming. I soak the flask in vodka every now and then, and I'll take a swig of the real deal when I need the evidence on my breath."

"All those years..." Charles remembered something. Nadia had told him that Boris recovered soon after her mother left them and that he stayed sober until she went to college. "Why have you been faking it all this time?"

"Cover, Mr. Charles. As far as the world is concerned, alcohol destroyed any chances Boris Petrov had of working in intelligence. Every now and then I'll have a public display. I've had some brilliant performances over the years, especially the ones that get me fired from cover jobs. Believe me, you have no idea how liberating it is to look some slave-driving supervisor in the eye and tell him in slurred speech that he's nothing but a smoldering pile of unexcreted human putrescence!"

Charles set the bottle in a cupholder beneath the dash. "I still don't see why you didn't tell Nadia. Do you realize how much she suffered because of it?"

Boris sighed. "That was my greatest sacrifice. I'll never be able to make it up to her, but I had no choice. My work is dangerous, Mr. Charles, very dangerous. If someone gave her a lie detector test and asked her if I was a salesman, she'd say yes and pass with ease. She'd tell them I was a drunk and never could hold down a job. To her, it's the absolute truth, as it must be. They must believe her."

"Why are you telling me?"

"I need you to trust me. And maybe I'm ready to get out of the game. A final dance with Magnus, then Boris makes his exit, stage right. Perhaps."

Boris flipped on the sound system. Bizarre voices and instruments began creeping out of it.

"Um, Boris, what are we listening to?"

"The Incredible String Band. Soul of the Sixties, my friend."

"Hey, I think Nadia told me about this. Peter's favorite band, right?"

"Yes, but I'm a little partial myself. I hate the mundane, Mr. Charles. These patchouli-soaked flower people weren't afraid to be themselves. No prunes and prisms for the hippies."

"Are they playing a kazoo?"

"Yes, and why not?" Boris eyed him. "You have a problem with kazoos?"

Charles somehow survived the entirety of *The Hangman's Beautiful Daughter.* By the end, he was enjoying it, which made him wonder if all the stress and chaos had shoved him beyond the borders of sanity.

On the other hand, how often does a biologist get to hear music written from the perspective of an amoeba?

"We'd better find a place to sleep." Boris turned off the hippies. "Nothing fancy, just a roadside motel."

He turned onto an exit a few miles later, and Charles soon found himself lying under crisp, cool sheets next to a window unit that buzzed to life with alarming frequency. But he was exhausted, and even the addition of Boris's chainsaw snores from the other bed couldn't keep him up for long.

He awoke to find Boris sitting on a dingy, striped couch and tapping on his tablet.

"You awake?" Boris set the tablet down.

"What time is it?"

"Almost one in the afternoon. We should get moving."

"Let me shower first."

He grabbed some clothes and went into the bathroom. Water hissed as it sprayed from a showerhead caked with mineral deposits. The steam mounted, rising, blanketing him. It wasn't enough. No outer warmth could pierce the numbness inside him.

He put on his clothes and brushed his teeth. He stepped out into the frigid room. "There's something I forgot to tell you last night."

"What?" Boris asked.

"We got a buyer for our scanner."

"Alpha Financial?"

Charles nodded.

"When?" Boris crossed the room with quick strides. "When did you learn this?"

"Yesterday afternoon, a few hours before I went to the airport. Thompson said they'd called him."

"Ah, Thompson again. That's very good news, Mr. Charles. I congratulate you. How much will they pay you?"

"Thompson said it would be around a hundred million by the end of the year."

"A hundred million? Very good." The excitement that had swept over Boris's features vanished just as quickly. He went back to his bed and zipped up his suitcase. "Come on, Mr. Charles. Let's grab some lunch and hit the road."

"Any chance you can drive a little slower today?"

"Nope."

Charles packed his bag and threw it in the trunk. They drove to a diner near the hotel. He wasn't hungry, but he forced himself to eat half a sandwich and down some coffee. When he climbed back into the car, he latched onto the leather grab handle with both hands.

Boris pulled onto the interstate and turned on the radio. A piano reproduced the complex layers of Bach's *Well-Tempered Clavier* in surreal counterpoint to the racecar-style driving as they hurtled past eighteen-wheelers and minivans.

"You must get a lot of tickets."

"Never had one, Mr. Charles. I get pulled over every now and then, but I don't get tickets. It's a job perk for top-level salesmen like me."

"Ah."

"Could you light this for me?" Boris handed him a cigar, then fumbled around in his pants pocket for the lighter. The car swerved from side to side, which had the interesting side effect of making the sandwich Charles had just eaten resurface at the back of his throat. Boris found the lighter and handed it to him. It took Charles a few tries to get the thing lit.

"Thank you, Mr. Charles." Boris cracked the back windows to keep the smoke out and cranked up the air conditioning. "If you want something to do, there's a notebook in that bag behind your seat. I think you'll find it enlightening."

"What's in it?"

"Nadia's unpublished papers."

"Really?" Charles reached behind his seat and grabbed the bag.

There was a lined notebook with a red cover inside. It was filled cover to cover with Nadia's flowing cursive, which was an art form in itself.

"Take your time," Boris said. "It's a side of her very few people know anything about."

Charles nodded and began to read.

Boris got pulled over a half-hour later. The officer was a hefty brunette with her hair tied back in a severe ponytail. She glared at Boris as she took his license, then went back to her car to process it.

"I think you might actually get a ticket this time," Charles said.

"Nonsense."

The policewoman came back.

"Unreal." She handed Boris his driver's license. "Never seen that before in my life. Not right, if you ask me."

"You have a nice day, officer." Boris grinned at her as he rolled up his window. "We lost some time there. Better grab that handle again, Mr. Charles."

The sun was dipping below the western horizon when Charles finished the notebook.

"I had no idea." He shook his head. "It's incredible."

"Of course it's incredible. She's my daughter, isn't she?"

They had driven for almost nine hours before Boris pulled off onto a gravel road. The wooden sign at its entrance was illegible in the darkness. The road wound around and branched a few times before Boris turned into a makeshift driveway and parked the car.

A solitary incandescent bulb illuminated the framed porch of a weathered cabin. Charles opened his car door and stepped out into a star-filled night. He'd never seen so vast an array with the naked eye. He picked out a few of his favorite constellations and then hunted for the elusive contours of the fell Glousermorg.

The door to the cabin opened. The elderly man who emerged wore a black robe with a skull cap perched over his deep brown face. As he held up his hand in greeting, the sleeve of his robe dropped down to his elbow.

"Father Anatoly!" Boris ran up to the monk and knelt in front of him with his hands held upward in supplication. The monk made the sign of the cross over him, pronouncing the blessing in words too soft for Charles to hear.

Boris kissed the monk's hands, leapt to his feet, and ran back to Charles. He grabbed him by the arm and led him to the monk. "This is him, Father. This is the world-renowned Dr. Charles Ferguson, the man who will marry our Nadia. Mr. Charles, this is Father Anatoly. He's an old and trusted friend of the family. He helped Nadia through the darkest hour of her life."

Father Anatoly took Charles's hand, looked him in the eye, and smiled with the unfeigned pleasure of a child. The hair beneath his cap and in his straggly beard was silver and white with only a few flecks of youthful darkness. "I've heard many good things about you, Dr. Ferguson. You are very dear to our Nadia. They told me she died in that terrible plane crash, but I don't believe them. You don't either, do you?"

"I don't want to believe it, but I have no choice. She was on that plane."

Anatoly nodded. "Come inside, children."

They followed him into the cabin. The furnishings were spartan— an angular pine desk with a row of books on it and stacks of books beneath it, a square, worn table with chairs, and a standing cupboard with an assortment of teacups, saucers, and bowls, some of which were chipped. Three icons hung on the eastern wall. Christ in the center. On the left, Mary holding her Child. On the right, John the Baptist.

"Do you like my windows?" Father Anatoly motioned toward the icons. "Windows on the outermost walls of the universe. And what lies beyond? When we discover that, we find that these are not just windows, but also mirrors."

Boris leaned over and whispered in Charles's ear. "Don't worry, Mr. Charles, I have no idea what he's talking about, either."

A teapot whistled over the fireplace. Father Anatoly grabbed it with a towel and poured three cups of tea.

He gestured toward the table. "Come, you're just in time for tea. You have been through a great deal. I pray for you very often, Dr. Ferguson."

"Oh!" Charles cleared his throat. "I don't really, um—thank you, Father. And you can call me Charles."

Anatoly reached into one of the pockets of his robe and pulled out a black, looped rope tied with a multitude of small knots. It was an Eastern Orthodox prayer rope, like the one Nadia always kept in her purse.

"Please take this." Father Anatoly handed it to him. "Maybe you just see an old rope? An elder who is now a saint has taught us otherwise. This is in fact a gun, and you can take it everywhere you go. Open carry! And the little knots—your prayers—those are your bullets. You are heading to war, so you need to be armed."

He accepted the gift with as much grace as he could manage. How could he tell this kindly old monk, who from the sound of things had made such an impact on Nadia's life, that he wasn't sure there was a God in the first place?

Anatoly noticed his hesitation and broke into his disarming grin. "Don't worry, dear one. We learn the truth by doing it. God is a Person. Talk to Him. Take your gun, fire your bullets, see what happens. *Lord Jesus Christ, have mercy on me.* There's your ammunition."

Boris roared with laughter. "I've missed you, Father Anatoly. What a world this would be if we all lived like monks. Ah, but then there's the women, thanks be to God! We can't all do without them, can we? If we did, we'd run out of monks in no time, eh, Father?"

Father Anatoly swirled his tea with a spoon. "You mean to embarrass me, but I've had sex, too, you know."

Charles choked on his tea and spent the next minute coughing and sputtering. Even Boris was, for once, stunned into silence.

"In a way, it's how I became a monk," Anatoly continued. "I've only told this story twice, once to a priest, once to my spiritual father. That was many years ago. But the person it involves has now asked me to tell it to you, Boris, if you have no objection."

Boris kept his eyes on his teacup. "Of course not, Father. Whatever you want."

Father Anatoly took a sip of tea. For a few moments he was silent, apparently gathering his thoughts. "As Boris knows, I grew up in inner city Chicago. I was in high school in the late seventies, and for a young black man, the times they were a-changin'. I worked hard and earned a scholarship. When I got to college, I joined a fraternity."

"Okay, that's enough, Father." Boris winked at Charles. "I think we know the rest."

"I'm sure you do. The fraternity had an off-campus party to start the semester. All those years growing up, I'd resisted so many temptations to get to college, but there I was, and the privileged kids were doing the same drugs and drinking the same booze I'd seen on the streets, only they weren't getting arrested. I gave in. I smoked marijuana and got drunk for the first time. I met a girl, Julia. Things moved too fast. I didn't even know her last name. When I awoke the next morning, she was gone."

"Julia?" Boris's mirth had vanished. He sat up in his chair, his eyes locked on the monk.

"The frat boys made a game of it," Father Anatoly went on, "but one of the other freshmen, Joseph, said that he and Julia had grown up in the same suburb west of Chicago. Her last name was Bennett. Her parents were very strict, very religious."

"Julia Bennett?" Boris almost shouted the name. "You mean *our* Julia?"

Father Anatoly nodded. "The same."

"Sweet Saint—" Boris coughed into his hand. "Forgive me, Father. This is a lot to take in. Please, go on."

"We looked for her on campus. Her dormmates told us that Julia had thrown her belongings in her car that morning and gone home. I promised myself that I would contact her soon and make sure she was okay. I never did."

Boris grunted and shrugged his shoulders. "It worked out in the end. Don't be too hard on yourself."

"But that was only the beginning. Months later, Joseph came up to me one day after class. He told me—"

Father Anatoly's teacup rattled as he set it on its saucer. "He told me that Julia had just had an abortion. Forgive me, it has been many years since I've talked about this. It feels like I'm hearing the words for the first time. That would have been our child. Do you understand? Julia, she could have been my wife. I failed her. How afraid, how utterly alone she must have felt."

"Wait a minute." Charles finally put it together. "Julia Bennett… is she Julia Pearson? The caretaker Nadia told me about?"

"The same," Boris said. "Bennett was her maiden name. She's much more to us than a caretaker. She's family."

"I would have spared you this," Father Anatoly continued, "but she insisted that you hear everything. It's easier for her this way. Forgive me. After I graduated, I came here to join the monastery. The abbot refused. He insisted that I find Julia and make things right first, even if it meant marrying her."

"Good for him," Boris said.

"Yes, and good for me as well. She was living in her hometown, divorced, dating an abusive man who was cheating on her. The moment we began to talk, I realized how easily things had gone for me, how little I had suffered for my sin. After the abortion, her closest friend spread the story through town. Julia's father kicked her out of the house and hadn't spoken to her since. She went to Chicago, lived on the streets, and for a while, she became a prostitute."

"A prostitute!" Boris leapt from his chair. "Julia Pearson was a prostitute? And you had me bring her into my home? To let her take care of my children, of my own daughter?"

"Do you regret taking my advice?" Father Anatoly's voice had an edge to it. "Perhaps she hasn't lived up to your expectations? Or did she lead your daughter into a life of sin?"

"Well, no, it's nothing like that." Boris frowned and sat down again. "But Nadia, she was only a teenager."

Father Anatoly nodded. "And Julia was a very different person by the time you met her. We believe in second chances around here. Even for hypocrites like me, and we religious hypocrites are always the worst cases. Can you imagine? I was writing a thesis paper on ethics at the university while the woman whose life I had so casually destroyed was selling herself on a street corner a few blocks away."

"But you didn't know that, did you?" Charles asked.

"Only because I didn't want to know." Father Anatoly sighed. "When I finally met her again, I asked her what she had wanted to become when she went to college. She'd had a disabled uncle who made an impression on her growing up. Her father always had something more important to do than playing with his own kids, but Uncle Frank had time for everybody. She wanted to return the gift by working with the disabled."

"There, you see? The woman was always a saint." Boris was as solemn as a judge delivering a verdict.

"Yes, prostitutes can become saints," Father Anatoly replied. "I knew what I had to do. I got a job near the monastery. When I earned my first paycheck, I cashed it and drove straight to Julia's house. Her boyfriend had left her by then. I put the money in her hands. 'Go to college. I'll pay for it all. God be with you.'

"Four years later, she got her degree. The next day, I became a monk. We've kept in touch through the years, writing letters. She wrote to me when her second husband died, a Mr. Pearson. She had no children. She'd been volunteering with a special education program, but now she needed a paying job. I knew just the thing, a family that was suffering terribly. Julia Pearson was exactly what they needed."

"She never told us." Boris ran his finger along the rim of his teacup. "All this time, and she never said anything."

Father Anatoly smiled. "She worried about what you would think of her, and, perhaps even more, what you would think of me. I realized all those years ago that I could say with the patriarch of old, 'She is more righteous than I.' Julia has suffered much, and from that suffering has come an even greater love. You'll meet her tomorrow, Charles, and Peter as well."

He rose from his chair. "Now forgive me, but there is a vigil tonight that I must attend. The guest room is ready for you. Good night, dear children."

He blessed them and left the cottage.

"Monks!" Boris downed his tea. "More layers than an onion. I hope you sleep like the dead, Mr. Charles. I know I will."

A half hour later, Charles gazed up at the wooden beams in the ceiling and tried to filter out Boris's snores as they cut through the steady chorus of insects chirruping and humming through the open window beside his bed.

He'd stolen a peek at the books stacked under Father Anatoly's desk and discovered everything from spiritual works to recent books on cosmology and astrophysics. There were paper napkins repurposed as bookmarks in all of them. One set, *The Philokalia*, looked particularly worn.

He picked up the cell phone Boris had given him and tiptoed to the front porch. He sat on a coarse wooden step and fired up a web browser. Mobile Internet was spotty out in the wilderness. It took half a minute to load the front page of his favorite news site.

War and politics. He skipped the politics and glanced at the war. The Hand of God was committing unspeakable acts of brutality, the U.S. and her allies were droning targets in a half-dozen countries and training up local resistance to fight the terrorists.

In other words, business as usual.

He clicked on the Science and Technology section and breathed in sharply when the page loaded.

A picture of Thompson and Rius took up the top half of the screen. They were grinning from ear to ear and shaking hands for the camera.

OneScan Medical Device Goes Global. His eyes raced over the article. Multibillion-dollar production contract. United Nations and World

Health Organization offer full backing. Silicon Valley juggernauts provide mobile Internet for the scanner's use in third-world countries.

He read snippets from an interview with Thompson. "We just hope it makes the world a better place. I can't tell you how excited we are." The interviewer asked a question about Charles. "Yes, that's right, unfortunately he had to take a leave of absence for personal reasons. Our hearts go out to him, horrific tragedy…"

The co-inventor of OneScan, the article explained, had been dating Nadia Petrova, a geneticist who was a victim of the Flight 109 bombing. A brief recap of the bombing zeroed in on Fazal al-Najjar and his fanatical relatives.

He closed the browser.

He was now officially a millionaire. The thought brought him no comfort. All he wanted was Nadia. Could Boris and Father Anatoly be right? Could she still be alive?

The moon was out, pale and waning, a dwindling crescent. A few days more and all would be darkness.

Chapter Seven

Saints and Angels

CHARLES WAS AWOKEN by flecks of sunlight darting into the window through the branches of a hickory tree. A breakfast of fruit with bread and honey was waiting for him at the table, but there was no sign of Father Anatoly or Boris. After a brief meal and a shower, he stepped outside into a brisk, late summer morning.

His aging sedan was parked next to Boris's BMW in front of the cottage. The doors were unlocked, and a copied key was still in the ignition.

He sat in the driver's seat and removed the key. "This doesn't make any sense," he said to himself. "Who could have driven it here?"

He got out of his car and slipped into the woods, giving only the slightest thought to the direction in which his footsteps led him. He needed the subtle working of nature in his soul, the blades of wild grasses bending under a whispering breeze, the curves and sinews of tree limbs straining heavenward, the boisterous chittering of squirrels and birds, the spotted rabbit nibbling on foliage and eyeing him with swift, furtive glances.

He heard Boris's familiar voice somewhere ahead. He spotted him about fifty yards away. Boris was apparently talking to a bush. The bush suddenly emitted a puff of smoke.

"Having a chat with God?" Charles shouted.

"Not quite, Mr. Charles," Boris yelled back. "Come and meet one of the angels."

The bush turned out to be a soldier in camouflage who was squatting on his heels. He stood as Charles approached. He was a few inches shorter than Boris and looked to be in his early twenties. He gazed at Charles with calm, sober eyes that shone dark and gray as thunderclouds. An assault rifle, also camouflaged, was slung over his shoulder. He removed his head covering, an army green helmet beneath a canopy of twigs and leaves, to reveal a head of black hair shooting up in numerous chaotic spikes.

"I am Gavriel Abramovich." The man spoke with deliberation, his accent far more pronounced than Boris's. "Very good to be meeting you, Dr. Ferguson."

"The pleasure's mine," Charles replied. Gavriel tossed the remnant of his cigarette on the ground and shook hands with him.

"Gavriel leads a small team that's been keeping an eye on Peter," Boris said. "They'll do the same for you while I'm gone. But please, Mr. Charles, don't tell the monks. These aren't the sort of angels they're looking for here at the monastery."

Gavriel grunted and lit up another cigarette.

"That's my car back there, right?" Charles asked. "How'd that happen?"

"Yes, yes." Boris muttered. "That's your miserable, moth-eaten four-cylinder. Ah, but it's reliable, isn't it, Mr. Charles? Like tooth decay. I had one of the junior angels drive it over last night. Now that's a job for the rookies, worse than latrine duty. You know what that car reminds me of? Nursing homes. Prune juice. Social Security checks."

"Thanks, Boris. Glad you approve."

Boris chuckled. "I'll take you to meet Peter and Julia. They should be at the farm by now. To tell you the truth, Mr. Charles, I'm afraid of these monks! What would happen to me if I started listening to them? A slight hesitation at the wrong time, a little mercy on the wrong person, and Boris is a dead man. Maybe we'll find religion when we retire, eh, Gavriel?"

He rattled off something in Russian that brought a grin to Gavriel's stony features. The soldier nodded to Charles, shook Boris's hand, and tromped off into the forest.

"He's getting antsy." Boris said. "I'll have to reassign him soon. Smokes like a train engine, and he's only twenty-four. Nasty habit." He flicked away some ashes from the end of his cigar. "Let's have a look at the holy farm. Don't let the pious robes and moss-covered aphorisms fool you, Mr. Charles. These sanctimonious types are always cutthroat entrepreneurs, especially the nuns. Gavriel told me they just gobbled up some more acreage for their little project."

He wasn't kidding. Charles had expected the garden project to be small-scale, maybe the size of a football field. According to the newly repainted sign that shot up like a scarecrow amidst a grass-covered parking area, the Monastic Farm of the Brothers of St. Anthony the Great and the Sisters of St. Mary of Egypt now comprised fifty-seven acres. At the moment, every square inch appeared to be swarming with school children.

"Merciful Saint Monica!" Boris parked the BMW next to a tightly bunched herd of dusty, yellowish-orange buses from a Chicago school district. "There must be hundreds of the little imps, all scampering around out there like a plague of locusts. Our Peter will be having one of his good days. He's a child himself, Peter. Before we get out, Mr. Charles, I want you to promise that you'll say nothing about Nadia or the bombing to him. Not a word while you're here at the monastery. Can you do that for me?"

"Sure, Boris, if that's what you want."

Boris nodded. "I'll tell him one day if I must, but not until we're certain."

Charles spotted an unusual pair of adults harvesting carrots with a throng of schoolchildren. One was a woman in blue jeans and a sweat-shirt, her long black hair woven into dozens of braids that rested on her back. She waved at them as they approached. Upper sixties, maybe, but she wore the years well.

The second of the pair was a clean-shaven twenty-something who looked up with a boyish grin, hurled the carrots he was holding into the air, and bolted towards Boris at full speed.

"Papa, Papa!" His voice was wild in its eagerness. He threw his arms around Boris and capered about in excitement.

"Peter, my darling boy."

There was no mistaking the gentleness with which Boris returned his son's embrace. Nor could Charles miss the signs he had expected—the peculiar tone of Peter's voice, the distinctive facial features. Peter had Down syndrome.

"Peter, this is Mr. Charles, the one our Nadia loves. She told you about him on the phone, do you remember?"

"Hello," Peter said shyly, his eyes flitting towards Charles's face and then turning to the ground. He extended a hand.

"Good to meet you, Peter." Charles returned the handshake with warmth. "I've heard a lot of good things about you."

"Yeah." Peter clasped his hands behind his back. "I better get back to work." He flashed a sudden grin before he raced back to carrot-picking with the kids.

"I love that boy," Boris said. "But where are my manners? This, as I'm sure you've guessed, is Mrs. Julia Pearson."

Julia moved right past Charles's handshake and wrapped him up in a hug.

"So you're the one?" She held him at arm's length and looked him over. Her motherly tenderness instantly struck a chord deep within him, resonating with something long buried, long forgotten. "I've been praying for you since the day I first laid eyes on Nadia. Give her a good one, Lord. That's what I always asked, and I knew He would. And there's the old rascal!" she added as Boris gave her a peck on the cheek. "Peter's missed you something fierce. You should come out and see him more often."

"Ah, yes, Farmer Boris." Boris folded his arms over his chest. "I'll live here and pick carrots and try not to terrify your impressionable little friends. But I doubt the PTA will approve of me. I went to a PTA meeting once. Do you remember, Julia?"

"All I remember is CPS showed up the next day and nearly took your children."

"That's right, I forgot about Mr. CPS! We had a nice little chat in the backyard, me and Mr. CPS. He was a dapper government man with an aluminum nametag on his starched shirt pocket. Prunes and prisms, Mr. Charles, just your type. We talked about proper etiquette and PTA meetings and stray bullets and premature funerals, and then he decided to let the kids stay with me. An excellent choice under the circumstances."

"Lord have mercy!" The aquamarine hair clips on Julia's braids rattled against each other as she shook her head. "You've been telling that old story so long you probably believe it yourself."

"And why wouldn't I?" Boris rumbled defensively.

"Well, for starters, you know as well as I do that *Mr. CPS*, as you keep calling him, was just old Bill Avery that used to live over on Hawthorn Lane."

"So what if it was Bill Avery?" he said. "Mr. CPS sounds better."

"Yeah, well here's the thing. Now you did take Bill out back and talk crazy to him, I'll give you that. But you seemed to have forgotten about what happened next."

"Nothing happened next!"

"Is that a fact?" Julia put her hands on her hips, her espresso brown eyes dancing with mirth. "Let me set the record straight, *Mr.* Boris Petrov. You just about scared that poor man to death. Put yourself in his shoes. He weighed a hundred and ten pounds and never harmed a flea, and now some six-foot-four Russian says he's about to bury him in the backyard."

"What does that have to do with anything?"

"I'm getting there. Bill came trembling into the house—it was neat as a pin, mind you—and told me he didn't know what he was supposed to do. He said you were a lunatic, said maybe it was his duty to take your kids away before they ended up having one of those premature funerals. That man was convinced you were going to kill him if he did it, but he said he had to think about the children first, and besides, he figured he'd already lived long enough anyhow."

"He said that?"

"Mm-hm." She stared down Boris like he was a reprobate five-year-old. "So let me tell you how it really went down. I don't want Charles here to get the wrong idea. I told Mr. Avery to have a seat at the dining table and we'd talk it over. I brought him a piece of double fudge pie with ice cream on the side—"

"You gave him the double fudge pie?" Boris's eyes widened.

"You know that's right. Sometimes you got to bring out the big guns. I sat down next to him and told him straight up that you were just an oversized puppy dog, all bark and no bite."

Judging from his ominous silence, Boris did not appear to be flattered by her character portrait.

"Yessir, that's what I told him," she went on mercilessly. "Said you were just a big fuzzy Russian bear, that you could growl with the best of them, but deep down you were a forty-year-old kid that still liked to eat popcorn and cheer for the White Sox."

"I hate the White Sox."

"I was improvising!" She flung her hands in the air. "Trying to save your children, remember? I said you were just acting ridiculous, and then I told him that if Nadia and Peter wouldn't be safe with Boris Petrov, they wouldn't be safe anywhere in the world."

"Hmph. That part was true, anyway."

"Well, by the time John finished a second helping of pie—Lord knows where those skinny people put it!—he was ready to drop the whole thing. 'Besides,' he said, 'as long as you're around, Mrs. Pearson,

I guess they'll be all right.' And that, Mr. Boris, was that. Had nothing to do with your Godfather nonsense and everything to do with my grandma's double fudge pie."

Boris glared at her for a moment and then broke into his deep-chested laugh. "I surrender, you win! Watch and learn, Mr. Charles. Never tangle with women. And whatever you do, don't buy that nonsense about gender equality. We're outgunned and outflanked in every encounter. But Julia, what's this I hear about you and Father Anatoly? It seems your quaint little tale about Mr. CPS and double fudge pie isn't the only thing you've been hiding from me."

He was so flippant about it that she was stunned.

"He told you, then?" Julia gave Boris a searching look and her features softened. "And you're not mad. Thank you, Jesus. You should have known from day one, but I was afraid. Too many people never look at you the same way once they know. I love working with Peter, being a grandmother to Nadia. I didn't want anything messing that up. And I sure didn't want you looking down on Jack. I mean Father Anatoly. You understand, don't you?"

Boris shrugged. "You're my second mother. As for Peter, what would my son be without you? And Nadia…"

"Is there any news?" Julia lowered her voice.

"Only hints," Boris said. "Don't give up hope."

She nodded. "I've been trying to keep myself calm for Peter's sake, but it's tearing me up inside. Especially seeing you, Charles. She and I had a good long talk on the phone just last week. She sounded so excited, so full of hope. She said she was going to bring you out to meet me and Peter. I just knew you two were going to get married. And now—"

She faltered and stifled a sob.

"Please, Julia." Boris glanced over at Peter, who was well out of earshot.

"I'm sorry." She dabbed her eyes with the back of her hand. "I'll be all right now. Don't you worry."

Peter and the boys around him burst into laughter.

"Looks like they've turned the corner," she said. "The first few weeks of school, the newer boys always tease Peter and pick on him when they come out here. He never fights back, though it hurts him more than he'll ever show. The older ones stick up for him, though, and eventually they're all friends. He loves the children. Always has."

They joined in the leisurely harvest, picnicking in the grass for lunch with sandwiches and chips that Julia had brought. The weather was warm and fine, the air fresh and rejuvenating. They heard the lowing of the cows from a nearby field. Some ducks wandered over for handouts.

The kids lined up and tramped back to the buses at two o'clock, every one of them taking home a grocery bag filled with handpicked vegetables and fruit, eggs from the poultry, and cheese curds from the dairy.

"The kids are the whole reason for the farm," Julia told him. The two of them were harvesting a row of beets together, a monotony that Charles found inexplicably satisfying. Boris and Peter were working on a row of carrots a few yards away. "This place wasn't cheap, either. It's those sisters over at St. Mary's." She leaned close to him. "They're loaded."

"Really?" Charles arched an eyebrow. "A little odd for nuns, isn't it?"

She straightened herself and stretched her back. "Well, they're in the chocolate business. Not that cheap junk they sell on the grocery aisles. High-dollar stuff, the kind with funny names on the outside and alcohol on the inside. Only they don't call it alcohol. They call it *liqueur*. The rich old ladies like to pretend it's dignified, but I'll tell you one thing, you drink a pint of the sauce those sisters put in their chocolates and you'll be howling at the moon. They got a brand going, got a partner in manufacturing, and now their convent pulls in five million a year. Can you believe it? Five million dollars a year!"

"I went into the wrong line of work."

"You and me both!" She laughed and went back to picking beets.

He suddenly remembered that he was a millionaire himself, assuming the money from Alpha Financial had come through.

"Funny thing is," Julia went on, "every blessed one of these monastics took a vow of poverty. So what in the world are they supposed to do with all that money? They tossed around some ideas, but nothing stuck until they heard Jack's plan. Now, you'll have to forgive me. I know it's supposed to be Father Anatoly, but he's always been Jack in my mind. Besides, I'm Methodist, so I guess they can't do much about it, now can they?"

"Do you see him much?" Given the couple's past and Anatoly's present, he didn't know if this was thin ice or not.

"Not really." There wasn't a hint of regret in her voice. "The abbot knows our story, and he figures it's best if we kept to our letters for the most part. I see Jack on holidays and such. Fact is, we've been pen pals so long I hardly know what to make of him when he's standing right in front of me. Those letters changed my life. Especially early on, back when he was putting me through college. Lord have mercy! I didn't have a lick of sense back in those days. But I'm just yapping now. What were we talking about?"

"You said he had a plan for the money."

"That's right. First off, he said they should toss a little up to the diocese since they're always whining about being broke. Send half of what's left over to help all those refugees they keep praying for and use the other half to build a farm. Now Jack, he grew up on the streets of Chicago. He knows how few of those kids will ever see anything in their entire lives but gangs, guns, and concrete. So he gets an idea to bring the kids out of the city. Teach them about something everybody used to know, farming. Give them some time in God's playground. Let them see the miracles for themselves. Spring rain falling on the crops, sunshine on a patch of wildflowers, planting seeds, the turning of the seasons. Who knows? Maybe a few of them will get a new perspective on life."

"There are worse ways to spend a fortune."

"You got that right. But the schools weren't so sure about it at first. It's a messed-up world we're living in. They came around, though. The teachers come out with the kids, and we've got quite a few parents now, too. And the monastery pays for some extra security, mostly off-duty cops. The nuns can be out here when there's kids, but not the monks. That was the deal, and it seems to be working."

They came to the end of the row. Charles wiped the sweat from his brow and fanned his shirt.

"I should do this more often." He stretched out arm muscles that were beginning to ache.

"You and me both. Seems like everything I eat goes straight to my thighs."

They sat down under the shade of a maple tree and guzzled iced tea from a cooler. The work had brought a calmness to him, mind and body.

"Maybe this farm of ours is just a drop in the bucket." Julia leaned back against the tree trunk and shut her eyes. "But you know something? Put enough of those drops together, and you've got yourself a flood."

Boris, Peter, and Charles ate dinner with the seventeen monks who lived at the monastery. Most of them were older, foreign, and brimming over with expansive facial hair. Their meals were as sparse as their furniture. Charles's first dinner—or so the monks called it—consisted of two chunks of bread with olive oil, a bowl of soup with freshly picked vegetables, and a whole cucumber.

There was no conversation. A younger, balding novice read a passage from a sacred text while the rest of them listened. The language was plain enough, but for some reason the actual meaning was hard for Charles to follow.

Instead, he was drawn into an unusual state of heightened awareness. It was a phenomenon that deepened during his time among the monks. The dull scraping of a chair against the concrete floor, the silvery clinking of spoons against pewter bowls, the repressed coughs and snuffles of a spindly old monk with hay fever, the parabolic contours of the reader's solitary voice—every individual event was thrust into the foreground by the overarching stillness of the monastery.

He and Boris walked back to the cottage alone while the monks began Compline.

"How do these people stay alive?" Boris lit a cigar. "At least Julia's around to make sure you don't starve to death. I'll have to hit up the Panda King on my way out of town. Their Szechuan chicken will put hair on your chest."

"You're leaving?"

"I'm a busy man."

"Where are you going?"

"Where I'm needed. Don't worry, Mr. Charles, I'll be in touch. Make the most of your time here. The devils are coming, so you'd better prepare yourself. And don't let these old men turn you into a monk. Remember Nadia!"

Boris ducked into his car and drove off. Charles caught a blur of motion in the distance as a militant angel stood and tromped off into the woods, a machine gun strapped to his back.

Chapter Eight

Double Cross

Boris Petrov peered through a slit in the blinds with a pair of military-grade binoculars. "That's him, right? The black shirt?"

"Affirmative." Kenjiro Nakamura's voice sounded even more formal than usual through Boris's earpiece.

They only had one shot at this. The local team's intel said that the target would be leaving any day now. Joining the hunt for Mr. Charles.

"Any ghosts?"

"One."

"ID on the ghost yet?"

"Negative. Should get it soon."

Boris bit back the word that leapt to the tip of his tongue. A ghost would complicate things. They would have to pull it away from the target long enough for the pitch. Five minutes at least, and it would have to be discreet. Even the ghost couldn't realize what had happened.

"Send me a visual," he said.

Seconds later, his phone emitted a soft chirp. He checked the message. The attached image was of a short, stocky man with close-shaven hair. Ex-military.

"Are those burn marks on his cheek?" he asked.

"Affirmative," Kenjiro said. "We're hoping that will speed up the ID."

"There's not enough time. We both know Magnus wipes them off the grid. It could take hours."

Boris turned from the window and sat on the edge of the hotel bed.

The ghost was a middle-aged male on assignment in a college town. Surrounded by an ocean of youthful energy, he would have had no time to socialize. Their orders were always strict. Who knows how long he'd been away from his home territory, how many days filled with nothing but the tedious work of stalking the target?

A Magnus Foundation ghost typically held two jobs. They protected Magnus assets, but they also monitored them. If there was even a hint of treachery, the ghost had orders to kill the asset.

The plan of attack was obvious. The Chemist would hate it, but she knew how the game worked. You did whatever it took to win.

"Kenjiro?"

"Sir?"

"Where's the target going?"

"Lunch, sir. Coffee shop a block down on Third Street."

"I know the one. He eats there every day?"

"Most days."

"How long will he be there?"

"At least an hour. He doesn't go back in until three. Looks like he had a book with him. For the most part, if he's not working, he's either playing an MMO or reading fantasy."

"Playing a what?"

"MMO. Online video game, sir."

This was it, then. Their only chance. The ghost wouldn't follow the target into a small café like that. It would be too obvious, risk exposure.

"Is the Chemist in town?"

"Affirmative. I believe she's on her shift at the restaurant."

"Contact her, tell her we need her on this one. She'll know what it means. There's an apartment building across the street. Get her a ground floor unit, one that's facing the street."

"Yes, sir."

The Chemist was brilliant, the best in her field of expertise. She had a passion for her work, but when push came to shove, she had to use every resource at her disposal. It was the same for all of them. Still, she wouldn't give in without a fight.

His phone rang a minute later. It was the Chemist. He answered in Hokkien.

"This is Boris."

"I don't want to do this."

"I know."

"Isn't there someone else? Sarah, maybe? She…doesn't seem to mind this sort of thing."

"Sarah's in D.C. right now. Top priority intel."

A pause.

"I don't want to have to do anything with him," she said at last. "These kind of people—they're always disgusting."

"You won't have to go very far. We only need five minutes. Ten, if you can."

"That's a lot of time."

"True, but I have an idea." Boris drummed his fingers against his knee. Who should play second fiddle? There were several options.

"What's the plan?" she asked.

"Do you remember that assignment in Guangzhou? With the loan shark?"

"Wait, you mean—"

"Exactly."

Another pause.

"All right." He could almost feel the tension flowing out of her. "I can do that. Who's my love interest?"

"I think we'll go with the Queen's man," he said. "It would mean that you like older men, and the ghost looks like he's in his early forties.

Kenjiro will call you with the details. I need you there in exactly seventeen minutes. Do you have clothes that will work?"

"I was planning to hit the gym after my shift, so I'll go with that. And Boris?"

"Yeah?"

"You owe me."

"I'll keep that in mind."

⁂

Derrick Jennings tapped his foot against the pavement and checked his watch. The egghead was just sitting down inside, which meant Derrick would be stuck here on this park bench for a very long time. The egghead had lugged a brand new, thousand-page book about elves and unicorns into the café. Nothing on the man's schedule, nothing better to do. Probably never been on a date in his life.

Derrick hated being on the Outside. Hated jobs like this.

It was different in Headquarters. He was with Security, and Security could do whatever they wanted if they stayed inside the lines. Keep the old man happy, don't mess with Control, don't talk to the Progress pansies unless you've got orders. Do those three things, and you would live like a king. And the women—well, most of them were plenty healthy when they first came off the ships. Before Control got involved.

He'd been on the Outside for a month now. Four weeks of eighteen-hour shifts tailing assets. Not a chance to breathe. He'd get to do a little hunting after this, he and the egghead and the Chief. That was a change, anyway.

"Mind if I sit next to you?"

A young woman's voice. He glanced up.

College age, maybe mid-twenties. Asian. Beads of sweat on that smooth forehead. Must have been jogging. Her form, figure, face—his mouth went dry just looking at her. She seemed distracted. Barely paying attention to him.

"Sure, you can sit here. Be my guest."

"Thanks. I always take a breather before I head indoors."

She sat on the far side of the bench, then she crossed her long, slender legs. He could feel his heart beating in his chest.

Her phone erupted into a rave music ringtone. She swiped on the screen to answer. "What do you want?" She sounded angry.

Derrick looked the other way and pretended he wasn't listening.

"I told you to stop calling me," she snapped. "It's over, Mike. It's been three weeks. Leave me alone."

So she was single.

"You always say that, and it's always the same. Stop calling me." She hung up and stretched her arm across the top of the bench. Her fingertips were nearly touching his shoulder. "I hate my life."

"I'm sorry to hear that," he replied.

He could have slapped himself. He used to be good at this, but he'd lost his touch. It was too easy in Headquarters. No work involved, no playing hard to get. They just wanted to survive.

"He's such a jerk!" she said. "He acts like he owns me, but when we go out he's staring at all the other girls."

He grinned. "Young men are fools."

"He's not a young man. He's forty-five."

So she liked older men.

She was looking at him with soulful brown eyes. "I don't know what to do," she said. "I shouldn't be with him. But when I'm not, I get…lonely, I guess."

"It's tough. I know how that goes."

She bent over and tied her shoe. Her T-shirt was loose around her shoulders. She was wearing a black sports bra underneath. He exhaled through pursed lips and glanced across the street at the diner. If it wasn't for the asset…

"Are you married?" she asked suddenly.

He blinked. "Me? Nope, never have been."

Those brown eyes were locked onto him. There were some sparks here.

"Do you want to do something together?" she asked.

He rubbed his hand against the stubble on his chin. He really wanted to do something together.

"I—hey, listen, I'm really sorry. I wish I could, but I can't. I'm, ah… waiting for someone."

"Is it a girl?"

"Hardly. Business meeting."

"When are they coming?"

"I don't know. Might be a while. At least another half hour, probably longer."

She rose and pointed at the apartment building behind them. "I live right here, on the ground floor. See that window there? Why don't you come in for a drink? You can look out the window if you want."

He took a deep breath, cast one last glance at the coffee shop, and got to his feet. "All right, but only for a few minutes."

She smiled at him, warm and inviting, her teeth like pearls. The women he had access to in Headquarters were never this confident. The Reaps kept their eyes to the ground. As they should.

She pulled a key out of her shorts pocket and worked the lock for a few moments. "I hate this thing. It always gets stuck."

"Mind if I try?"

"Go for it."

He slid the lock open. "Nothing to it."

She patted his arm. "You must have the magic touch."

She sailed past him. Her ponytail lightly brushed against the scar on his cheek as it swung to one side. Women usually gaped at that scar, but it didn't seem to bother her at all.

It was a one-bedroom apartment with an open layout. The decor was urban and top-notch.

"Have a seat." She pointed to a black leather couch. "Martini?"

"You serious? I'd love one."

He leaned back and watched her moving around in the kitchen. He could watch a woman like her all day. The window blinds were closed. He wasn't about to open them.

It took her a few minutes to get the drink ready. She sat down next to him, so close her thigh was touching his. She handed him a wine glass. He took a sip and set it on the coffee table. Dry martini with a pair of olives. High quality stuff.

"Man, that tastes just right."

She rested her hand on his knee. "What's your name, anyway? I forgot to ask you earlier."

"Derrick." The word was out of his mouth before he realized what he'd done. At least he hadn't told her his last name. He needed to get control of himself. He reached for the martini. "Derrick Foster. What's yours?"

"You didn't come in here for a drink, did you, Derrick?"

The glass in his hand froze halfway to his lips. He set it down again. She reached over and began removing his suit jacket.

"A gun!" She scrambled to her feet and backed away toward the kitchen. She cupped her hands over her mouth, and those deep brown eyes turned wide with shock.

For a split second, he considered using the gun. It would be so easy. He'd just point it at her, and she'd do whatever he said.

But that was too much like Headquarters. It felt better this other way. The real thing for a change. Nothing forced, nothing coerced.

"No, it's not like that, nothing to worry about," he said in a soothing voice. "I'm kind of a cop."

"Do you have a badge?"

"No."

She crossed her arms over her chest. "I don't like guns."

"It's fine, relax." He got up and walked over to the doorway. He slowly removed the handgun from its chest holster and placed it on an end table. "I'll leave it over here, okay? I forgot I had it on me, sorry."

"You said you were a cop?"

He exhaled. "I work in private security. To tell you the truth, the only time I've used that gun is for target practice."

A bald lie, but it worked. She lowered her arms. "I didn't mean to get so upset. They just make me nervous. Here, let me turn this off first. Last thing I want right now is another phone call from the jerk."

She picked up her cell phone from the counter, tapped it for a minute, then sat back on the couch and patted the cushion next to her. "Let's try this again, shall we?"

"Sounds good to me." He went over and sat beside her. She grabbed his martini and took a long swig.

"Where were we, Derrick?"

She handed him the martini. Her fingers toyed with his shirt collar as he took another sip.

"Are you done?" she asked.

He set the glass down. "Yeah."

She leaned close to him. He could feel her warm breath on his face, smell the fragrance of perfume on her neck. She kissed his lips gingerly and backed off. They locked eyes. Suddenly her mouth was covering his, her kisses fierce, her hands running along his chest—

The front door slammed open. The girl shrieked and pulled away.

Derrick looked up to find himself staring down the barrel of a 9mm Glock. A Glock with a silencer.

"I knew it!" the man yelled from the doorway. Middle-aged, British, receding hairline, face like some old-time butler. Holding that gun like he knew what he was doing.

The man edged inside and kicked the door shut with the back of his foot. "I knew you were cheating on me."

"How could I be cheating on you?" the girl shouted back. "We're not even dating."

Derrick stood up slowly, his hands in the air. "Hey, pal, let's just calm down."

"Shut up."

The newcomer aimed the Glock straight at Derrick's forehead. Steady hand, too, despite the antics.

"Take it easy," Derrick said. "I'm leaving right now, all right?"

His own gun was right next to the front door. All he had to do was pretend to leave, and then—

As if reading Derrick's mind, the man grabbed the gun and tucked it under his belt. "You won't be needing that."

Derrick shook his head. "Hey, mister, I'm with the police."

"Good for you. You're police, I'm special forces."

The guy probably wasn't lying about being in special forces. He had some kind of military-looking tattoo on his forearm, and he wasn't showing a trace of fear.

"It's not what it looks like," Derrick said. "I just met her a few minutes ago. I don't even know her name, swear to God. She asked me to come in here, she gave me the drink, then she was all over me."

"Oh, so my girlfriend's a prostitute now, is that what you're saying? You think I'm an idiot?"

"I hate you, Michael," the girl screamed. "It was me, you hear? I wanted a real man for once instead of a manipulative psychopath."

The man shifted his aim. He was pointing at the girl now, at her chest. He came farther into the room, still watching Derrick out of the corner of his eye.

"You're not really with the police, are you?" he said.

Derrick swallowed. He needed to think fast. "Nope, I'm just security. Rent-a-cop, you know?"

"Well, listen here, rent-a-cop. You're going to sit down on that couch for a few minutes while I decide what I'm going to do with you. With both of you."

"Sorry, but I—I got to get going." Derrick took a step toward the door. There was a sharp, high-pitched pop as the stranger's Glock fired through the suppressor. The bullet could have shaved off the tip of Derrick's nose. Two inches away at most, judging by the hole in the wall.

Derrick sat down on the couch.

"That's your last warning, rent-a-cop." The man's voice was calm. Not a good sign.

Derrick could hear a clock ticking on the wall above his head. The minutes passed by with agonizing slowness. The girl sat on the kitchen floor, leaning back against one of the cabinets, stone-faced. The man just stood there, looking at Derrick, looking at the girl, gun lowered but ready.

Derrick started to sweat. If anything happened to the asset while he was stuck in here, he'd be a dead man. Heimler would do it himself. He'd throw one of those Garden Parties of his, only this time Derrick would be on the other side with the Reaps. Part of the entertainment.

"All right," the man said at last. "I believe you, rent-a-cop. She's got a way about her. Keeps me on edge. You can leave but listen up. If you tell anybody what's going on in here, I'll blow her brains out. Keep your mouth shut, and she'll live. You never saw her, you never came here."

Derrick stood up with his hands raised. "Yeah, sure, whatever you want. I'll be out there, right on that park bench. You can watch me, okay?"

"Go." The man had turned back to the girl. He raised the gun and pointed it at her. "As for you…"

Derrick rushed out of the apartment, slammed the door behind him, and hustled back to the park bench. He checked his watch. Almost thirty minutes had passed. Was the asset still there? He got up, crossed the street, and looked through the window as surreptitiously as he could manage.

He was there all right. Lost in Nerd Paradise with the elves and the unicorns. Derrick let out a deep sigh, crossed the street again, and sat on the park bench. The girl probably wouldn't make it out of that place alive, but that was none of his business. As long as Magnus and Heimler never found out about this, he could survive. He'd dodged a bullet, no two ways about it.

Speaking of which, he'd better find himself another gun before Heimler showed up.

✺

The Chemist's phone rang as she stepped out the back door of the apartment. She'd already called her uncle to let him know she was okay. Not that he was worried. Boris and her uncle went way back. They trusted each other.

She answered the phone. "Hello, boss."

"You all right?" Boris asked.

"I'm fine. Well, I had to kiss him, but I tried not to think about it. Kind of like when you eat a snail. Sanderson was Oscar-worthy."

"He's a man of many talents."

"I didn't know he could shoot like that." She glanced back over her shoulder, but there was nothing to worry about. Sanderson was cleaning up the apartment and patching the bullet hole in the wall. The ghost was back on his park bench. "I think the ghost's first name is Derrick. Not so sure about the last. He said Foster, but he was being careful by then."

"Excellent work," Boris said. "Kenjiro's here with me. They're on it."

"Did you have enough time?" she asked. "Did it work?" She knew how it went. If any part of an operation went south, all the effort was for nothing.

"Enough time?" Boris switched to his Russian accent. "Ha! Kenjiro, did you hear that? The Chemist wants to know if we had enough time. I could have snuck in a few games of chess with the target, read him my favorite chapter from *War and Peace*, and signed him up as a contestant on *The Next American Genius*. The man was clay in our hands. He has taken a solemn oath and transmogrified himself into a thirty-year-old Boy Scout."

The Chemist grinned. "You're nuts, Boss. But you still owe me."

"I'm sure you'll think of something."

"Mom and Dad like Palm Beach. I don't mind it myself."

"Fair enough. Next time we get a breather."

"Dad's never flown first class, you know."

Boris broke into his deep laugh. "That poor, deprived man."

Chapter Nine

Paradise Lost

THE SOUND OF a fist banging on the front door jolted Charles out of a dream. He rubbed his eyes and checked his phone. Six in the morning. Day four at the monastery.

Father Anatoly was already at the chapel with the other monks for one of the services. It was either the Midnight Office, which, oddly enough, took place at five thirty every morning, or the Divine Liturgy that followed.

The pounding on the door continued, insistent. Another pilgrim wanting to see Father Anatoly. The elderly monk was apparently a minor celebrity in some Eastern Orthodox circles. These people never left him alone.

Charles swung his feet off the bed, stretched his arms and back, and ambled to the front door. He worried about the visitors. They could be anyone, and they could come from anywhere, including the Magnus Foundation.

He opened the door. On the front porch stood a man in his late thirties or early forties, hair showing streaks of gray, face downcast. Purple rings encircled his eyes, splotches darkened his lightly tanned skin.

"Where's the monk?" The man ran a hand through a head of black curls. Greek, perhaps, but it was hard to tell. Many of Father Anatoly's visitors were immigrants from the Orthodox world—the Mediterranean, the Middle East, Eastern Europe, Russia. Others were the offspring of immigrants, and a handful were dyed-in-the-wool Americans, whatever that meant.

"I think he's at one of the services."

The man sniffed. "Are you going to let me in or not?"

"Oh, um, sure. Be my guest." Charles stepped aside.

The visitor barged into the room, yanked back a chair, and sat with his arms crossed over his chest. "When will he be back?"

"Usually after breakfast, sometime around eight. You're welcome to go down to the service if you want." Pilgrims usually crammed all the church services they could into their brief visits.

"No." The man shook his head with vehemence. "No services."

"Ah." What was he supposed to do with this person? "Listen, I'm not with the monastery or anything, so I guess you can just make yourself at home. I'm going to take a shower and get dressed. They'll have breakfast down at the refectory around seven thirty."

The man inclined his head in acknowledgement but said nothing.

Charles went back to the guest room and cleaned up. Then he took a walk in the woods and headed to the refectory. Breakfast was like all the other meals at the monastery, enough to eat, but never too much.

The spiritual reading that morning involved a favorite topic among the monks, something they called watchfulness.

Attentive, the mind having descended into the heart, observe your thoughts as they come and go. In this way, your Prayer never ceasing, you will learn how to guard the inner heart, how to repel the evil thoughts...

After the meal, he and Father Anatoly walked back to the cottage together.

"You have a visitor," Charles said.

"I'm not surprised." The skin beside the elderly monk's eyes wrinkled into crow's feet as he smiled. "For your sake, I was hoping for a vacation! You've been here four days now, and we've barely had a moment to talk."

"You're a popular man."

"The world is hungry. Here you can find bread."

The visitor was right where Charles had left him, his brows lowered like a pair of storm clouds, his jaw clenched firmly.

"Good morning, child," Father Anatoly said as he entered the room.

The man stood but did not move forward to receive the monk's blessing. He sat down again abruptly.

Unfazed by the unusual behavior, Father Anatoly walked over to the table and took a seat. "Don't leave, Charles. Come and join us."

Charles took a deep breath and went inside. He'd already had enough of their insolent guest.

"Would you like some tea?" Father Anatoly asked.

"No tea," the man snarled.

"You have a question to ask me?"

"Not a question. A declaration. I've lost my faith. I'm no longer a Christian. I don't believe in God."

Charles shifted in his chair. Had Father Anatoly known what the man would say? Is this why the monk had asked him to stay?

"Most gods are unworthy of our trust," Father Anatoly replied. "They must all be abandoned if we are to find the One who is."

"You think that?" The man's laughter was harsh and abrupt. "Worthy of our trust? Tell me this, monk. Does God control everything that happens?"

"If you're asking whether God causes everything to happen, my answer is no."

"None of that, priest!" the man shouted, waving an arm in protest. "None of your religious games. I've heard about you, I know you're a clever man. I want a straight answer. Is God in control, or not?"

Father Anatoly lowered his head. He remained silent for a few moments. "I am sorry for your loss, Alexey," he said at last.

The man was thunderstruck. "How could you—"

He stood up and walked to the other side of the room, his back toward them. "My wife, my daughter—they were killed because of my sins, weren't they? There were so many things I hid from them. The car wreck was my punishment from this God of yours."

Father Anatoly rose and swiftly crossed the room. He placed a hand on the man's shoulder and spoke to him in a whisper. Alexey trembled and began to weep. The two of them spoke for several minutes in hushed voices while Charles thumbed through a book of St. Athanasius's writings.

Alexey lowered his head. Father Anatoly prayed over him and blessed him.

"Come, Alexey, now you must have some tea with us."

The three of them sat around the table together, drinking tea and nibbling on crackers.

"You are too kind to me, Father." Alexey scratched the permanent furrows on his brow. "If you knew the things that I've done…"

"Our crimes are terrible indeed," the monk replied. "And yet, as a handful of sand thrown into the ocean, so are the sins of all humanity in comparison with the mind of God. Saint Isaac the Syrian taught us this." Father Anatoly glanced up at the icon of Jesus on his wall. "Christ came to save sinners, and I am the worst of them. If I want to see all the evil in the world, Alexey, I have only to close my eyes and look within. By the grace of God, if I want to see all the beauty the cosmos can contain—even the absolute Beauty—I can find it in the same place."

"Surely not!" Alexey's eyes widened. "All the evil in the world? You are a true monk, a holy father!"

Father Anatoly's eyes were tinged with sorrow. "At its best, the Church is a hospital. The diseases we treat are the passions that dominate people's lives. I too have been a victim. The sickness digs into the heart, puts down roots, spreads. We lose control of our will and become slaves to our own desire. We are dehumanized. Sin turns us into machines, but grace would turn us into gods."

Charles took a sip of his tea, lightly sweetened with honey from one of the convent's beehives. "If you don't mind my asking, Father, why did you become a monk?"

"That's very simple. I met Someone beautiful and fell in love."

Charles set down his teacup and fidgeted with the corner of a napkin. "I don't want to seem rude," he said, "but that sounds too simplistic. In fact, it seems almost childish."

Father Anatoly nodded. "There are some ways in which children are wiser than all of us. I was struck with wonder, and I never recovered. You know something of this as well, don't you? Hasn't your life changed since you met Nadia?"

"Well, sure, but that's different."

"Indeed. One is the Original, the other its icon. Dostoevsky was right, Charles. Beauty will save the world."

Alexey grunted. "Beauty, you say? Let me tell you, Father, there are many beautiful things in this world that are poison. I would know."

"You're right, of course," the monk replied. "We speak only of the beauty that is also truth. This is the heart of our humble God, a love that consumes the darkness within us."

⤎

Charles and Peter were ruling the roost. On top of other minor holdings and investment properties, Peter had just constructed a pair of high-dollar hotels on Park Place and Boardwalk. To him, these twin edifices represented the epitome of all earthly power and dominion. On the other end of the social spectrum, Charles shuffled along with an ever-expanding conglomerate of cheap housing over in the dark purple and pasty blue slums.

"You've done it again, Peter." Julia shook her head. "I don't know how you get those two hotels every time we play this game. If you don't land on them, you start working those sad eyes and sweet talk me into trading. Next thing I know my car's getting repoed and you're tossing me out on the curb."

"I wouldn't toss you out on the curb!" Peter looked horrified.

"Is that a fact?" Julia laughed. "We'll just see what happens the next time I take a stroll down on the Boardwalk. I'm just kidding with you, Peter. You've been nothing but good for me from the day I met you. In fact, you're the only reason I haven't gotten old yet."

"I am?"

"You know, Julia," Charles chimed in, "if you're not up for the high life, I can book you a room down at the Roach Motel."

"Thanks, but no thanks, Mr. Slumlord," she replied. "For one thing, you've spent way too much time in the slammer to be an honest man. For another, I know all about the wrong part of town. Don't get me wrong, there's no shame in living there. I've just spent too much time out here in the fresh air to ever want to go back."

Peter went to bed a rich man. In less than two hours, he'd created a monolithic realty empire that annihilated everything in its path, including the slumlords and the freeloaders. Julia and Charles sat outside on the front porch with cups of steaming cocoa, listening to the crickets.

"We've sure been through the ringer, haven't we?" She smoothed out the wrinkles in her dress with her palms. "I'm amazed at how well Boris was looking the other day."

"Yeah, well, he thinks she's still alive."

"I know he does. I'd say it was just denial, but Jack told me the same thing in a letter right after it happened. I don't know what to think. I do know Boris is a strange one. He's got to be the only man in the world that gets himself drunk off water."

He met her gaze. "You know about that?"

"I live here, remember? One day I took that sweaty old jacket of his down to the dry cleaners. He accidentally left the bottle in it. I hate to admit it, but I was downright curious. What is this nasty stuff he's been guzzling for the last decade? Nadia, she said it was vodka, and he always kept the bottles around, but somehow it didn't add up. So I took a tiny little sip, and what did I taste? Water, straight from the tap. I figure he must be into some funny business, lying to Nadia and me for all these years."

"Oh, well, I don't—"

She patted his arm. "Don't you worry, Charles, I'm not digging around for any secrets. But I will say this. You best be careful. You're not like him. I always figured that man was born with a cigar in one hand and a pistol in the other. For what it's worth, I'll be praying for you, same as I always do."

He checked the news on his phone when he got back to the monastery. The page eventually loaded and images appeared. He stopped breathing.

There he was, front and center. It was a picture of him and Thompson smiling and shaking hands. They'd gone down to a photography studio to get a professional shot for a newspaper when the scanner was still in the running for the Nobel Prize.

A little farther down the article was a portrait of Liu Xiang, General Secretary of the Communist Party of China, President of the People's Republic of China, and Chairman of the Central Military Commission. The man who held absolute sway over the fate of one point four billion human lives.

He'd thought Rius was crazy when he'd promised this would happen. Now it was a reality. China was all in.

The journalist's incredulity bled through her objective wording. China's goal was ambitious. Within four months, Liu Xiang promised, every man, woman and child in the People's Republic would undergo a scan with the device.

⁊

Sheets of rain lashed the windowpanes in sudden bursts, peals of deafening thunder rattled the dishes in the cupboard. Charles and Father Anatoly sat across the table from each other, both absorbed in books. Ten days had passed since the encounter with Alexey.

The scientist was reading a treatise by a seventh-century Syrian monk. The monk was reading a history of the theory of cosmological expansion.

"Listen to this part, Charles." Father Anatoly began reading aloud. *"The evolution of the world may be compared to a display of fireworks that has just ended: some few red wisps, ashes, and smoke. Standing on a cooled cinder, we see the slow fading of the suns, and we try to recall the vanished brilliance of the origin of the worlds..."*

"Did you hear that?" Charles asked suddenly.

"I can't hear anything over all that thunder," Father Anatoly replied.

There it was again. A gentle rapping sound, faintly audible before another magnificent boom rolled through the atmosphere.

"I think somebody's out there." Charles set down his book and went to the front door.

"Careful with the door. The wind's blowing from the east."

He nudged the front door open a few inches. A spray of rain and mist slipped through the crack. There was a visitor outside, short and broad-shouldered, his raincoat drenched, his wet, close-cropped hair plastered to his forehead. He held a gloved hand over one side of his face as if he had been injured. Charles opened the door wider.

"Sorry for bothering you," the stranger said.

"Come in!" Father Anatoly called from inside. "No need to wait in the rain."

"Thank you, Father." The man nodded to Charles and shuffled past him into the cottage, where he peeled off his raincoat and stood dripping and shivering in the entryway. Charles followed and shoved the door closed against a howling blast of wind.

"I've come to ask for your blessing, Father." The man sidled up to the table with halting steps. "After years of thinking it over, I've finally decided to join the Church."

Father Anatoly watched the newcomer with his lips pressed together firmly. His gaze lost its warmth and turned cold and distant.

"I'm struggling with distractions," the newcomer continued. "It's such a sinful world out there. It seems like I just can't keep away from it all."

"Why have you come here?" Father Anatoly's chair scraped against the floorboards as he stood. His eyes flashed like lightning.

The man edged back a few steps. "But I've already told you that, Father. I've come here for your blessing."

"Where is your tail?"

"What?" The man glanced at Charles, wide-eyed. "What do you mean, Father?"

"And your horns, what about those?" Father Anatoly shouted, waving his arms. "Did you saw them off before you came to the monastery?"

"Father, you're being cruel!" The man clasped his hands against his chest devoutly. One of his cheeks looked like it had been burnt. "Is it because I'm a sinner? Is that really so unusual? Surely the Holy Scriptures command you to be merciful to sinners."

"So you want scripture, do you?" Father Anatoly ran to the cupboard and flung open the cabinet. He stuffed his hand into a box of crackers and pulled out two of them, one of which he crammed into his mouth. He hurried over to the man and handed him the other cracker. "Here's a scripture for you. What you are about to do, do quickly."

Charles was stunned. Had the old monk lost his mind? There was a loud, crackling hiss as a bolt of lightning flashed outside. A bellowing thunder like the roar of a cannon quickly followed. The lights in the cottage flickered out for a few seconds and then kicked back on.

The visitor stood with his arms crossed over his chest and an ironic grin playing over his lips. "Clever old goat, aren't you?"

He crushed the cracker Father Anatoly had given him and tossed the crumbs onto the floor. "Any other day, I'd put a bullet through your skull, monk, but you lucked out. No blood, the old man said, and orders are orders. Not that it matters. We've found what we're looking for." He turned and nodded to Charles. "Take care, Dr. Ferguson." He strode out of the cottage and slammed the door shut behind him. A few seconds later they heard tires peeling as a car screeched out of the driveway.

Father Anatoly sighed. "It seems your time among us has come to an end. If there is anything you wanted to ask me, child, you should do it now."

Charles ran a trembling hand through his hair. The Magnus Foundation had found him. The calmness he'd grown accustomed to in this place was shattered, gone like it had never existed.

"You did want to ask me something, didn't you?" Anatoly prodded. "Or perhaps I misunderstood."

"No, you're right." He had been thinking about it for days, but what did it matter now? It wouldn't stop what was coming. "I want you to prove to me that there's a God. Like Alexey, only I want something intellectual, something scientific. Absurd, I know."

A hint of a smile flashed across the old monk's features. "Your sanity demands that reality must be undivided and whole. That isn't absurd, it's healthy. At the same time, you must realize that this question involves not only our minds but our entire being. The path to *theosis*, to union with God, is open to everyone regardless of their mental capabilities. But there is something that may help you."

"What is it?"

"The remembrance of death."

Charles shuddered. "What does that mean?"

"From the human body to the human race to the farthest reaches of the cosmos, these words hold true over all things: *You shall surely die.* Entropy works against all systems and brings them all to their knees. The mechanistic processes of my body will break down. The molten fires of every star will burn out, the atmosphere of every planet dissolve—everything will be united in a vacuous eternity. Our pride may be limitless, but no matter what our technology accomplishes, there can be no final hope for the human race without some great change. What happens to every one of us as individuals will one day happen to the species. That day may be closer than we think."

"Thompson talks like that when he's in a dark humor," Charles said. "Universal expansion, heat death of the universe, not with a bang but with a whimper. He doesn't think we'll ever leave this solar system, and even if we did escape to some distant planet, of course we couldn't survive if the whole universe turned into a vacuum."

"Hearing all that from Thompson is one thing," he went on, allowing his frustration to seep into his voice, "but hearing it from you—are you really saying that we should just give up, that we shouldn't even try? Is your God just a void, an emptiness? Or maybe you're hoping for a spiritual future that has nothing to do with this world, Thompson's pie in the sky. It's almost like you don't believe in anything after all."

"I do believe, and therefore hope," Father Anatoly said quietly. "Either there is Nothing, or there is Someone. In the end, there are no other possibilities."

Charles rubbed his eyes with the palms of his hands, trying to focus. Too much was happening, too many other things pressing in. "I don't understand."

"Perhaps you will one day," the monk replied. "Don't be afraid, our hope goes beyond some disembodied bliss. God has forever united himself to our physical nature through the Incarnation. Through the Resurrection, he assures us that this world, the world we all know, the real world of flesh and bone and blood, will be renewed. The great work has begun, and our highest calling is to take part in it. But I must ask you to forgive me." Father Anatoly lowered his eyes. "On his deathbed, Saint Sisoës told his followers, 'I have not yet begun to repent.' So it is for me, and because of my inadequacy I cannot answer your question properly. Pray for me."

He drew close and embraced Charles warmly.

"If you see Nadia," he added, "give her a message from me, the words spoken to Saint Silouan. 'Keep your mind in hell, and do not despair.' Remember that. It is my message to her, and to you as well. 'Keep your mind in hell, and do not despair.' Whatever you do, don't forget about your gun and your bullets. They are more powerful than you can imagine. And if it brings you comfort, dear child, know that I will always keep you in my prayers."

The monk fetched his umbrella, glanced at Charles one last time, and went out to attend the evening prayers.

Charles sat down heavily in a chair. Outside, the thunderclaps softened to distant murmurs as the storm moved on. Father Anatoly's words had slipped like seeds into a dark, quiet place deep within him.

Other things were more pressing. That man with the burned face—what was he doing now? He needed to talk to Boris. Why hadn't he heard from him yet? Gavriel, that was the answer. Gavriel would know.

He rushed to the door and flung it open. A fine mist was all that remained of the torrential rain. A large tree limb had split, the broken half hanging downward into the empty driveway.

Empty. His car was gone.

"Dr. Ferguson!" Gavriel Abramovich stepped out from behind the trunk of a hickory tree, assault rifle at the ready.

"I think they found me, Gavriel."

"We know." A walkie-talkie at Gavriel's waist erupted into sharp static followed by a woman's voice speaking in Russian. He picked it up, rattled off a reply, and switched it off. "Your car, they take it."

"Who?"

"Magnus people."

"And you let them?"

Gavriel shrugged. "We follow orders. Boris, he says, 'Maybe it's good thing. They steal lousy car, now Mr. Charles gets new one.' They come for you soon. You go with them."

"Go with them?" He stared at Gavriel as if the young soldier had gone mad. "Why don't we run away, hide somewhere else?"

Gavriel shook his head. "They find you eventually. It's best this way. Trust Boris. He knows what's good. Now listen. I need you to give closest attention to what I say, Dr. Ferguson. You can do this? Calm yourself?"

"Okay." Charles rubbed his hands against his arms. It wasn't cold, even with the storm, but he couldn't stop shivering. Trust Boris. Oh yes, that had gone wonderfully so far. "I'm listening."

"Good. Video games, you play?"

"What?"

"Video games!" Gavriel slung his gun over his shoulder and pretended he was pushing buttons on a controller. "You play?"

"I, uh—no, not much anymore. Thompson's into them. Is that a problem?"

"When you go to Foundation, you play video game. Crimson Reaper 3. Play map—Dead Man's Waterfall. Behind waterfall is cave. The back of cave, that's where you go. You remember this, yes?"

"Yeah, I think I've got it. Crimson Reaper 3, Dead Man's Waterfall, back of the cave behind the waterfall."

"Tell no one. Magnus, they come soon." Gavriel placed his hand gently on Charles's shoulder. "Goodbye, Dr. Ferguson. Best of luck."

He turned and slipped back into the woods, chattering into the walkie-talkie as he went.

Charles sat on one of the porch steps. It was something he had done many times over the last couple of weeks, drinking in the quiet murmurings of Nature, pondering the things he'd read or heard among the monks. His heart rate was finally beginning to slow when he heard gravel crunching beneath a set of tires. A black SUV turned the corner into the driveway and came to a stop a few feet in front of him. The night stalker, Franz Heimler, climbed out of the driver's seat, pulled back the flap of his jacket, and slid a sleek handgun from a holster over his chest.

Chapter Ten

Into Darkness

Franz Heimler aimed the gun at Charles's head. "Are you armed?"

Charles held his hands in the air. "No. Just take it easy."

Heimler glanced around, then slipped the gun back into its holster. "Your phone. Let me see it."

Heart pounding, Charles pulled the phone Boris had given him out of his pocket. He edged toward Heimler with the phone extended in one hand. Heimler snatched it as soon as it was in range.

"Where did you get this?"

"I bought it," Charles lied. "I dropped my old one in the toilet, so I got a replacement."

"Why change your number?"

"After what happened, I just wanted to get away from everything."

Heimler looked up from the phone and gave Charles a searching glance. "What's the PIN number?"

"One four eight two."

Heimler keyed in the numbers and tapped on the phone for a moment. "You haven't called anyone since you got this?"

"Like I said, I wanted some privacy."

Heimler handed him the phone. "You'd better not be lying to me. We have ways of finding out. Get your things. You're coming with us."

His bag was already packed. Heimler took it from him and threw it in the back of the SUV. Charles opened one of the rear doors and started to climb in. He froze with his foot on the running board.

He had caught a glimpse of a familiar face in the rearview mirror.

"Thompson!" he cried. "What are you doing here? Did they kidnap you, too?"

Thompson was sitting in the passenger seat. He looked pale, his hair was disheveled, and there was a few days' growth darkening the lower portion of his face. "Not exactly," he said.

Charles looked at him in disbelief. If they hadn't kidnapped him, that meant—

"You're with them."

Thompson glanced at him in the mirror and looked away.

"Thompson, how could you?"

"Don't get all high and mighty on me," Thompson shot back. "They pay me a hundred thousand a year on top of my salary. I did it for the money, Charles. Money, and something else, something even better. Just get in. I'll explain everything."

Charles climbed into the back seat and closed the door behind him. Franz Heimler started the engine, backed the SUV out in a quarter turn, and hit the accelerator.

"My question," Thompson said, "is what are *you* doing here? Good God! I didn't expect to find you out cavorting with a band of medieval fanatics."

"They grow on you," Charles replied tersely. "But seriously, Thompson, shouldn't you be teaching freshmen biology or cruising Italy in a Maserati?"

"Ah yes, freshman bio. The department didn't take me up on my kind offer. I can't imagine why." Thompson sighed. "As for the Maserati, it's tragic, but it'll have to wait."

"Where are we going?"

"Chicago. Now brace yourself." Thompson turned around in his seat to look at him. "Ready for some bombshells?"

"What?"

"One. I've been with the Foundation for nine years, starting the week after I finished undergrad. They gave me the job at the university so I could keep an eye on you.

"Two. What you did on Phoenix and Alpha was phenomenal, Charles. You didn't realize it because you're so charmingly naïve about your own capabilities. The only reason they pulled you off those projects was to give the researchers in the Foundation time to figure out what you'd done and apply it to their own work. It's taken them almost six years.

"Three. Nearly every researcher in the Foundation besides myself is presumed to be dead out here in the real world.

"Four. Nadia is alive. She's waiting for you at Magnus Headquarters as we speak. Are you ready for five, or shall we take a break?"

"Nadia—" Charles couldn't say anything more. Boris had told him to hope. To some extent, he had. But hope and certainty were two very different things.

"Delightful news, isn't it?" Thompson broke into his eccentric laugh, which always struck Charles as having more than a hint of the maniacal. "She's alive, but she could be doing better. Depression. Guess it's a problem she's had for a while. She won't take medication, won't see a Foundation therapist. Magnus wanted to wait longer to bring you in, but I convinced him that it wasn't worth the risk. We're hoping you can cheer her up. Get her back in the game."

"I can't believe it," Charles murmured. "I think I'm in shock, Thompson. But what about Flight 109?"

"Ah, yes." Thompson shook his head. "Now there's a sad tale. The Foundation has a business partner in the Middle East who has proven to be a little—how shall I put it?—unstable over the years. He called us the day of the flight and said that the plane *might* be bombed by some old friends of his. He's done that sort of thing before and it came to nothing. We didn't consider it credible enough to scare the authorities, but we decided to protect our potential assets just to be cautious. Even the worst sources get it right once in a while. Nadia was escorted off the plane just before takeoff. We know now that we should have warned them, but we were afraid to cry wolf too often. Tragic, really."

"So the Foundation had nothing to do with it?"

Franz Heimler gave Charles a sharp look in the rearview mirror.

"What?" Thompson exclaimed. "Of course not. The Foundation's just a bunch of researchers and business leaders. Now let's get back to the bombshells. Five. Congratulations, Charles, you're now the head of another Magnus research project. Aeternum. Nothing major. All you have to do is turn human beings into immortals. You'll get a whole year to pull it off."

"Tell me you're kidding."

"Finally," Thompson went on, "number six. In about fifteen minutes, your house is going to explode. Sorry about that. Leak in the gas line. Your neighbor, the gossipy old witch across the street, saw a taxi drop you off late last night. Your car broke down on the way home yesterday, so you got a lift with one of those ridesharing services. The records are all there for the authorities to see. They'll find your charred remains and pronounce you dead on the spot. They won't bother to check your DNA. It would be a waste of embarrassingly limited funds, and this is an election year.

"So, to recap, I'm with Magnus, Nadia's alive and moping, and you're about to become a zombie and discover the Fountain of Youth. Any questions?"

"Give me a sec." Charles felt like hyperventilating. He took a series of measured breaths—in and out through the mouth—and rubbed his temples with his fingertips. These really were bombshells, every one of them. "So you were *spying* on me all these years?"

"Spying is such a nasty word. I always thought of it as…friendly observation."

"Right, so you were spying. Oh, man. I thought you were my friend, Thompson. I really did. What do you really think of me? No, I can guess. The blind, socially impaired idiot who can't figure out that his best friend is getting paid six figures to tolerate his presence."

"I am your friend, Charles," Thompson said quietly. "I know you won't believe this, but I feel like human trash right now. It all sounds terrible, but it wasn't just the money. You want to know what I think of you? I think you're the most gifted biologist the world has ever seen. Sometimes I would just stand back and watch you in awe, and sometimes—you said you wanted the truth—sometimes I wished you didn't exist.

"Do you know how intimidating it is to work with someone like you? Someone who remembers everything, who knows everything you know and a thousand times more? I felt like a dead weight when we worked together, but I didn't care. It was so exciting just to be near you, to see your mind ripping through problems that would take the rest of the world years to solve."

"But what about the scanner?" Charles asked. "You had a lot of great ideas on that."

"Those weren't my ideas." Thompson turned back in his seat and looked out the front window. "I had a whole team of scientists at the Foundation helping me out. And still, even when you were outnumbered twenty to one by some of the best minds in the field, you were the one who came up with all the breakthroughs. That's why they're finally bringing you in. Magnus has big plans for you, Charles."

Charles folded his arms over his chest. "So I heard. He honestly expects me to cure *death* in, what, twelve months?"

"Is that too long? Anyway, you won't be working alone. You'll be teaming up with an old friend, Raj Bhandari. Nadia, too, if you think she'll be helpful. You'll have access to everything. All the research, all the resources. You need it, Magnus provides it. And you won't be starting at square one. We've been working towards Aeternum for a long time now. Leap past a few critical gaps and we're done with it."

Charles spent the next few minutes looking out into the darkness and sifting through everything Thompson had told him. Some of it he had expected, but not all. Not by any means. Despite what he knew about the Magnus Foundation, despite Ali Hamid, even despite the bombing, the scientist in him was excited.

To be back in that world, harnessing the power of their advanced AI system, accessing years of research that was nonexistent outside the Foundation, daring to tackle the most difficult problem imaginable—in some ways, it was a dream come true. And a nightmare. Could the goal be accomplished? Could the science of life lead humanity to the negation of death? What would happen to the world if he succeeded?

"Madness," he whispered under his breath.

"What was that?" Thompson asked.

"I said *Magnus*. I'm just thinking, if Nadia has been there ever since the bombing, why didn't she tell me? For that matter, why didn't you tell me? I went through hell, Thompson. You could have at least given me a clue. Anything would have been nice."

"How was I supposed to tell you? After you disappeared, I didn't have your phone number, remember? And it's not like I would have thought to mail a letter to some monastery in the middle of Nowhere, Illinois. Even if I could have contacted you, there are rules that can't be broken, rules that now apply to you. No contact—absolutely none—with the outside world. We've worked too hard to take any chances. It's a sacrifice, but it's worth it. Don't worry, though. Like I tell all the others, it won't last forever. We're getting down to the keystone projects, the lightning bolts that will come crashing down from the heavens to usher in a new era. When all is said and done, we'll open the doors and let everyone see exactly what we've been doing."

"I have trouble buying that."

"Oh, come on, Charles." Thompson grinned at him. "Would I lie to you?"

෴

They boarded a private jet at O'Hare that was fit for a sultan. It felt surreal after two weeks of the spartan life with the monks. The main cabin held plush leather recliner seats near the front and a U-shaped couch rounding a dinner table in the back. There wasn't a single window in the passenger area.

Charles sank into one of the seats and heard the gentle stretching of the leather beneath him. It felt even better than the cozy, well-worn furniture in his own home, furniture which, he realized with a twinge, had been reduced to cinders by now. Thompson sat in the chair across from him. Heimler went into the cockpit and closed the door behind him.

"Where are we headed?" Charles asked.

"Magnus Headquarters. And that's all you'll find out about it from me. The location's secret."

"Secret location? Couldn't anyone at Headquarters with a cell phone figure out exactly where they were?"

"You're welcome to try if you'd like," Thompson replied. "The newcomers always do. Everything flows in, nothing goes out. Magnus Communication Policy in a nutshell. No emails, no calls outside the organization, no checking in with the satellites and cell towers everyone else uses, no logging in to anything. We can communicate with each other internally but nothing beyond that."

The phone Boris had given Charles had already connected to a wireless network on the plane. There was no mobile Internet access, which meant the signal was either out of range or the plane was blocking it somehow. He tapped on a location app.

"That's odd. It says we're in Manhattan."

"We're always in Manhattan. Get on any device within a Magnus environment and you're immediately in Manhattan. I don't know how the magic works. That's Landry's business. He's our resident digital deity, and you'd have to sacrifice your own offspring to pry his secrets out of him. I'm going to get some shuteye. It's a long flight, and I wasted too many precious nights of sleep hunting you down. That blasted monastery was on our list of places to check, but I never would have dreamed you'd actually go there of your own free will."

Thompson yawned, then rolled up his jacket and stuffed it behind his head as a pillow. His eyes, however, remained open.

"Did you ever meet him?" he asked suddenly, leaning forward in his seat. "When you worked on Phoenix and Alpha, did *he* ever meet with you? I mean Alexander Magnus, the owner."

"No. Tom Murrow said he'd talked to him once, but I never did."

"I suppose he doesn't travel much these days. Always at Headquarters. When you meet him, you'll understand. People like Magnus weave history around themselves. The rest of us get pulled in whether we like it or not."

Thompson fell asleep within minutes. Charles tried to bypass the restrictions on his phone, to access anything that would let him communicate with the rest of the world. It was hopeless. He eventually admitted defeat and scanned through a few news sites. No mention of the scanner, but there was one article that drew his eye.

Boris had told him that the Foundation was working on a top-secret military contract. The news story, citing an anonymous source, was about a high-ranking general at the Pentagon who had boasted that the Hand of God would be completely wiped out by the end of the year. The journalist went on to outline the difficulty of accomplishing such a feat and suggested that a full-scale, boots-on-the-ground invasion could be in the works.

He read a handful of movie and book reviews, caught up on the news, played a game of chess against a laughably unskilled computer opponent, and finally joined Thompson in the oblivion of sleep.

When Charles awoke, he was no longer on the plane at all. He was lying in his bed in his own bedroom.

At least, that was his first thought.

The furnishings were the same, the paint colors identical, even the picture of Nadia seated at the piano was there on the dresser, tilted just enough so that he could see it. But something wasn't right.

The fan. His bedroom had an old-fashioned ceiling fan that had begun rattling a few months back. The one above him was a sleek silver and whirred softly as a whisper.

He noticed other anomalies. The missing A/C vent in the ceiling. The synthetic hue of the light spilling through the window above the desk. The lack of even a mote of dust on any surface. He liked to keep things tidy, but he'd been away for several weeks now. There should have been dust.

A knock on the bedroom door roused him from his mystifying observations. He was still dressed in the same clothes he had worn on the flight. He climbed out of bed and opened the door.

It was Thompson, bearing a breakfast tray with covered dishes and a steaming cup of dark-roasted coffee whose rich fragrance drifted up and beckoned to Charles.

"Breakfast for the newest arrival. What do you think of the place?"

"Where are we?" Charles snatched the cup of coffee and took a sip. It singed his tongue, but it was worth it. It was always worth it. "I feel strange, Thompson. A little groggy."

"That happens with tranquilizers. Secret location and all. Which, of course, answers your other question. We're in Magnus Headquarters."

Charles stepped out of the bedroom. It was the exact same layout as his house, everything was there, right where he had left it.

"I don't understand. *This* is Magnus Headquarters?"

"A small slice of a very large pie. Impressive, though, isn't it? They had to work overtime to finish up since we brought you in early. It's hard to live underground, so we go out of our way to make our higher-ranking members feel right at home…literally. Your house was small enough that they could recreate the whole structure within the space allotted for you. A team swapped out the furnishings in your real house a few days before they burnt it down. They were, of course, discreet. Even the old crone across the street saw nothing."

"And you said that we're underground?"

"Precisely. This is Level Three, the residential level. Two is where most of the research takes place. One, near the surface, is the Garden, which, by the way, is absolutely incredible. You'll have to see for yourself when you get a spare moment.

"Clean up and wolf this down as quick as you can. You have a meeting with Magnus in about forty minutes. It will be held in his office. That's an extraordinary honor for anyone and unheard of for a newcomer. He's a very private sort of person. He holds a high opinion of you, though, and I've assured him that you'll more than meet his expectations.

"Now, then, one orange, two pieces of toast, one egg sunny-side up. Dark coffee, one glass of water. Did I miss anything?"

"How did you—"

"I've been keeping tabs on you for years, remember? Painfully tedious work, I might add. You have to be the blandest polymath in history. I know this is all a catastrophic change, especially for someone with your temperament. Take it in stride. Or, if that's impossible, at least try not to crack up on us. See you in half an hour. Make sure you're ready on time. Magnus isn't patient with that sort of thing."

Thompson handed him the tray and turned to leave.

"Wait! What about Nadia?"

"Don't worry, she's here. Pining away for you, no doubt. After the meeting, Charles. Magnus's orders."

Charles made short work of the breakfast, which was, as Thompson knew all too well, exactly what he'd eaten nearly every morning for the last five years. He took as long of a shower as he could afford. It did feel good to be home, surrounded by the familiar, even if he knew that this version of home was buried beneath the earth's surface.

His clothes had been organized with compulsive perfection, arranged first by type and then by color from darkest to lightest. He wore his perennial favorite, a dull pair of loose-fitting light khaki pants, an unremarkable gray dress shirt, and drab brown shoes. Comfortable, and in his book, comfort trumped fashion seven days a week.

Thompson banged on the front door exactly thirty minutes after he had left.

He cast a scrutinizing glance at Charles's attire. "Ah, *that* shirt again. Guess it's your blasted safety blanket. Come on, then. Don't worry about locking the door. When you want to enter, just place your hand on it and it'll open. We use scanners for access here."

The hallway outside his quarters was quiet and comfortably lit. There was a slight resistance underfoot from an immaculate white carpet with random geometric patterns in gold. The soft, indirect lighting tucked away above the crown molding illuminated the Surrealist and Deconstruction artwork that lined the walls. It felt like they were exploring the corridors of some five-star, avant-garde hotel.

He glanced at a few of the paintings. A woman's face in psychedelic colors with a keyhole instead of a nose. A ladder rising up from the midst of a graveyard and going nowhere, propped up against nothing. They wandered along for several minutes and passed by two people, one a middle-aged man in a charcoal pinstripe suit and a maroon tie, the other a young Hispanic woman in green medical scrubs. Both walked at a good clip and were fixated on the screens of their tablets.

"All work and no play, is it?" he asked Thompson.

"Something like that."

Thompson made a few turns and led them to a lobby lined with elevators.

"This place must be enormous," Charles said.

"You have no idea."

A set of chrome doors parted. They stepped into one of the elevators.

"Level Six," Thompson said.

"One moment please." It was the same feminine, British voice that Charles remembered from his earlier work with the Magnus Foundation. "Eugene Thompson, identity confirmed. Charles Ferguson, identity confirmed."

"Have a seat, Charles," Thompson said. "The elevators are a bit different around here."

The elevator was spacious and lined with leather seats along the interior walls. Circular hand rings were suspended from the ceiling, as if they were in a miniature subway car. He took a seat across from Thompson.

The doors slid closed. The elevator began a rapid descent, then slowed to a halt after a few moments. There was a mechanical clanking and hissing outside the elevator and then it suddenly felt as if they were moving sideways.

"Headquarters is enormous, so the elevators move along the X, Y, and Z axes," Thompson explained. "Intricate system, but it saves us a lot of precious time."

"Efficient."

Thompson scratched his ear. "Listen, Charles, it's a different world down here. Things don't work the same way. Whatever happens, promise me one thing."

"What's that?"

"Don't think badly of me. I deserve some blame, but you've got to understand that we're dealing with a tidal wave. You either move with it or get swept away."

The doors slid open. Franz Heimler was waiting for them, flanked by a pair of heavily armed guards.

"Follow me, gentlemen," he commanded.

They walked along a cold, dimly lit stone-paved hallway that terminated in twin golden doors engraved with the old heraldic symbol of the lion rampant. Heimler placed his hand on one of the doors, and they both slid open without a sound.

The spacious room within was thirty feet wide and twice that in length. Ceiling-high bookshelves were lined with rare, antiquarian editions. Original artwork from masters ancient and modern hung among elegant boiseries, the same style of ornate wainscotting that adorned the Palace of Versailles. Not that he'd ever been to Versailles, but he'd watched a documentary about it with Nadia.

A roaring fire blazed behind the grate of a massive marble fireplace, its light flickering over the busts of Roman emperors and senators who observed the world through pale gray eyes devoid of pupils. Every nuance of the decor and architecture was a calculated expression of the inexhaustible wealth of its owner.

At the far end of the room, Alexander Magnus sat behind an enormous desk made from some exotic hardwood. He was absorbed in reading a copy of the London Times. He didn't so much as cast a glance in their direction when they entered the room.

Heimler led Charles and Thompson to the desk. There were no seats for them, so they were forced to wait on their feet like soldiers at attention. The silence was broken only by the crackling of the fire and the crisp rustling of paper as Magnus turned a page.

His appearance was nothing like Charles had envisioned. The wealthiest man in the world was short and portly with a round face, muddy brown eyes, and a thick head of silvering hair that curled at the tips. His face was mottled and pockmarked, his indistinct eyes a little too distant from one another.

A portrait on the wall behind the desk depicted a stern, brooding figure dressed in late Victorian fashion who glared down at them with an air of magnificent superiority. Beneath it the following words hung in gilded letters just legible from where they stood:

THE REAL PHILOSOPHERS, HOWEVER, ARE COMMANDERS AND LAW-GIVERS; they say: "Thus SHALL it be!" They determine first the Whither and the Why of mankind, and thereby set aside the previous labor of all philosophical workers, and all subjugators of the past—they grasp at the future with a creative hand, and whatever is and was, becomes for them thereby a means, an instrument, and a hammer. Their "knowing" is CREATING, their creating is a law-giving, their will to truth is—WILL TO POWER.

Magnus made them wait so long that Charles's legs began to fall asleep. Finally, the Foundation's namesake set down his newspaper and peered up at them with an unexpectedly warm and winsome smile.

"Here you are at last, Charles Ferguson in the flesh! I'm honored to meet you."

He took Charles's hand and shook it vigorously.

"I just read that they've replaced ninety-five percent of the work-force in a Chinese factory with robots. Twenty human workers instead of four hundred. These Outsiders have come a long way, haven't they? But now it's our turn. They got it down to twenty workers, but I can get it down to one. It'll happen everywhere. Every industry, every profession. What do you think of that?"

"What happens to the workers?" Charles asked.

Magnus clapped his hands together. "Precisely! That's the heart of the matter. Do we subsidize them? There's your modern, democratic answer. Billions of people transformed into human leeches so they can suck the life out of a monstrously bloated welfare state. The solution is obvious. Why subsidize them when we can cull them?"

"Cull them?" Charles looked at Thompson, but his friend's face was inscrutable.

Magnus grinned. "The New World arises, and we are its masters. Tell me, what do you think of the portrait behind my desk?"

Charles took another glance at the painting. "To be honest with you, I don't like it. And I'm not sure where you're going with all this. I have a feeling I don't want to know. I just want to see Nadia."

"Always be honest with me, Ferguson," Magnus replied. "Never lie to me. This portrait was a gift from my father on my seventh birthday. He taught me that there is only one thing worth having in this world, and that thing is Power. His were brutal lessons. I believe I've learned them well. You want to see her? Computer, give us a video feed of Nadia Petrova."

A screen came to life behind a blank section of the wall to the right of the desk.

"Nadia!" Charles rushed over to her image. She sat alone at her dining table in what looked like her apartment by the campus, though he knew it must have been reconstructed somewhere within Headquarters. Hair unkempt, face haggard, purplish rings beneath her eyes—the contrast with her normal appearance startled him. Her breakfast lay before her, untouched. She gazed listlessly toward the screen.

Magnus came and stood next to him. "We had to give her something of an orientation. Our newcomers are occasionally forced to make a few adjustments to fit in with the worldview here at Headquarters. I'm afraid she hasn't responded well."

Charles's fingers curled into fists. "What have you done to her?"

"Don't worry, Ferguson, it's nothing like that. I'd have to check the reports to get the exact details. From what I understand, she managed well enough the first few days. Toured Headquarters and made a few friends. To my surprise, she even wasted some time on video games like you young people are always doing. Then she took a dive, and now she just stares at the walls or types sentimental nonsense into her private journal. No surprise given her history."

"Her history?"

"You mean you don't know?" There was a glint in Magnus's eyes. He couldn't tell if the man was genuinely surprised or just mocking him. "Nadia slit her wrist when she was fifteen years old, a few weeks after her mother ran off. Quite a man, that Boris Petrov, isn't he? Classic Russian male. Drinks enough vodka to drown himself and everyone closest to him."

He knew it was true. He had seen the straight-line scar on Nadia's wrist and had wondered, but it had never seemed like the right time to bring it up with her.

"She hasn't eaten in two days," Magnus went on. "I have my own chef preparing her meals, and she won't touch them. Ah, but look at the devotion in your eyes! You're a cardinal, Ferguson, always have been. You'll mate for life, poor thing. We're very different in that respect.

I'm something more of a…lion." He flashed twin rows of perfectly set teeth. "I always have my pride, so to speak. Still, I can appreciate your faithful temperament. In fact, I'm going to manipulate you with it. You won't mind that, will you?"

"What?" Charles felt a chill come over him.

Magnus barked a staccato laugh. "No, you won't mind a bit, Ferguson. I know you. You need to grow up a little, learn your lessons just like I learned mine. We'll start today, this very instant, and then I'll let you go fluttering off to the chaste embraces of your saintly maid. Thompson, tell Raj Bhandari to pick his team and be ready to start Aeternum in two days. You come with me, Ferguson. Class is in session."

Heimler led the way back to the elevator. The doors opened automatically as they approached. Magnus, Heimler, and Charles went in. Thompson stayed outside the door, fidgeting with the top button of his polo. He looked at Magnus, at Heimler, at the floor. He wouldn't look at Charles.

"Control holding rooms," Heimler said after Magnus and Charles had taken a seat.

The doors closed, and they descended for several floors before the elevator came to a gentle stop. Then, without warning, it lunged forward with the speed of a commuter train.

"Kinks still crop up in the system now and then." Magnus massaged the side of his neck. "Heimler, have Grummonds fix that connection."

"Yes, my lord."

The elevator stopped again and shifted to a leisurely sideways motion before it came to a halt. The doors opened, and they stepped out into a sterile white hallway with glaring fluorescent lights and heavily armed guards on patrol. Metal doors with small slits at eye level lined both sides of the hall.

"Before we go any further, I have something I want to tell you, Ferguson." Magnus rested his hand on Charles's shoulder. "I always hoped that when we met, you would respect me, but I knew it wouldn't be the case. There's a part of me that despises what I do, what we are all doing here. Even now, I can feel the pull of the sticky, silken web of human empathy."

Magnus leaned close. Charles could feel the man's breath on his face. "It's easy, isn't it? You just lay down in the middle of the herd and sleep, but that sleep would be the death of us all. We are rational beings, the lords of this world. Logic, pure and inflexible, must be our guide. And logic now demands of us a most difficult path."

He let go of Charles's shoulder and followed Heimler down the hallway. "You will despise me, Ferguson," he called over his shoulder, "but that is unavoidable. What matters is that you obey, and for that to happen, you need to fear me, to fear what I have become."

Heimler stopped at the fifth door on the left, glanced through the opening, and laid his hand on the center of the door. It slid open to reveal a prison cell furnished with a bed and a steel toilet. A prisoner sat on the mattress, hair disheveled, wrapped in a long-sleeved gray shirt and matching pants. Both were sizes too large, which gave him a comical, childish appearance. He looked up at them with terror in his eyes.

"You remember old Tom, don't you?" Magnus sidled into the room. "Tom Murrow. Clever little rogue, wasn't he? Where are your manners, Tom? Say hello to your old friend. Say hello to Dr. Ferguson!"

"Hello," Tom said in a mechanical tone. His furtive gaze shifted between Magnus and Heimler.

"Tom learned a secret last week, didn't you, Tom? A secret none of those kind little do-gooders in Progress know anything about. Progress, Ferguson, is a rosy-hued outpost where we assign altruistic researchers like yourself. But there are two departments in my Foundation. Progress is one, the other is Control. Or, as I like to think of them, Life and Death. Tom already knew a little about Control, but he discovered all the rest when he went sneaking about on our network. Impressive work, Tom, but Landry sniffed you out. Landry's a bloodhound."

Tom rocked back and forth on the bed. "Oh God, I'm sorry, Magnus! I'll never do it again, I swear."

Magnus's pressed his lips together as he listened. "You see, Ferguson, we need all the kindhearted people in Progress to believe that they're saving the world with their breakthroughs. But we also need the realists in Control who understand that very few people in this world deserve to be saved. When we found out that Tom was in on the whole game, we warned him to keep silent. We gave you a fair chance, didn't we, Tom?"

"Yes!" Tom pounced on this point. "You were fair. You were good, you've always been so good to me. You are the best of masters!"

"That's right, Tom. I was fair, but you still disobeyed me. You tried to sneak behind my back and tell the others. You thought I wouldn't notice, but my eyes and ears are everywhere." Magnus threw his arms wide open. "Look around you, Tom. The very walls are listening!"

"But the Reaps…they're human beings!" Tom cried out in a wild voice.

Magnus walked over to the bed, knelt in front of it, and grasped Tom's right hand.

"And what is a human being, Tom?" His words were soft and gentle. He patted Tom's hand. Tom gazed back at him in mute horror.

"Speak, Tom!" The sudden fury in Magnus's voice cracked through the room like a whip. "You've learned how we look at things in Control. Reason, reason alone, Tom! Now tell us, what is a human being?"

Tom whispered something inarticulate.

"Louder, Tom. We can't hear you."

Tom's expression became flat, his stare glassy and vacant. "A human being is an animal."

"Very good, Tom." Magnus stood up and tousled Tom's hair playfully, like an old grandfather coddling a repentant child. "I'm glad you've come to your senses. Now that you acknowledge the truth, you'll understand how important it is that nothing hinders our work. I'll be good to you, Tom. We're always good to our own. We'll keep you safe in one of the cryo-chambers. And then, one day, when we've learned all the secrets, we'll find a way to bring you back. The struggle will be long over by then. Now we must face the labor pains—the tears, the screams, and the blood. But after that comes the beautiful child. Just think of it, Tom, a world renewed! You'll see it with your own eyes, I swear to you. So let's not call this goodbye forever. Only goodbye for now."

Magnus stepped back, thrust a hand into his coat pocket and withdrew a small glimmering object that looked like a mechanical insect. Tom snapped out of his daze and scrambled back against the wall in terror.

"I said I'm sorry, Magnus!" he shouted. "Oh God, oh God help me! Please Magnus, I swear, I won't say anything. I'll keep it all secret. Please!"

"This is a Harvester, Ferguson." Magnus said, ignoring Tom altogether. "It's a type of biomechanical drone. Control manufactured this newer model last week. As you may have noticed, they're patterned after the desert locust. The world needs a good reaping now and then, doesn't it?"

He tossed the device into the air. It flapped its tiny wings until they hummed and turned into a blur.

"Computer, Tom Murrow is the target."

"Confirmed," replied the soft, feminine voice, which seemed to emanate from all directions.

Tom screamed as the Harvester shot toward him. His voice cut off abruptly, and he sagged against the wall. There was no sign of injury, not a drop of blood, nothing but a deathly stillness. Magnus extended his hand. The Harvester returned and landed lightly on his palm.

"So painless, so effortless." He walked over to Charles and patted his arm. "All the same, I'm sorry you had to see this, Ferguson. I know your tender constitution must be in agony. It's a necessary evil. It takes time to remold our view of life, to steel ourselves against the necessity and usefulness of death."

"You…just murdered him," Charles said quietly.

Magnus shook his head. "No, Tom murdered himself. Don't go and do the same. You see, we have a problem. Like Tom here, you already know a little about Control. Phoenix was a Progress project, but you've also worked on Alpha. It's nearing its completion, and it has come a very long way since you last saw it. We warned Tom about it, and he did keep quiet until he learned the rest. Raj Bhandari has been more discreet. The things you learn about Control from me, the things you see while you are with me—none of it must ever be repeated to anyone in Progress. Do you understand?"

Charles nodded. He couldn't take his eyes off Tom Murrow's body.

"Computer, notify everyone in the Garden that they must leave within the next ten minutes. It will be reserved until further notice."

"Confirmed."

"And have a team take Tom Murrow to a cryo-chamber."

"Confirmed."

"Good, good." Magnus turned to his Head of Security. "Heimler, after Ferguson recovers, take him to Nadia Petrova's quarters. You may have a break after that. In fact, you and your friends can have a Garden Party after Charles is done with it."

Heimler bowed his head. "Thank you, my lord."

Charles felt Heimler taking hold of his forearm, none too gently, and leading him away from Tom Murrow's cell.

"Progress is a very comfortable environment." Magnus rocked on his heels as they waited for the elevator to return. "You may be tempted to forget about today's lesson, Ferguson. Don't give in to that temptation. I'd hate for a lovely young woman like Nadia to end up in one of these cells—or worse."

The words snapped Charles out of his stupor. "You wouldn't. Not to her!"

"I would do that and much more if I felt it necessary. She is a beautiful woman, after all."

"Monster!" As he shouted the word, Charles tore free from Heimler's grip and lunged toward Magnus, his outstretched fingers straining toward that corpulent, vulnerable neck. The next thing he knew, he was on the ground with Heimler's knee planted on his back and his arm twisted in an excruciating hold.

"Enough!" Magnus shouted. "Gentle, Heimler. I won't have you breaking him on his first day."

Heimler stood at once.

"*Beware that, when fighting monsters, you yourself do not become a monster,*" Magnus intoned. "More sound advice from the man in the portrait. I'm not a monster, Ferguson, believe it or not. That's why I'll succeed where all who came before me have failed. Everything will be sanitized, every action swift and impersonal. We'll please the modern conscience as far as possible. Still, the work must be done."

"I hate you." Charles staggered to his feet and rubbed his sore right arm.

"That's always the starting point. I hated my father when my lessons began. Heimler's going to bring you to my Garden now. Take all the time you need. There are many pretty little things up there, squirrels and rabbits, trees and flowers, maybe even a cardinal! When you've calmed down, he'll take you to Nadia. You'll see me again in a few weeks for your next lesson. I look forward to hearing about your progress with Aeternum. You will give us your absolute best on the project, won't you?"

Charles remained silent.

"Of course you will. And if there's anything that you and Nadia need to be happy here—within reason, mind you—you have only to ask."

An artificial sun slipped behind the billowing clouds that drifted along the domed expanse of the Garden. The place was a technological masterpiece, a vibrant, diverse ecosystem entirely underground, a vast island of life within the manufactured confines of Headquarters. But Charles had no appetite for wonder at that point.

The scent of fallen leaves, the living fragrance of every forest, drifted into his awareness. Oak leaves. Tiny, dry corpses that rustled and crunched beneath his feet.

He wandered until he came to a purling stream whose waters were clear as a diamond. He lay down beside it, closed his eyes, and watched as Tom was murdered over and over again in his mind.

Chapter Eleven

Reunions

"Her quarters are there, second on the right." Heimler pointed at the door in question and left without another word.

Charles was in a different wing of Level Three, about a ten-minute walk from his own quarters. It was, as Heimler had explained to him on the ride down from the Garden, impossible to get lost in Headquarters. If ever you didn't know where you were, all you had to do was ask the omnipresent Computer.

He knocked on the door. A moment later it slid open.

Nadia looked up at him. Her eyes widened, and then she was in his arms. He heard her voice murmur his name and savored the soft pressure of her lips against his.

She hooked her arm through his and led him inside. Her quarters were a replica of her apartment by the college. The living room went pitch black as soon as the front door slid closed. He fumbled over to an end table and switched on a lamp.

"Cold in here." He looked around. Her living room was immaculate. No heaps of clutter, not even a hint of the immortal laundry pile.

"Would you like me to raise the temperature?" the Computer asked.

He and Nadia exchanged an uneasy glance.

"Go ahead," Nadia answered.

"Confirmed."

They sat beside each other on the sofa. A soft whoosh from the vent above them was followed by a current of warm air.

How many video cameras were watching them? How many microphones listening to every word they spoke?

He reached over and clasped her hand. "Are you okay?"

"No." She leaned against him and ran a finger along his cheek. "I've been here two weeks now. They put me to work on one of their projects. Gene sequencing. I ran away and locked myself up in here like a bird in a cage. This place—it looks like my apartment, but they've changed it. They're trying to take my soul."

"What do you mean?"

She stood. "See for yourself."

He followed her down the hallway and into the guest room.

"There." She pointed to the wall in front of the bed.

In place of her icons hung three paintings that mimicked the Orthodox style. Gone were the aureolae, gone the golden light shining outward from the figures. The tones of these new images were dark and forbidding.

The painting on the left showed the story of Jesus and Peter walking on the water. Only in this version, Jesus was sinking beneath the waves. He reached out his hand, begging Peter to rescue him. Peter had his arms crossed over his chest, his face a mask of indifference. The disciples in the boat pointed at Jesus and laughed at him. Charles read the title, written in bold, crimson letters on the bottom right of the painting.

The Ascension.

In the middle painting, Peter and John were rushing into the tomb. But the tomb wasn't empty. Instead of graveclothes, they discovered Jesus' corpse. It was exposed. Rats scurried across the cold stone floor. Worms crawled out of the ears and mouth of the body. Charles felt bile rising in the back of his throat.

The Resurrection.

In the last painting, a middle-aged husband rushed into a Roman-era bedroom to find his young wife in the arms of a man her own age. The title was itself a mockery, written in the sharp, sticklike letters of a child's hand.

The Virgin Shall Conceive.

"What is this?" he cried.

"My punishment. They called it a lesson."

Furious, he snatched one of the paintings off the wall and lifted it over his head with both hands.

"Don't!" Nadia lunged toward him and grabbed his arms. "You can't."

He looked at her in amazement. "Why not?"

"Because of what he said." Her eyes turned from his. "He'll come for me."

"What?" He staggered back, his hands still clutching the painting. "Who will come?"

"I'll tell you everything." Her words were rushed. She looked terrified. "My first morning here, the front door opened while I was getting dressed. It was a team from Security, six or seven men. They told me that my apartment was in violation of protocol and that they were going to fix it. My icons, my books—they took anything that had to do with my faith. And then they brought in these other things. Their paintings, their books."

"Can't we just hide them somewhere?" he asked. "Bury them in the closet?"

"That's what I asked the guard. He told me that I was a lucky girl, that the old man was watching out for me that day. He said this was my first lesson. I have to leave their pictures up and keep their books in plain sight. If I don't, the old man will give him permission to come back in the middle of the night, to sneak into my bedroom while I was asleep and to—"

Her voice broke. She clapped her hand over her mouth. She still wouldn't look at him.

He carefully hung the painting back on the wall. He went to her and took her in his arms. He could feel her trembling with every breath.

"It's all right," he soothed, but they both knew his words were empty. "We're together now."

"I didn't mean to fall apart like that." She leaned back and looked up at him, her eyelashes glistening. "Nothing happened, he never came back. They've taken the outward things, but they can't take what's inside. I've been praying, Charles, praying all the time. I won't give in. They can't make me."

He took her hands in his. "You're better than them. Stronger, too, you know that? Come on, it looks like they left the living room alone, anyway."

She curled up next to him on the couch. He put his arm around her and turned on one of her favorite pieces, Mozart's 19th piano concerto. The airy and optimistic strains enfolded them. After a while, her breathing grew deeper and more rhythmic as she drifted off to sleep.

He watched her as the minutes ticked by and wondered how he could keep her safe. How he could get her out of this place.

At precisely twelve o'clock, the Computer informed them that lunch had arrived.

Nadia sat up and stretched. "How long was I out?"

"Maybe an hour."

"That's the best sleep I've had since I got here."

She went to the front door and opened it. An automated cart outside bore a stainless-steel platter laden with a variety of Indian dishes—lamb kebabs, chutney, chapati, tandoori chicken, basmati rice, others he didn't recognize. Enough to feed a half-dozen people with leftovers to spare. Two glasses of mango lassi and a carafe of steaming tea rounded off the feast.

"Whoa," he said. "Do they eat like this all the time around here?"

"It doesn't look bad, does it?"

"It looks incredible."

They spread the dishes out on her dining table, sat next to each other, and dug in. She rarely ate much unless there was chocolate involved, but she had some catching up to do.

"When I went to the airport that day, I thought I'd lost you," he said. "I thought I'd never see you again."

She reached over and placed her hand on his. "I begged them to let me talk to you, to let anybody talk to you and tell you that I was okay. But they're heartless."

"It's not your fault. After the bombing, I needed to get away from everything. I went to the monastery and stayed in Father Anatoly's guest room for a few weeks."

"The monastery!" Her eyes widened. "You met Father Anatoly? And Peter?"

"Julia, too."

"You have to tell me everything." She put down her silverware and pulled her legs up to sit cross-legged on her chair. "What did you do there? What did they say? How is Peter?"

He laughed. "That's a lot of questions. Let's see. Peter's doing great. I think he may have a future in agriculture."

"The holy farm, right? I wish we could be there right now."

"You and me both. It felt like I was still close to you when I was there, and that was all I wanted. It's all I ever want, you know." He leaned over and kissed her on the lips. She pushed him away playfully.

"None of your funny business until you tell me everything that happened, *Mr. Charles Ferguson*." She said his name with a flawless imitation of her father's accent. "Now come on, hop to it."

"All right, all right. What do you want to know?"

"What did you think of Father Anatoly?"

"He's one of the most interesting people I've met. I can't imagine making that kind of decision, giving up everything you own, renouncing even marriage."

"Especially marriage." She patted his leg.

"Right…so, getting back to the monks." He sat up a little straighter in his chair. "I guess I always assumed people like that had to be insane. Why else would they do something so extreme?"

"I imagine some of them are."

"Maybe, but Anatoly wasn't what I expected."

She took a sip of lassi. "I used to visit the convent when I was in high school. I'd talk to the nuns about prayer and sacrifice and wonder what it would be like to join them. It just wasn't for me. I could never let go of that old dream of marrying a prince and raising adorable children with him. Lots of adorable children."

He coughed and wiped his mouth with a napkin. "I, um—you know, I forgot to tell you something. Father Anatoly wanted me to give you a message."

"A message? Didn't he think I was…dead?" She glanced at the walls, a not-so-subtle reminder of the omnipresent Computer.

"Actually, no," he replied slowly. "It's a funny thing about those monks. They don't seem to draw a very thick line between the living and the dead."

"What was the message?"

"Keep your mind in hell and don't despair. Not exactly a Hallmark greeting, is it?"

"He always knows." She stirred the lassi with a straw. "Thank you for telling me."

"Sure, but what does it mean? Why would you want to keep your mind in hell?"

She chewed her lower lip for a moment. "There's this story I heard about an old man who visited an Orthodox monastery. He said he'd known the psychiatrist Victor Frankl, that they were prisoners in the same concentration camp during World War II. One day while they were out digging a trench for the Nazis, Victor looked over at him and said, 'This is where you've got to find your happiness—right here in this trench, in this camp.' I think that's part of what it means."

"That's a sobering thought."

She nodded. "There's also the hell we all face, the darkness within us. We come to grips with our own shallowness and addictions, our indifference to the suffering of others. We need help, we need a resurrection. We need God."

Was that true? Was he shallow and indifferent? There were times when he despised himself, times when he hated the things he'd done. Wasn't that normal?

"I'm not the poster child for living it out," she added. "It's a tough road to follow."

He absently picked up a small, diamond-shaped confection and took a bite. And another, and then another.

"Do you know what these are?" He held one of them up. "They're amazing."

"I think they're called *barfi*."

"Barfy, huh?" He shrugged and popped it into his mouth. "A rose by any other name…"

He wanted to get her out of the apartment, so after a steaming cup of hibiscus tea, they ventured out for a tour of Headquarters. Or, to be accurate, a tour of Progress. He assumed that Nadia knew little or nothing about Control. After what she'd been through, he wouldn't be the one to clue her in.

"I've been sitting alone in a dark room or staring at a computer screen for most of my time here," she said, "but they gave me a tour when I arrived. Computer, how do we get to the mall?"

"Continue down this hallway until you reach Elevator Six," the Computer replied. "I will direct that elevator to the mall."

"Thank you."

"You're welcome."

"That thing terrifies me," she whispered.

Elevator Six awaited them with open doors. After getting shifted about in every direction but down, they ended up in a spacious, circular courtyard with shop fronts and a sizable restaurant along the perimeter. There was a modest crowd, maybe a hundred in all, milling about the stores or eating lunch at the restaurant. In the center of the courtyard stood an enormous fountain in which three Roman-style statues were frozen in an eternal conversation.

They went over for a closer look at the fountain. The inscriptions identified the figures as the Roman god Apollo flanked by the ancient physicians Galen and Hippocrates. It took a moment for Charles to realize that Apollo's facial features had been subtly patterned after those of Alexander Magnus.

"I can't believe they've built all this underground," he said.

"It is something, isn't it? They told me that Magnus's great-grand-father bought the land before World War II. It was a mine back then, but he started converting it into an underground facility. There's a lot more than this—a sports complex that looks like it could host the Olympics, a virtual reality movie theater that's packed out after hours. Oh, and the Garden."

"I've seen the Garden." He shuddered as the memory of Tom Murrow's execution returned in full force. "It's impressive, isn't it?"

"It would be a lot nicer if the Computer wasn't up there, tucked away behind every tree and bush."

"Do you know how many people are here?"

"A lady that works in robotics—Tanaka, I think—she was my tour guide. She told me there were over a thousand researchers in all. Many of them have spouses and children, so the total population is quite a bit higher."

"So many? Are all of them are presumed to be, you know…"

"Dead?" she asked. "Awful, isn't it? Like the bombing. Everyone on the Outside is still blaming it on Fazal al-Najjar, but he and I were removed from the plane before takeoff. That was unreal! Three FBI agents came on board, called us by name over the sound system, and rushed us to a limousine on the tarmac. Fazal was in a wheelchair, and they just hauled him out of it, shoved us both in the car, and slammed the doors shut. We were trapped. We couldn't open anything—the doors, the windows. Then the air started feeling heavy. The next thing I remember is waking up on my own bed in the new apartment, only it wasn't my apartment at all. I haven't seen Fazal since then. He must be here somewhere."

He nodded. "That's a little like my story. I was drugged on the flight here. Thompson was with me."

"I know." She lowered her voice. "I saw him once during the tour, talking to some researchers. I don't think he noticed me. I'm not sure he would have said anything if he did. He was so friendly when I first met him at that conference last year, but he always seems so cold and standoffish when you're not around. I guess I'm just not his type."

"I'm sure you're right." He was actually sure of the exact opposite. Thompson hadn't bothered to mask his jealousy when Charles and Nadia had started dating at the beginning of the summer. But if she didn't know, he wasn't about to tell her.

They went into a clothing store, which led to his first encounter with Magnus Foundation robots. There were three of them inside, all with human proportions. One was folding clothes, one talking to a customer, and the third standing behind the counter. They were identical with their black camera eyes, their thick, four-fingered prehensile hands, and the smooth, gray-toned surface that passed for skin. All three spoke with the soft, feminine voice of the Computer.

"Welcome!" the robot behind the desk said. Its slit of a mouth twitched upward in a ghastly attempt at a smile. No fear of these machines crossing the uncanny valley. "We have some men's pants that are twenty credits off. Today only, so don't miss your chance."

"Credits?" Charles asked.

"They give you credits for your work here," Nadia said. "From what I was told, if you finish your project early or make a big contribution, you'll get bonus credits. They send you basic meals and supplies for free, but the perks cost you."

"Do you have any credits?"

She sniffed. "I doubt it. Something tells me they don't give out bonuses for hiding away in your quarters."

"I wonder if I have any."

"I can check your credit status if you would like, Dr. Ferguson," the robot piped in.

"Um, sure. Why not?"

"Very well, accessing your records. It seems you currently have thirty thousand credits. A ten thousand credit deposit is pending."

"Not a bad start." He recognized the voice at once. "Long time no see, Charles."

He turned and found himself shaking hands with Raj Bhandari. Raj was just the way he remembered him, impeccably dressed with careless suavity, eyes sparkling with a youthful and mischievous *joie de vivre*. The man was something of an anomaly among scientific researchers, a natural leader who would have made a killer salesman.

Tom Murrow used to look on Raj's carefree attitude with thinly veiled contempt, but Charles had learned very quickly that, despite outward appearances, Raj was every bit as methodical in his research as his more somber colleague.

He also knew Raj had once worked with Boris Petrov. Did he still?

"You don't look like a man who just survived a house explosion," Raj continued. "Why, you don't even look singed!"

"So they really did—" He froze. "I mean, is it okay to talk about that sort of thing?"

"Relax." Raj laughed. "Most of us are presumed dead in one way or another around here. We have our own personal ghost stories. I sailed off into the abyss a few years ago. Wasn't on my to-do list, but I think it's working out for the best."

There was something more to that last line, but Charles couldn't put a finger on it. It was like an undercurrent flowing beneath Raj's words and expressions and leading in a very different direction. Raj shot a swift glance at Nadia and continued with his banter.

"So you two worked together?" she said.

"Oh, yeah," Raj replied. "We were on a Foundation project a few years back. Top secret, hush-hush, all went nowhere. I'm sure Charles would have told you all about it if he could have."

"I wish I had." Charles cast an apologetic glance at Nadia, but she was watching Raj like a hawk.

"Hey, I saw your funeral service this morning," Raj said. "It's a form of perverse entertainment among the natives here. The Foundation hires someone to go out and secretly record the funerals. When we get the video, we all eat popcorn and drink smoothies while the friends and family of the newest arrival make up all sorts of nonsense about how kind and saintly the poor missing stiff used to be.

"It's usually lousy entertainment, but yours was incredible. It's even gone viral on the Outside. There was this crazy guy—what was his name? Something very Russian. Ivan, was it, or maybe Gavriel? No wait, Boris, that's it!"

Charles caught his breath.

"So," Raj went on, "this Boris guy stumbles up to the podium with all the grace of a town drunk, and then he launches off into this insane quasi-patriotic diatribe, ranting and raving and pounding the podium like a maniac. Here, see for yourself. I've got it on my phone."

He pulled out a sizable smartphone, tapped around on it for a few moments, and showed them the clip. There was Boris, all right, swaying back in forth in front of a podium with fire in his eyes. Fire that, to all appearances, bore a direct connection to the so-called Russian water.

"They took my daughter," Boris bellowed, "and now they've taken him. Oh, I know they told you it was a gas leak, but that's a lie. It was terrorists! Terrorists in the gas pipes. It's war those devils want, so I say we give it to them." He pounded the podium with his fist.

"Raise the black flag!" he shouted. "No quarter for the enemy. Let the unquenchable bombs of our great and glorious Republic fall like rain upon the barbarians! May they all be blown up into a state of enlightenment so that they can enjoy the peerless liberties we so dearly prize. Let freedom whistle with every flying munition into the depths of dark and dire oppression. May the unassailable gates be hurled open to receive the tender caresses from the bayonets of our gallant brigadiers. To victory, my friends, to victory!"

Boris yanked the silver flask from his jacket, took a long draught, and smacked his lips.

"In short, God bless you, Mr. Charles Ferguson. The world loves you. The world misses you. The Grand Republic weeps for the charred and cindered remnants of her noble son!"

An awkward silence followed, punctuated by a handful of timid coughs. Boris's gaze roamed through the crowd with feverish defiance. An usher climbed up to the podium and begged him in hushed tones to give way to the next speaker. Boris threw the man aside with frightening ease. A child in the audience burst into loud wails and chairs screeched as people took to their feet in alarm.

"And I'll tell you something else!" Boris slurred at the top of his lungs, stumbling backward a few steps. "There isn't a blasted one of you—not a one—who's half as decent as the burnt-up corpse of our dear friend Mr. Charles Ferguson. As for my darling girl, all I can say is, wait for me, my dear one, and I'll fly up there to find you! They're both there now, out there." He pointed vaguely toward the ceiling. "In that better place. May the angels come for them. I'll see you again, my dears. Won't be long now. I'm devastated, a broken man. Won't be long…"

He staggered to one side before tumbling to the ground. Ushers rushed the stage and hauled him off between them. The mild-faced minister—chaplain at Charles's campus—hurriedly reclaimed the podium, wiped the perspiration from his forehead, and falteringly continued the extraordinary memorial service with an old-fashioned hymn.

"Fantastic, wasn't it?" Raj grinned until he noticed Nadia's expression. "My goodness, you're crying! Did I do something wrong?"

"No, no." Nadia wiped her eyes and smiled. "It's not your fault."

"It is my fault, I'm sure of it. Forgive me, I should have introduced myself earlier. I'm Raj Bhandari."

"Nadia." She briefly shook the hand he extended.

"If you don't mind my saying so, Nadia," Raj added, "I sincerely hope you are one of Charles's relatives. Close relatives. His sister, perhaps?"

Charles cleared his throat. "She's my…" He couldn't find the right word for her. *Girlfriend* sounded childish. *Fiancé* felt better but wasn't true. "We're, um…together."

Brilliant way to put it, caveman. Smooth as sandpaper.

"Of course." Raj heaved a sigh. "Story of my life. Well, you picked a good one, Nadia. But these tears—was it something I said?"

"No." She lowered her eyes. "It's just that the man in the video, Boris—he's my father."

"Are you serious?" Raj raised his eyebrows. "I'm such an idiot."

"It's not your fault, really."

"That's kind of you. Rumor is we're going to be working together again, Charles. I heard about Project Aeternum the day I came to the Foundation. It's incredible, isn't it? Can you believe that one year from now you and I will hold the keys to everlasting life?"

"You really think we can do it?" Charles asked.

Raj darted a glance at Nadia. "Maybe it won't even take a year," he said. "Things are moving so quickly here, there's so much we've already learned. If everything falls into place, we could wrap the project up in nine months."

"I see you're still an optimist," Charles said. "But what about Phoenix? Did they ever finish it?"

He assumed that this was safe to talk about since the Phoenix project belonged to Progress. He had been thinking about it for years, wondering who, if anyone, had broken through the obstacles that had remained.

"Afraid not," Raj replied. "Phoenix ended the day we were removed from it. They still have a handful of them—the Phoenixes, I mean—in storage. They haven't seen the light of day in years. I think we were never meant to solve it. The real aim was to find breakthroughs for other projects. Biotechnological parasites, mimicry, adaptive gene manipulation—they've come in handy in all sorts of other research."

"But isn't Aeternum the same idea as Phoenix, just on a bigger scale?" Charles asked.

"Not quite. It's less ambitious in some ways, more so in others. We're not worrying about gunshot wounds or car wrecks with Aeternum. The goal is to stop—maybe even reverse—cellular aging. We'd love to dive into cancer and heart disease while we're at it, but keeping the cells young may take care of all that anyway. Of course, Phoenix also gave the Foundation a chance to vet some new recruits, didn't it?"

"And here we are," Charles replied. "But what about Tom?" It was a risky question, but he wanted to find out if Raj knew the truth. "Did they end up hiring him, too?"

"You mean Tom Murrow? He was here for a while, right up until a few weeks ago. I guess they must have transferred him. It happens sometimes to colleagues here, and when it does, we never end up seeing them again. I imagine they get promoted and reassigned back on the Outside. Now *that* would be nice! Life is great here, don't get me wrong, but I sure miss being out on the water with sunlight sparkling on the waves and wind filling the sails."

"You always were talking about sailing."

"I miss it like crazy. There's hope, though. I've heard rumors that Aeternum will be the last project before the Foundation goes public and we all go back to the Outside. Zombie Scientist Invasion—there's a headline I can't wait to read. But listen, I'd better get back to my current team. It's my last day with them, and we've got a ton of ground to cover before I hand it over to the new team leader. A pleasure to meet you, Nadia, truly. See you around, Charles."

"He's a real charmer, isn't he?" Charles said after Raj was out of earshot.

Nadia examined the window display of the bookstore. "I guess so."

"Looks like I'd better treat you well. You've got options, you know. Good ones, too."

She looked up at him, surprised. "You're kidding, right? What does Raj have that you don't?"

"Oh, I don't know. A real haircut, Fifth Avenue clothes, Casanova personality, good looks."

"If you're done with your fascinating list, I'll tell you one thing you have that he never will."

"What's that?"

"Me."

They wandered through the bookstore, which had a severely curated selection of bestsellers along with mostly scientific nonfiction, bought Nadia some soaps from a bath and beauty shop, and peeked through the window of a hair salon. Not once did they see a single human employee. Even the restaurants were completely staffed by robots, some little more than the self-propelled food carts that delivered meals and cleared tables. Others, like the cooks, stockers, and cashiers, seemed capable of incredibly advanced behaviors.

When they'd finished with the mall, they took an elevator to the other side of Level Two for a look at some of the research labs. The first stop was Robotics, the largest subdepartment in Progress. The first lab they visited had a digital sign above it.

New Era Infrastructure and Development.

"Sounds intriguing," Nadia said.

"And vague."

He placed his hand on the door. It slid open.

A disheveled, spiky-haired youth in a half-buttoned lab coat spun around in his office chair. "Come on in, the show's about to start." He turned back to his work, drawing with a stylus on a tablet mounted to a drafting table. A twenty-foot-wide bay window beside him revealed a pair of inert, multi-limbed robots surrounded by heaps of bricks, lumber, and other construction materials.

"What's all this?" Charles asked.

"The end of another career path," the youth replied without looking up from his tablet. "And good riddance. It won't be long now before our work goes mainstream, and when it does, the only jobs left will involve creativity, comfort, and research. That's all modern people should be doing anyway, not this kind of mundane nonsense."

"But what happens to all the workers?" Nadia asked.

The youth finished drawing his architectural design. "When it comes to construction, we'll need a few humans around to give our buildings an artistic dimension, at least in the early phases. But we won't need people to slap bricks on top of each other or wire a house or set up the plumbing. That's predictable, no creativity needed. In other words, it's machine work. Soon our bots will be able to build anything we throw at them. They'll run the entire electricity grid, fix all the power outages, install and repair all the plumbing, roofing—you name it. The bots will do it faster, they'll do it better, and they'll do it cheaper. See for yourself."

He set the stylus down. "Computer, build what I just drew."

"Confirmed."

The lumbering robots sprang into action, snatching boards, sawing them, and then nailing them together with a speed that took Charles's breath away. Their myriad limbs worked in perfect harmony, every action flowing toward the unified goal.

Within ten minutes, they'd finished constructing a square wooden frame, twelve feet high and fifteen feet long. They installed insulation and drywall, added flooring, built a roof, and slapped down shingles. Finally, they enclosed the outer walls with a brick veneer.

From start to finish, the miniature home took them just under an hour to complete.

"Beautiful, aren't they?" the youth cried as the final bricks were set in place. He stood and leaned closer to the window. "Everything they do is perfect, every detail according to plan. Every nail in that building is precisely spaced, every angle exact. Humans can't compete with this, and they shouldn't try. There'll always be other things for people to do."

"What if there were people who couldn't do more sophisticated work?" Nadia asked.

"Look around, lady," the youth said. "The kind of people you meet here in Headquarters are the only ones who belong in the world we're building. As for the rest, I figure they'll either adapt or get phased out one way or another. I don't know, that's not my job. My job is figuring out how to get my bots to use those new sustainable materials from the Green Team, so if you don't mind, I've got work to do."

He turned his attention back to his tablet. Nadia and Charles slipped out of the laboratory without another word.

The hallway ended in a complex of offices and laboratories that focused on disaster recovery. The teams they met tackled potential catastrophes ranging from nuclear war to drug-resistant plagues to the return of an Ice Age.

One project involved the use of robots to eliminate human corpses as quickly as possible. The hypothetical scenario was a global pandemic with a significantly higher mortality rate than COVID-19. Human contact with the dead would increase the risk of the plague spreading further, so the team had created machines to dispose of the victims.

"How are all the robots here getting power?" Nadia asked one of the researchers. "I haven't seen any wires or external cables."

"To tell you the truth, we don't know." The middle-aged Italian researcher peered up at them over a pair of hot pink, horn-rimmed glasses. She and her colleagues were prepping a test run in which one of their robotic undertakers would dispose of a life-sized dummy made of biodegradable materials. "Embarrassing, is it not? All we know is the Foundation provides us with these power cells. We are shown how to interface with them and how to monitor the amount of charge they have remaining. They come in all sizes. I've heard there are some that are only a few centimeters wide."

"Power cells?"

"They will not tell us how the cells work. They give us strict orders not to tamper with them. There is one thing I have noticed. If you look at them under a microscope, there are always two tiny letters, E and P, in the bottom right corner. I heard someone in Infrastructure Management took a power cell apart in her quarters a few months ago. She was transferred out the next day. We haven't seen her since."

"Does that happen often?" Charles asked. "The transfers, I mean."

"There are times when people are coming and going in waves and other times when there is very little movement at all. There have been many waves lately, but I'm not sure why. Working at Headquarters is a privilege. Once they decide to kick you out, you're out for good."

Oh yes, he thought grimly. Out for the count.

"Those power cells must be incredibly efficient," Nadia said.

The researcher nodded. "One small cell can power our robot unit for months on a single charge. It's hard to believe that I used to get excited about the robots on the Outside. We had to deal with so many limitations, always writing out proposals and trying to get grants and funding, always waiting for some breakthrough power source. Here, it feels like the only constraints are the ones we bring with us, our human need to eat, sleep and, once in a great while, socialize. Now watch, I will show one of our machines in action. We call them Corpse Processing Units. CPUs, yes?"

The robot looked humanoid, much like the ones working at the mall. As soon as it was activated, it approached the artificial corpse and leaned over it. It opened its mouth, and tens of thousands of tiny black machines came scuttling out. They covered the corpse, enveloping it under an undulating blanket of darkness. Seconds later, they scampered away, crawling up the robot and reentering through its open jaws.

The corpse had vanished. All that remained was a mound of pinkish-gray matter that the machines had excreted.

"We are working together with the Green Team on a system to reuse the remains," the researcher informed them. "Not the worst material for a garden. It's nice to know that if there ever is a catastrophe on the Outside, we will be ready and able to put all those extra bodies to good use."

"How many of these CPUs are there?" he asked.

"I don't know the number," she replied. "My team was given a huge bonus after Mr. Magnus watched a demonstration. We are solving a very practical problem, and Mr. Magnus always prides himself on being a practical person."

"Let's get out of here." Nadia grabbed Charles's arm and pulled him away.

As they headed back toward the elevators, he envisioned an army of Corpse Processing Units roaming through city streets cluttered with the corpses of Harvester victims, vomiting swarms of mechanical insects, converting the dead into compost.

⁓

Charles and Nadia lay next to each other on a blanket in a secluded clearing in the Garden. The night sky, a vast domed display, brimmed with glittering, simulated stars.

"What did you think?" he asked.

"Of what?"

"The projects we saw today."

She leaned up on one elbow. "Do you really want to know?"

"Of course."

"I think the world is about to become a very frightening place."

"It always has been." He ran his hands along the deep green, perfectly manicured grass. Not a single weed in the entire Garden.

"That kid over in construction was right," she said. "It's coming, and nothing will hold it back. There isn't much left for people to do here at the Foundation, is there? Nearly all of us are scientists, and then there are those brutes in Security and a few chefs for the higher-ups. The only other human being is Magnus himself. One of the ladies in robotics told me that machines take care of the Garden now. They used to have gardeners, real ones. Now bots crawl up here in the middle of the night and trim the bushes, water the plants, fertilize, pollinate—all of it. Can you imagine a world without gardeners? Without farmers or cooks? A world where one machine does everything. It's here right now, watching us, analyzing us. Hello, Computer."

"Hello, Nadia!" Its cheerful voice sprang out at them from an unseen speaker in the bushes. "May I help you?"

"Not exactly."

She lay on her back again. "Do you realize that we're sitting in a

Garden that never feels a single breeze, that never comes to life after a sudden thunderstorm? I know what you're thinking. It's all so innovative, so breathtaking. But there's no soul, Charles. It's steel and wires, ones and zeroes. It's hellish."

"Won't argue with you there." He stood and stretched his back. "It's been a long day. Maybe things will look up in the morning."

"At least I've got you." She started folding the blanket.

"Listen, Nadia, I'm going to sleep on your couch tonight."

She hugged the blanket tightly in her arms. "I know you're worried, but I'm okay. Maybe it was all just a joke."

"Talk like that is never a joke, especially when it comes from the man holding the gun. But I may have a way to take care of it."

"What do you have in mind?"

"If it works, you'll be the first to know."

Chapter Twelve
The Reaping

THE NEXT MORNING, Charles's phone alarm went off at six. Nadia was still asleep in her bedroom. He ate an early breakfast and left a note for her on the kitchen table. He spent the next several minutes pacing up and down the hallway outside her quarters, mustering the courage to take the next step.

It was the only way.

"Computer?"

"Yes, Dr. Ferguson?"

"I need to talk to Magnus as soon as he's awake."

A pause. "That may not be possible."

"I need you to tell him that it's urgent."

The silence stretched on so long that he thought the Computer had forgotten him. Then it spoke. "Very well, he will meet with you in ten minutes. Please turn right at the next hallway and take Elevator Eight."

He drummed his fingers against his pants leg while the elevator zipped down to Level Six.

Magnus was behind his desk, feasting on a generous serving of crepes, bacon, quiche, and fruit. A pair of royal blue parlor chairs had been placed in front of the desk.

"Come in, Ferguson, have a seat. What can I do for you?" Magnus looked like he'd already been up for some time. His grin was warm and amiable, his eyes twinkling. Santa Claus meets Mussolini.

Charles rehearsed his line of attack and reminded himself to keep his voice level. That was crucial. He couldn't be emotional, couldn't appeal to the wrongness of the thing. Ethics were irrelevant here, traditional morality anathema.

"You told me yesterday that if Nadia and I needed anything to be comfortable here, you would provide it," he began.

"Yes, yes. Within reason, you'll remember."

"Of course, within reason." He fought down a sudden rush of anger. Steady voice, steady emotions. "I've thought of a few things that might help. First, you don't threaten to put Nadia in prison. I need to be calm to focus on my work. I won't be calm if I'm always worrying about what you're going to do to her."

"You'll find a way to focus." Magnus speared a few pieces of crepe and a bite of quiche on his fork and stuffed them in his mouth. "Do your job and she'll never be in any real danger. I need you to understand that I will do whatever is necessary to finish the task, but you can also rest assured that I'm aware her well-being is inextricably linked to yours. That's why I have you working in Progress instead of Control. It's better for both of you."

Charles took a deep breath. "Okay, let's move on to two. You were worried about her depression, right?"

Magnus guzzled a glass of orange juice and wiped his mouth. "I always want my researchers to perform at their highest level, so yes."

"Forgive me for being blunt here, but you're the one who caused her depression. You knew her past. What did you think would happen when you tried to destroy the very thing that's at the center of who she is? And then you—" He got out of his chair and ran his fingers along the line of his chin. Logic, balance, a steady voice. "Then you had Security threaten to…to sexually assault her."

"What did you say?" Magnus's soft voice held a dangerous edge. "What are you talking about, Ferguson?"

"I'm talking about that monster from Security. He said it was all your orders, that if she so much as moved one of those paintings of yours, he'd sneak into her apartment while she was asleep and—"

"Enough!" Magnus snatched the plate in front of him and smashed it on the ground. His face was bright red, his eyes bulging. "Computer!"

"Yes, Lord Magnus?"

"What Dr. Ferguson just said—is it true?"

"Confirmed."

Magnus sat there, panting, his fingers curling into fists and then uncurling again. Then he leaned back in his chair and let out a breath. "I sometimes allow our Security members certain liberties," he said in an even tone. "But those liberties only take place within strictly defined contexts. Progress is not—can never be—one of those contexts. I want you to know, Ferguson, that I had nothing to do with this. It was unauthorized. There is no need to worry about someone from Security harming Nadia. I will assure you of that. From now on, you need only be concerned with me. Computer, get me Heimler."

A projection of Heimler's face suddenly appeared against the side wall. The head of Magnus Security looked exhausted but wary.

"Yes, my lord?"

"We've had an incident, Heimler. Arrest every member of the security detail that was assigned to Nadia Petrova's orientation. Lock them up in holding rooms. I'll meet you there."

"Right away, my lord." The image vanished.

"Computer," Magnus said, "which member of Security threatened Nadia?"

"Jacob Kingsley."

"Very well."

Charles bit his lip. This was his chance, it was now or never. "What about her belongings? She's been through a lot, you know."

Magnus pressed his fingertips together and rested them against his lips. "You want me to give them back, is that it?"

"That's it."

"And you'll want your magic rope back as well?"

"Magic rope?" Of course, the prayer rope Father Anatoly had given him. It had been in his suitcase when he left the monastery but not when he unpacked at the Foundation. "Yeah, I do, actually."

Magnus swore. "You of all people should know better. A coward is too feeble to reap his own justice in the here and now, so his slavish mind conjures up heaven and hell, angels and eternal judgement. There's no need for it. We'll turn ourselves into gods by the sheer strength of our determination. We'll gift ourselves immortality. We'll learn until we know everything, and then we'll control everything with our knowledge."

Charles stared at him. The man had the calm composure of a zealot. Or a lunatic. "You really believe that, don't you?"

"Of course I believe it. Humans are animals, and that's all. No divine image, no angelic choir, no pie in the sky. People prattle on about equality and inherent rights, but when push comes to shove, they remember what they really are and behave accordingly. You think I'm a monster? Here's reality, Ferguson. In a world like ours, I'm the savior.

"If we keep allowing anyone and everyone to breed like rabbits, the day will come when half the world will have to turn themselves into real monsters and slaughter the other half. We're trying to spare everyone that terrible decision. It goes against their instincts to preserve the herd, so we'll do it for them. The strongest, the most intelligent, the most beautiful—they'll all survive. When the world is freed of the burden it now carries, those same survivors will thank us for what we've done."

"That's ridiculous," Charles cried. "No one in their right mind would want this. No one!"

"Is that so?" Magnus shot him a mirthless grin. "Here's a nice little children's story for you. On the Outside, they perform a test for Down Syndrome on fetuses. Two-thirds of the mothers who test positive abort the fetus. Sixty-seven percent, and these are the mothers! The truth is that we don't want unnecessary people. We don't want the disabled, the mentally ill, the refugees. We pretend we want them because we're all getting crushed beneath centuries of nonsense about *imago Dei* and inalienable rights. Given the opportunity, we immediately fall back to our true nature, which is Nature itself. The Down Syndrome population has already been reduced by over thirty percent in America. Don't you see? The wolves are good for the herd. We're going to trim the fat that's weighing down the collective human organism. We're giving them what they want more than anything else. They're just too weak to admit it."

"How many?" Charles asked quietly.

"Around seventy percent of the global population needs to be culled. If the mothers can do it, so can I."

"*Seventy* percent?"

"Yes, but not all at once. We'll preserve some genetic undesirables—Reaps, as Security likes to call them—for infrastructure, at least in the first stage. All we're doing is pruning the barren branches of our genetic tree. The tree may go into shock, but it will survive. It will adapt, recover.

"We'll also avoid ethnic groups with lower populations. They could have some useful knowledge buried beneath their primitive ideologies or even some key lurking in their DNA that will one day unlock a breakthrough. I'm not a racist, Charles, as you might have gathered from what you've seen of Headquarters. We're very intentional in our diversity here. The only measure of a human is their genes, pure and simple. I think of people as strings of information that may or may not be useful for the future of our race. The redundant data will be eliminated, but I have no intention of removing any distinct expressions of the genome.

"Thanks to your work on Alpha, we now know exactly what to look for in a desirable human. Control is now on pace to launch within nine months. The first wave will eliminate four point eight billion people."

Charles was shaking. He felt like throwing up. "But how? How could you possibly know everyone's DNA?"

"My dear Ferguson! We owe it all to you." Magnus withdrew a folder from his desk and handed it to him.

Alpha Financial was written in red letters on the cover of the folder. He opened it. The contract for the OneScan device. Not a copy, but the original.

"Of course." He closed the folder. "It was you all along."

"It still took a bit of work," Magnus said. "We had to cajole some politicians with bribery and blackmail, the usual tactics. They're all on board now. With few exceptions, every man, woman, and child on the planet will use that scanner of yours in the coming months. But it wasn't just Alpha. I'm the one who got you your job at the university. I'm the one who funded your research on the scanner. I've owned you for a very long time now. And there's more, but that will have to wait until your next lesson. The point is made. You are mine."

"I still don't see how you could pull it off," Charles said. "Even if you had all those blood samples, there's no way you could match them to their owners."

Magnus grinned. "You vastly underestimate the power of modern surveillance. We have had very little trouble linking the blood samples to their respective owners, even in the most remote locations. Our modern world, so deeply interconnected, so comprehensively monitored, makes child's play of it. We have access to every cell phone, every computer, every laptop, every Internet-connected device with a camera or a microphone. We have an army of satellites, drones, and spy planes traversing every region of the globe at every point in time. We know exactly who is getting each blood test. The Computer analyzes the sample, issues a verdict, and sends the appropriate information to our tracking database. Our Harvesters will know who they're targeting. We see them in surveillance cameras, we follow them with satellites and drones, we listen to their phone calls. It's almost trivial. I hear from Control that we could have two billion targets identified within the next three months."

"I still think it's insane," Charles replied stubbornly. "You say you're going to kill nearly five billion people all at once. How could you prepare for the aftereffects of something like that? We're talking entire cities almost vanishing, the whole world economy crashing to the ground, militaries instantly stripped to the bone. It would cause absolute chaos. Who's going to bury five billion people? How are the survivors supposed to keep going when all their infrastructure is broken? What if somebody launches nuclear weapons in retaliation? You could destroy everything!"

"Haven't you been listening?" Magnus chided. "Control has been working on this for years. Militaries will be disbanded, nuclear weapons will be disarmed. Once they experience the power of the Foundation's technology, the survivors will get in line and do what they're told. Peaceful compliance or death are the only possible terms.

"As for the corpses, yes, that will certainly be a pressing issue. I believe you saw one of our early plans when you were touring Progress. Those CPUs will come in handy in the crowded cities, but we'd need time to deploy them. One of our Control researchers has come up with a workaround. The same Harvesters that kill the Reaps will also embalm them, all with a single injection. I just saw a demonstration yesterday. A well-preserved human corpse, the porcelain features calm and at rest, the body freed of its endless struggle—truly, it was a thing of beauty."

Beauty will save the world. Father Anatoly's words echoed in Charles's mind, though they now seemed feeble and confusing. The brooding countenance of the man in the portrait glowered at them from the other side of the desk. He seemed real enough.

"I'll tell you what," Magnus went on, "since you're so interested in the Reaping, I'll keep you in the loop. We're planning a little demonstration, a dry run. You'll be here to watch it. As for your request, Nadia will get her fairy tales and talismans back, as will you."

Magnus reached into a drawer, pulled out the prayer rope Father Anatoly had given him, and slid it across the desk. "I was curious when they told me it was in your luggage. Perhaps you think it will conjure up a miracle for you from some intergalactic deity? Regardless, you have what you want, and I expect results from my leniency. Work hard and work quickly."

"Wait." It was risky, but it felt like the right move. "There's one more thing."

Magnus blew a long breath through pursed lips. "Out with it!"

"I want Fazal al-Najjar on Project Aeternum."

Flames spit and hissed in the fireplace. Magnus took a sip of coffee. "So she told you Al-Najjar is still alive, did she?" He gave Charles a penetrating stare. "Why, exactly, do you want him on your project?"

Charles wiped his palms against the sides of his pants. He had to appear calm even if his heart was pounding like a snare drum.

The key was in Nadia's unpublished papers. A recipe for revolution with advanced mathematics as a prime ingredient. "I read a news report about Fazal. It said he was brilliant, that he'd come up with a new approach for getting probabilities from data sets. With Aeternum, we're about to go looking for needles in a few billion haystacks. He'd be useful."

Magnus tapped his chin with his forefinger. "They'll be gnashing their teeth in Control, but I'll give him to you. He'll still have to report in on their side of the fence from time to time. He is a remarkable young man despite his flaws and his unfortunate disability. Thanks to him, the first demonstration will take place weeks ahead of schedule. But he wasn't at all what we expected. Too soft, too compassionate. Disappointing given the family tree. The cousin of the Butcher of Beirut, and he might as well be a pacifist!"

"That won't bother me."

"Fazal will come with a price," Magnus said. "Computer, change the schedule for Project Aeternum. They now have nine months to complete instead of twelve."

"Confirmed."

"Nine months?" Charles cried.

"I want you to match Control's pace. We'll finish both projects at once, just as it should be. And I don't want to hear any excuses, Ferguson."

Twelve months, nine months—did it even matter? Both numbers were absurd.

"Fine," he said. "Whatever you want."

"One last thing," Magnus added. "Jacob Kingsley. What is your verdict?"

He blinked. "My verdict?"

"He's the guard who threatened Nadia. This is a perfect opportunity to continue your training. Shall I kill him, or shall I let him go? You must realize that if I release him, he may very well follow through on his threat."

He looked at Magnus in shock. "You're asking me if I want him to be killed?"

"Precisely."

"Then no!" he cried. "I'd never want that."

"Even if his survival puts Nadia at risk? I've heard he has a very bad reputation."

Charles leaned back in his chair and rested his hand against his forehead. "I—no, I can't ask you to kill him. I don't want anyone's blood on my hands."

Magnus stirred some sugar into the remnants of his coffee. "Why are you shivering and stuttering like a scared little boy? He's your enemy, Ferguson. The man is a wolf, and he means to harm her. Do you want that to happen?"

"Of course not."

"Then say the word, say you want justice!"

"I don't want him to hurt her."

Magnus laughed. "Then you do want him to die."

"No!" Charles scrambled out of his chair. "Just stop him, keep him away from her."

"Enough." Magnus waved him away. "You don't deserve Nadia in the first place. Cowards shouldn't be allowed to mate in a world like this."

"But you'll stop him, right? You won't let him harm her?"

Magnus stood and tossed his napkin on the desk. "Who knows? It's not my choice, Ferguson. It's yours. I suppose you'll just have to wait and see what happens. The odds aren't good, I'm afraid." He walked toward the door behind the desk.

Charles gripped the back of his chair with both hands. He pictured Nadia, imagined what could happen to her because of this man, this wolf named Jacob Kingsley.

He hated him.

"Don't let him hurt her."

"Do you mean—"

"Don't let him!" he screamed.

"As you wish." Magnus bowed and left the room.

Charles stood rooted to the spot, his breath coming in heaves. Then, suddenly, he snapped out of his stupor and rushed toward the door as it slid closed behind Magnus. He set his palm against it to open it.

It didn't move.

"Computer, open this door. I need to talk to Magnus."

"You do not have access to that area," the Computer said.

"But I have to talk to him!" He pounded on the door with his fist. "Don't kill him! Do you hear me, Magnus? I was wrong, I changed my mind. Let him live!"

Silence.

"Let him live," he whispered.

He slid to the ground with his back against the door. He pulled the prayer rope from his pocket and clutched it between his fingers.

You just killed a man.

You didn't have a choice.

You murdered him.

"Computer, can you send a message to Magnus?"

A pause.

"Lord Magnus has asked not to be disturbed."

"Do it anyway! Tell him I've changed my mind. Tell him not to kill Jacob Kingsley."

"I will deliver your message as soon as Lord Magnus is available again."

"It will be too late."

The Computer said nothing.

Jacob Kingsley.

Forgive me.

⁓

Security had already arrived at Nadia's quarters.

"I can't believe it." Nadia watched as two of the guards carefully stacked her books and icons on the dining table. The others were hauling off the anti-icons. "Do you know anything about this?"

"I talked with Magnus this morning."

"You went to Magnus? And you demanded…" She ran up and threw her arms around him.

"I was just trying to help."

"Thank you." She wiped her eyes. "I feel so much safer now that you're here, even after what happened. You didn't tell Magnus about… that other thing, did you?"

He looked away and covered his mouth with his hand. He couldn't tell her that the guard was going to die. That he had, even in an indirect way, ordered the man's execution.

"What is it?"

"Nothing. Magnus promised that it won't happen again. You don't need to worry about that anymore."

She watched him in silence, then leaned up to kiss his cheek. "I don't need to know the rest if you don't want to tell me. I do know that you need to unwind. We don't start the project until tomorrow, right? How about we get something to eat and head over to the pool for a few laps?"

"Swimming? Sounds nice."

"You up for your standard breakfast?"

"You know me."

He picked at his perennial morning fare, eating as much as his frayed nerves allowed. Nadia blew on steaming spoonfuls of raisin cinnamon oatmeal before slipping them into her mouth.

He joined her as a silent partner for her morning prayers. It reminded him of the monastery—the calm alternation of sound and silence, the reverent tones, the gestures and genuflections. It lasted about fifteen minutes, like a highlight reel from the marathon services of the monks.

While she prayed, he thought about Jacob Kingsley. Was he still alive? Were they executing him at that moment, targeting him with a Harvester or pressing the cold barrel of a pistol to his forehead while Nadia whispered *Lord have mercy* and tapped a clenched fist against her chest?

What had been Jacob's crime? A threat, a dangerous one. Worthy of a court trial, maybe some time in jail. Not worthy of death.

The situation Magnus had put him in was impossible. What else could he have done?

She finished her prayers. They grabbed their swimsuits and rode an elevator to the sports complex. They changed in separate locker rooms and met up at one of the two Olympic-size pools.

"I've missed this!" She dove in, swam underwater like a porpoise, and surfaced a few yards away. "Come on, it's perfect."

Her cheerful voice echoed off the rippling, chlorinated water and bounced around the open room. A pair of swimmers toiled away at asynchronous laps on the other side of the pool, the no-nonsense side where green and white swim ropes separated the lanes.

He took a deep breath and dove, his whole body exhilarated by the rush of cold and the illusion of near weightlessness. He came up and wiped his hair off his forehead.

The moment he opened his eyes, she splashed him right in the face.

"Hey, what was that for?" He blinked and rubbed the water out of his eyes.

She splashed him again and burst out laughing.

"All right, you asked for it." He brought his arms back and shoved them forward again just under the surface of the water. The Ferguson tsunami, his favorite move as a teenager in swim class.

Nadia shrieked and sputtered as the miniature wave collapsed over her. Then she pounced on him, wrapping him up in her arms, trying to push him under.

"Okay, you win, you win!" He laughed and wrestled free from her grasp.

They swam a half-dozen laps together and splashed around. Then they toweled off and sat on the edge of the pool, kicked their legs in the water, held hands, and talked about unimportant things.

It was almost enough. If only they could walk out of there and leave Headquarters, go back home, forget everything they'd seen and heard. But that couldn't happen. There was no escape from this place, his home had been destroyed, and he never forgot anything.

⌇

The main entry to the Aeternum laboratory slid open. Fazal al-Najjar wheeled himself into the conference room. The nineteen-year-old wore a pair of thick, black-rimmed glasses, a pair of blue jeans, and a gray T-shirt. From the looks of things, he struggled with hair even more unruly than Charles's.

"Hello," he said in a soft, subdued voice. "I hope this is the right place." He recognized Nadia and gave her a self-conscious wave.

"Before I say anything else," Raj replied. "I want to get something straight. You didn't blow up that plane, right?"

"I would never…" Fazal levelled his tone. "Listen, I'm an American. It's true I have family over there, and yes, some of them are crazy people. They've made their choices, I've made mine. My parents and I became Sufis before we immigrated. We couldn't do that back there without getting persecuted, so we came to America. It's changed everything for our family. The enemies we now fight lie within, not without."

"I know what you mean," said Miguel Velasquez, a plump Colombian with delicate features and meticulously styled hair. He'd spent most of his adult life in the mechanized environs of Headquarters but had grown up on a coffee farm in the Andes. "One of my uncles joined the cartel when I was a kid. We never spoke to him again. There was nothing we could have done, but we still felt guilty. Come on in."

"Thank you." Fazal bowed slightly and wheeled himself next to Miguel's chair.

Their allotted space for Project Aeternum included an entire suite, a half-dozen rooms with a conference room at the center of the hub. The laboratory proper was over two thousand square feet and jam-packed with the Foundation's latest technology. On the other side of the suite, they had an open lounge with a small kitchen and some sofas and recliners, which eventually became their base of operations. And some thoughtful planner had added a bedroom of sorts with a couple of single beds in case one of them needed to crash after a binge of workaholism.

"So, Fazal, I hear you're a mathematician," Miguel said.

"Not really. I'm just a student."

"Good grief," Raj said. "You're as bad as Charles. You work with statistics, right? Probabilities?"

"Well, yes, I've done a little bit with that. It's nothing, really."

Raj rolled his eyes. "Listen, kid, if the Foundation hired you, you're the real deal. I bet we'll find something for you to do around here. Did anyone tell you what Aeternum was about?"

"Maybe, but I'm not sure I heard it right."

"Oh, you heard it right." Miguel grinned. "We're going to build the Fountain of Youth. In one year."

"Actually, nine months," Charles corrected him. "New deadline. Magnus just told me yesterday."

"We had better get to work, then," said Anna Mueller, a short and buxom German in her early thirties. She had a slightly irregular nose, a single dimple on her left cheek, and softened features that provided an unusual contrast to a blunt personality. Her specialty was cryogenics.

Their first step in the project would be ferreting out the existing research—within the Foundation and without—that had the most potential for Aeternum. This proved to be an enormous undertaking, one that could have eaten up weeks of precious time.

Fazal, however, proved his worth his first day on the job. Search algorithms were right up his alley. After the rest of the team came up with a list of the terms and concepts they were seeking, Fazal and the Computer hunkered down for an hour and compiled a hefty array of research articles and studies.

They divided into two groups and dug into the work, plowing through the mountain of research on tablets and digital readers. Fazal joined Nadia and Charles for one group, Raj, Anna, and Miguel formed the second.

Lunch showed up at noon on the dot, borne by a pair of automated food carts. Deli sandwiches, chips, and an assortment of fresh fruit with some chocolates thrown in for a sugar fix. The team brought the trays into the lounge and had a meal together.

"Guess they're done spoiling us," Charles said to Nadia as they bolted down their sandwiches. "So much for the five-star cuisine."

"What?" Miguel wiped his mouth. "You guys are getting five-star cuisine?"

They told Miguel about their Indian feast. He shook his head in disbelief.

"We all thought the real cooks were long gone," he said. "They must keep a few of them around for the higher-ups. If you have some credits, you can get something decent down at the mall, even if it is made by robots. If you don't have credits, well, this is about as good as it gets. Keeps you alive, anyway."

At around one o'clock, just as they were getting back to work, Fazal asked Charles in a hushed whisper if he could pray.

"I'm sorry, what?" Charles glanced up from a paper on the life cycle of Antarctic sponges.

"Pray. May I pray? Please?"

"Oh." Charles looked to Nadia for guidance, but she was lost in a study about the confining world of endoliths. Her hand, he noticed, had strayed into the pocket of her jacket, the pocket where she now kept her prayer rope. "Of course, Fazal. Why not?"

"Really?" Fazal's eyes lit up. He reached behind his wheelchair and grabbed his backpack, went off into the bedroom area, and returned about ten minutes later.

"They would never let me do that in my last assignment. Thank you, Dr. Ferguson."

❧

They called it a night at around seven. In a single day, Nadia and Charles had pored over the details of twenty-three research projects. There were around fifteen hundred projects on the list, which meant this initial stage could cost the team over a month even if they never took a day off.

"This is insane," Anna said flatly. "You tell me we have nine months to do this. Nine years would be more like it."

"It wasn't my call," Charles replied. "You're welcome to take it up with Magnus if you'd like."

"Magnus? Oh." She looked away. "That won't be necessary. We will do our best."

"Dinner at the mall in ten minutes." Raj tossed his tablet onto a coffee table. "My treat. We're in this madman's race together, so I say we get off on the right foot."

"Hey, thanks Raj!" Miguel sat up and stretched. "I almost ran out of credits last weekend. Can you believe it? Twelve years in this place and I'm still broke."

"Are you serious?" Anna frowned. "How could you spend them all? I always have more than I know what to do with."

"Well, I occasionally do a little bit of, you know, gambling." Miguel gave an apologetic shrug. "Some of us get together on the weekends and watch football. Soccer, not that weird American stuff. La Liga. We start talking, bragging, and, you know, betting. Stupid Barcelona has been killing my teams this year. And then, whenever I turn traitor and bet on them, they lose. It's ridiculous! I mean honestly, what are the odds that I don't win a single match I'm betting on for an entire season?"

"I can run the numbers if you'd like," Fazal replied eagerly. "I'd need to factor in the capabilities of the players on both teams, coaching records, personality indexes, matchup dynamics, injury reports…"

"You're kidding, right?" Miguel asked.

"Not at all. I did a probabilities test during the college basketball tournament a few years ago. It was a proof-of-concept for an approach I'd been working on."

"Is that right?" Miguel leaned forward in his chair. "How did it go?"

"Okay, I guess. The model correctly predicted the winners for fifty-seven of the sixty-three games. Roughly ninety percent accuracy."

"Ninety percent?" Raj repeated, wide-eyed. "Good grief, Fazal! If we ever get out of here, I'm taking you to Vegas."

"And *I'm* taking you to watch La Liga next weekend!" Miguel had an ear-to-ear grin.

The grin, however, didn't last long. While they rode in the elevator, Miguel interrogated Fazal about the minutiae of his March Madness project and stumbled across a startling discovery.

"You can't gamble? At all?"

"Well, I *could* gamble," Fazal said, "but I don't. We say that it's forbidden. Anyway, it's bad for you."

"Bad for you?" Miguel raised his eyebrows. "I guess the pope wouldn't approve, either, now that you mention it. Wait, does that mean you can't tell me who's going to win the match this weekend?"

"I couldn't tell you that even if I wanted to," Fazal replied. "These are only mathematical probabilities, not real-life certainties. Why don't you just ask the Computer? I'm sure it could do all this for you."

"I can't." Miguel sighed. "It's against the rules. They always check before we place bets to make sure you haven't tried. But listen, if it's just mathematics, something the Computer can do, it's not really gambling, right? It's just math, not chance, and the money goes to the best mathematician."

"Nice try, Miguel," Fazal said, "but no dice, so to speak."

Miguel drummed his fingers against the wall of the elevator. "Okay, I've got it! If I promise not to gamble on the match this weekend, will you tell me who's going to win? I want to see your magic in action."

"I…guess that would be okay," Fazal said. "If you promise you won't gamble, I'll do the math. But I'll have to get all the data first."

"Deal."

"Don't you boys have something else you should be doing?" Anna asked, a little too sweetly. "Like, you know, that minor research project we're working on?"

"Bah!" Miguel waved her off. "If I stopped watching La Liga, I'd turn into a foaming-at-the-mouth lunatic. I need that happy little place where I can jump up and down and scream at referees and throw things at the TV and cry out against all the injustice in the world. I get to do all that every single time I watch soccer. I don't even have to leave the living room!"

"Pathetic." Anna muttered. "Sounds like an ape at the zoo."

"Hey, we're all primates here, aren't we?" Miguel shot back. "Besides, there *is* injustice. Those refs are crooks, every one of them. They're all being bribed. Criminals! You know how many soccer officials are in prison now?"

Charles enjoyed the mindless chatter. It felt great to be back on a research project, to be surrounded by a motley group of colleagues with all their quirks and foibles.

They shared a feast that centered around prime steak and enormous coconut shrimp. Every bite had been prepped, seared, and served by robotic hands. Raj blew through several hundred credits on the meal, but from the sound of things, he had more than enough to spare. Miguel pigeonholed Fazal and was showing him data from La Liga on his phone. Anna, who was apparently a cellist of some caliber, was chatting with Nadia about Baroque music. Raj and Charles were too busy stuffing their faces to talk about anything.

Robot cooks or not, the shrimp were dynamite.

Chapter Thirteen
Chameleon

THEY PLOWED THROUGH a large swath of the reading list over the next two weeks. Thompson wasn't bluffing. The Foundation had already come a long way towards completing Aeternum.

Charles was mowing down the standard breakfast on a Tuesday morning, his mouth chomping up toast, his mind chewing on a study involving telomerase manipulation that he'd read the day before, when a realization struck him.

Magnus was right about one thing.

He had said that Progress would make Charles forget the things he'd seen. And now, after only two weeks, Tom Murrow's death had slipped out of the foreground, and he'd gone for days without a single thought about Jacob Kingsley.

Life had taken a new course, and the ruts were already forming. Research, strolls through the Garden, dinners at the restaurant, laps at the swimming pool. Best of all, evenings with Nadia, curled up on her couch with tea or hot cocoa or a glass of wine in hand, holding each other close, talking about anything and everything that came to mind.

At least, anything and everything that was safe to talk about when the walls had ears.

He finished breakfast, brushed his teeth, and opened the front door to leave. The path was barred. He staggered back from the hulking form of Franz Heimler. The head of Magnus Security had apparently been waiting for him.

"Let's go," Heimler said. "Time for your next lesson."

"I'm on my way to the laboratory." A feeble excuse, but he felt like a rabbit cornered by a wolf. "They're expecting me."

"Your team has been informed of your absence. I'm sure they'll manage."

Heimler turned and walked down the hallway. The guards with him waited for Charles to pass, then fell into step behind him. They marched him down the plush corridors lined with artwork, rode the elevator across and down to Level Six, and led him through the gilded doors into Magnus's office.

Magnus reclined on an ivory couch, newspaper in hand. He sat up and motioned for Charles to sit next to him. "How's the project, Ferguson? Making headway, are we?"

"It's coming along." Charles rubbed his palms together nervously. "There's a ton of research we need to dig through, but we're seeing light at the end of the tunnel."

"Excellent! I'm sure you've realized by now that Control has given your team access to their own research. It's being carefully filtered, of course, to make it sound like it originated from Progress. Not an easy task, particularly when it comes to the more unorthodox experiments on human subjects. Do you think you'll finish on time?"

Charles ran his fingers through his hair. "I can't make any promises."

"I have perfect faith in your abilities, Ferguson. No one in the entire world is as capable as you."

"You might be overestimating my abilities."

Magnus regarded him with a mysterious smile. "Before you leave this office today, you'll understand why I can say that. It's time for your next lesson. What did you think of the first ones, old Tom and that business with Jacob Kingsley?"

Charles lowered his eyes. "You already know the answer."

"It was all necessary. Kingsley was a given. I can't have loose cannons among my own personal security, and you can't have a monster like that around your chosen mate. Tom was a tougher call. Given the chance and the capability, he would have murdered me, and he would have felt like some mythic hero for doing it. He was blind to the truth. What we're accomplishing here is more important than any one person. The only crime is to get in the way of it."

Charles remained silent.

"Cheer up, Ferguson! Remember that I promised Tom I would bring him back. I meant that. We *will* bring back those who have served the cause. We can't do that for everyone, of course. Kingsley, for example, wasn't worth the effort. You'll forgive all the chaos when you see the result, an entire planet healed of its deepest wounds, thriving and flourishing again. A new and prosperous humanity, robust, civilized, its every nuance governed by the razor-edged steel of inflexible logic."

"I assume you'll be the one to govern them?" Charles asked.

"Who else?" Magnus folded the newspaper and set it on the cushion beside him. "It's time to bring us back to the old Leadership Principle, to *Führerprinzip*. You called me a monster after the incident with Tom. I'm firm, intractable, convinced of my assumptions. I'm willing to make sacrifices for the greater good. That doesn't sound very monstrous, does it?"

"What it sounds like and what it is are two very different things," Charles said.

"Do you think so? Whether we'd like to or not, we males always pattern ourselves after our father figures. Whether by imitation or the attempt to distance ourselves from him, those of us who have been blessed or cursed to grow up with a father can never fully escape the paternal orbit. Once you've heard my story, perhaps you'll understand me a little better."

Magnus leaned back on the couch and tapped his fingertip against his lips. "You are what those on the Outside would call a dependable person. I trust you can keep this to yourself?"

"If that's what you want."

"As far as I can recall, I have only one happy memory of my parents," Magnus said. "I was nine years old. My father, Philip—"

"Your father's name was Philip?" Charles said. "And he named you Alexander Magnus…Alexander the Great."

Magnus grinned. "History does repeat itself every now and then, doesn't it? One of my father's companies had just broken through to the top of its market. For most, that would have been the plateau, a place to stop and settle in, but not for him. It wasn't enough to have the most prosperous business of its class. He didn't want to rule an industry. He wanted to rule the world."

"Like father, like son."

"Exactly. He'd just found out that day that his top competitor was going down in flames, so he was unusually cheerful. He flew my mother and I to Paris to celebrate. We walked along the Seine, warm baguettes in hand. He suddenly took my mother in his arms, kissed her, and spun her around. He was not an affectionate man. I can't remember him ever hugging me or kissing me, and this was the only time I'd seen him kiss her. She was a beautiful woman, of course. My father would never have married anything less. But to me she never seemed so beautiful as she did right then. Such a brief moment, and it all changed so quickly."

Magnus lapsed into a self-absorbed silence.

"What happened?" Charles prodded.

"She died a year later, almost to the day. So, you see, Ferguson, there is something that you and I have in common. Only my mother didn't die a natural death like yours. She was…"

Magnus stood abruptly and walked to the fireplace. He paced back and forth, muttering to himself and wringing his hands spasmodically. Finally, he turned and gazed at the portrait behind his desk.

"All this time, all that has transpired, and am I still so weak?" His voice trembled.

"I'm sorry, Magnus," Charles said gently. "Sorry for your loss. I know how it feels."

"You know nothing!" Magnus whirled on him, eyes blazing. "You think I want your pity? She deserved it. She betrayed him! Betrayed my father, her own husband. In doing so, she betrayed *me*. She fell in love—*love*, the fools call it!—with my father's closest adviser. They plotted to kill my father and take over his empire. But he was on to them! He had spies everywhere. He always said the world was full of traitors, and they proved him right. When the time came to bring them to judgment, he did the deed himself, and he made sure I was there to see it. That was my first lesson, my first glimpse of the real world."

The transformation that came over Magnus as he spoke was terrifying. For the briefest instant, Charles beheld what few, if any, had ever seen. The child behind the man. The man behind the monster.

"Enough!" Magnus forced himself back into his usual outward tranquility. "You now see how my path began. You understand how privileged I was to have a father who understood how the wheels turn. You, on the other hand, had no such fortune. Allow me to tell you a story about your own father."

"My father?" Charles's eyes widened. "You knew him?"

"It's time this veil is lifted for you, Ferguson. You need to see things as they are, to wake and find yourself in the world where heroes and villains alike have feet of clay and price tags dangling from their necks. Where everyone you meet is either a conqueror or a coward, a killer or a victim. My father was a conqueror. As for yours..."

He strolled back to the couch and sat, his eyes lit with a cold mirth, his fingers intertwined and resting between his knees. "Tell me, Ferguson, what is the first thing you can remember?"

A strange question, but the answer, whispers of memory from his earliest years, brought comfort to him even in this place. "My mother. Nothing particular, just bits and pieces. Her voice as she sang, her arms wrapped around me as I was falling asleep."

"Never mind her," Magnus snapped. "I'm not asking for the

shattered fragments that survived your childhood amnesia. I want to know the first thing you can remember in perfect detail. I know all about your gift. Tell me, when did the camera start recording?"

Charles was speechless. Of course, Thompson would have reported on his unusual memory, but even Thompson didn't know the half of it. Magnus was right. It was like a camera, always on, always filming. Everything it captured could be replayed in full if he only took the time and focused hard enough.

But when had it begun? Why had he never asked himself that question? He closed his eyes and began the sinuous journey through time, before he met Nadia at the beginning of the summer, before his earlier work with the Foundation, before he earned his degree, before college, before his mother died, all the way back to…

"I can remember the day my father left us," he said. "I was sitting—"

"No!" Magnus's voice cracked like a whip. "There's more than that. A little farther, Ferguson. Just a little farther and you'll get there. No doubt you've repressed it. That's what *she* always thought."

Repressed? What could he mean by that?

"I'll try."

He focused again, beginning with that dreadful day his father walked out on them. He willed his mind to travel deeper, deeper.

"We were in a truck. It was just the two of us, my father and I."

"Good, yes!" Magnus leaned forward, a tiger edging closer to its prey. "And where were you, Charles? What can you see?"

"A building. Pale walls and tall, dark windows. Guards everywhere, guards in gray uniforms."

"You've found it!" Magnus cried. "Go on, go on."

"I don't know why we were there. And I can't remember anything before that, not clearly. We were driving away from the building. I felt cold. My father was weeping, and I couldn't figure out why. He kept asking me if I was all right. We drove up to a guardhouse. A tall fence with barbed wire—"

"And a sign!" Magnus shouted with fanatical glee. "The sign, Ferguson, what does the sign say?"

Charles could see it as if it were right in front of him. A black iron rectangle that hung just over the door of the guardhouse. Four golden words were written on it.

Magnus Foundation Research Facility.

"Wait…no, I don't understand." His mind raced to put the pieces together. "Why were we there? Why was my father crying?"

"He cried because he was a coward," Magnus said. "As for your first question, your father was a failure in every conceivable way. No matter how hard he tried, he could never land a job worth having, never get a raise worth mentioning, never so much as lift his head with a shred of dignity. He was ashamed of his lower-class home, his lower-class car, his lower-class prospects. All he had going for him was your mother, but he was even ashamed of that, ashamed he couldn't provide for her the way he wanted, couldn't give her one of those sprawling estates he drove by on his way to his dead-end job.

"You were already on our radar at that point. Seven years old with a mind far beyond your age. Your father was the weakest link in your family, so we went after him. It was a simple ruse. An insider tip on an investment that couldn't possibly fail. One of our smaller companies, on the verge of bankruptcy, though no one knew it. We convinced him it would be sold in one week for ten times its value. With enough money down, he'd be a millionaire within days! He took the bait, of course. People with his profile always fall for childish stratagems. He gambled everything—the house, the vehicles, the insignificant retirement savings he had somehow accumulated over the last decade."

The room felt like it was spinning. He wanted to deny Magnus's words, but he felt paralyzed. His father had always talked about money. How little they had, how rigged the system was, how a man only needed one opportunity, one golden ticket, and he could climb to the top of the pile.

"You see, Ferguson," Magnus went on, "despite all the automation here at Headquarters, I've always pinned my highest hopes on the human mind. We began tinkering, experimenting on inferior subjects. We made some headway and decided it was time for the real challenge, something I called the Paragon Project. For that, we needed brilliance. We made a few…acquisitions. Precocious children whose parents needed a leg up in the world. Children like you, Charles. But we had to be discreet, oh so discreet! The world isn't yet ready for these kinds of transactions, but it will be soon."

Charles couldn't breathe. He knew where this was going. He also knew it was true.

"Despite having such a clear line of attack," Magnus went on, "I thought we might run into trouble with your father. It was dangerous, a delicate operation to perform on a developing brain. We'd already lost dozens of children by the time we came to you. But your father was soft as clay. His price—the price for *you*, Ferguson!—was a trifle. We paid off all his debts, and after that, a mere two hundred thousand dollars was all it took for him to sell us his only child. He understood there were risks. To his credit, he didn't know the whole truth. We didn't tell him that nearly every child up to that point had either died in surgery or fallen into a catatonic state soon afterward. The three who fared better lost their sanity. But even if he had known, I doubt it would have changed his mind. He just wanted the money."

Charles closed his eyes. A storm of emotions tore through him. Anger, rage, shame, betrayal. Even hatred.

Then, suddenly, another memory ripped through his consciousness like a lightning bolt.

He was a child. He lay flat on his back, strapped to a metal table with a light shining overhead. A monitor beeped steadily, and a pungent waft of rubbing alcohol made his nose tingle. Shadows were all around him. A shadow leaned over him, the contours of a woman's face veiled in black. He heard a shrill buzzing and saw a surgical drill on the periphery of his vision.

"Your mind won't shatter like the others, will it?" said the voice behind the veil.

The whining of the drill grew louder. It shrieked in his ears as it drew closer, closer.

Charles snapped his eyes open. He was sweating, shaking, about to scream.

"Who is she?"

Magnus leaned back on the couch. "I'm surprised you remember her at all. You only saw her for a few moments right before your procedure began. Her name is Aryana Voss. When you were a child, she was a leading researcher in Control. Now, she is second only to me. You met her recently, though her identity was concealed as always. She was the woman in the black veil at your sales meeting with Alpha Financial."

"What did she do to me?" he said.

"The same thing she did to all the others. Our methods improved from our past failures, but the real difference was the quality of the material we had obtained. You were unlike any child of your generation. Even before your modifications, you were so astoundingly brilliant."

Modifications.

Charles looked at the floor, at the fire, at anything but those dark eyes across from him, the eyes of a man who had bought him like a slave.

"And look at what we've accomplished!" Magnus said. "A mind like yours, already dominant, but now enhanced, broadened. In the end, we had a seven-year-old who could remember absolutely everything, and that was only the beginning. There's more we did to you."

Magnus grinned at him, taunting him, every curve of that smug and sanctimonious face laughing at the spectacle of the inner torture he was inflicting on his victim.

"What do you want with me?" Charles rasped. "Why did you tell me all this?"

"I want what I will get. I created you so that you would serve me and complete the very work you are now doing. As I've told you before, you belong to me. You were bought and paid for long ago."

"That's a lie!" Charles screamed the words and tore himself from the couch. "I'm not yours. Do you hear me, Magnus? I'm my own, mine! I'm no one's property."

"And yet," Magnus replied softly, "here you are, right where I want you to be. Living in Magnus Headquarters. Working on Project Aeternum. Working for me."

"Not anymore." He paced like a caged animal. "Never again! I'm leaving this place, and I'm taking her with me."

"Don't be ridiculous!" Magnus snapped. "Have you already forgotten your first lesson? Consider the facts. If you don't do exactly what I say, she'll be the one who pays for it. The very reason I've told you all this is so that you would understand that there can be no question of escaping from me. From the day your father sold you, your entire life has been directed by my hand. Your world revolves around me, and nothing you can do will ever change that. Believe me, you have no idea how far I will go to get what I want. You can't imagine the suffering I would inflict on her. Perhaps, to prove my sincerity in this matter, I should give her to Heimler for a few days. He's been a very good boy and is overdue for a present. What do you think?"

Charles looked up in mute horror.

"No." He lowered his head. "Please, Magnus."

"Oh, very well, but only because you asked nicely." Magnus rose and picked up the newspaper he'd been reading. "But you shouldn't trust Nadia so blindly, you know. Have you ever wondered why she fell in love with you in the first place? Or why she happened to arrive not only at your university, but in your very department?"

Charles frowned. "What are you trying to say?"

"Only the obvious. She's a beautiful, talented, capable woman. She could have her pick of mates, yet she chose a dry, inexperienced male. Why? Surely it had nothing to do with the scanner you were inventing, a device that would certainly turn you into a millionaire or even billionaire. Think, Ferguson! She must have known quite well what was on the horizon. But women never marry for financial security, do they? They are above such mercenary tactics." Magnus laughed softly. "That will do for today. Go back to the sunny side of the fence, and remember that every smile of hers, every kiss from her lips, every embrace, every moment you have with her—it's all a gift from me, a gift I can take back with a wave of my hand. Class dismissed."

✦

Charles and Nadia spent what should have been a relaxing evening together. They dined alone in her quarters, rested in each other's arms, listened to Mendelssohn's *Songs Without Words*, sipped tea, and nibbled on cheese and crackers.

He had a feeling she knew something was wrong.

"It feels good to work in a lab again," she said. "It's a distraction from…everything else."

"Right."

"I'm not much use without a project to chew on," she added. "And our teammates are starting to grow on me."

"Are they?" He tried to focus on what she was saying instead of thinking about the building in the woods with its metal roof, barbed-wire fence, and gold-lettered sign. The table, the veiled face. The drill.

A gift I can take back with a wave of my hand.

"Anna's brutally honest," Nadia said. "I can respect that. Raj is like a smarmy used car salesman. For the sake of all unattached women in Headquarters, I hope he finds a girlfriend sooner than later. I like Miguel, though I've never understood sports mania. You should see Dad when he watches the World Cup. He shot our television when I was a kid. Emptied a whole clip into it."

"Did he really?" he blurted out with a weird, barking sort of laugh.

What else did Aryana Voss do to him when he was a child?

Nadia cast an uneasy glance in his direction, then kept up her banter. "Fazal is so quiet sometimes that I forget he exists. We're a motley crew. I hope our differences don't blow up in our faces before this is all over."

"Right."

"Charles." She reached over and laid the palm of her hand against his cheek. He drew back.

You don't know what I really am. You don't know what he would do to you because of me.

He wanted to tell her, but he couldn't. He had to obey Magnus. It was that simple. He had to do whatever Magnus wanted.

"Listen to me." She locked eyes with him. "Whatever happened, whatever you're going through, you need to remember that I love you. Do you hear me, Charles Andrew Ferguson? I will always love you, no matter what."

He let out a deep breath. If she knew he was a freak, that he had been *modified*, would she still say those words?

Even as the thought crossed his mind, he knew the answer.

She would say the same words, and she would mean them.

When he kissed her goodnight, her eyes held an unspoken question. Or was it a demand? What did she want him to do? He pondered it as he trudged back to his quarters.

The answer came to him an hour later while he brushed his teeth. He hurriedly spat out the toothpaste and bolted into the office. In his old house, he'd always kept a laptop on his desk. The Foundation had replaced it with a mouse, keyboard, and monitor, all wireless. The monitor turned on the moment he sat in front of it.

"Good evening, Charles," the Computer said. "May I help you?"

"I'd like to wind down a little before bed. Do you have any games I could play?"

After briefly trying a few other games, including a deep space simulation that could take years in real time to complete, he fired up Crimson Reaper 3. It was a massive, first-person shooter. He hadn't played anything like it in years, and he was shocked at how realistic the violence had become. He practiced on a few other maps to get the feel of things before he went to the Dead Man's Waterfall.

It was brutal. He took a few sniper shots to the head, was blown to bits by a grenade, then laid out flat by a shotgun blast straight to the chest. Finally, his indefatigable avatar limped up the winding stairway to the waterfall. A narrow, faintly concealed path led behind the waterfall and into a cave. He ran to the back of the cave, his heart—the real one—racing, and he discovered…nothing.

After a few seconds of inactivity, the camera panned out so that he could see the stalwart, muscle-laden soldier that he commanded. The soldier tapped his feet, yawned, scratched his head, and eventually began twirling his rifle like a baton. No one in sight, nothing to see but a single stalactite with water dripping from it.

Drip. Drip drip. Drip. Drip drip drip.

Charles leaned back from the screen. Was something supposed to happen?

Drip drip drip drip. Drip. Drip drip.

Four separate patterns. Quaternary, just like the old cipher Nadia's grandfather had invented. He watched until the sequence repeated itself. Was he supposed to use the cipher? If so, the pattern was just doling out a random array of characters. He shrugged and typed them into the keyboard.

The screen flickered and the game vanished. A new window appeared.

September 25th, 9:52 p.m.
Welcome to Chameleon

(Prof has joined the conversation. 2 of 5 users are online.)

Stargazer: You figured it out! I need to verify, though. What's my favorite constellation?

Prof: Glousermorg the Great?

Stargazer: You're the only person in the world who could know that.

Prof: What is this?

Stargazer: A diversion from depression. It's an old-school chat room that flies under the Computer's radar. You can type anything you want here and the local gestapo won't know about it.

Prof: What about their surveillance cameras? Couldn't he just look at our screens and see what we're typing?

Stargazer: He?

Prof: I meant Magnus.

Stargazer: Trust me, Magnus has better things to do than watch surveillance feeds.

Prof: So how does it work?

Stargazer: Believe it or not, the Computer does all the work. I've got it modifying our video feeds in real time while Chameleon is running. Anyone watching the feed will just see us working away like the diligent researchers we are. Typing notes, entering data, journal entries, that sort of thing. If they paid close attention to the feed, they could notice the disconnect between what our fingers are doing and what happens on the screen. It's a risk, but there are only seventy people in Security, and they're monitoring several thousand people if you count Control. They don't even watch video feeds anymore unless the Computer tells them something needs closer attention. The mics are still on, though, so make sure you don't talk while you type.

Prof: You've heard about Control?

Stargazer: A little. We're having a meeting tonight. The others will be coming on soon.

Prof: Others?

Stargazer: You'll see. Charles, what happened to you this morning? I've never seen you that stressed out.

Prof: I had another meeting with Magnus. "Lessons" as he calls them. I'll tell you someday, I promise. Let's talk about something else. Your father let me read your unpublished papers. Why didn't you tell me that you were a computer genius?

Stargazer: The same reason Langley never found out. I didn't want that life, remember? Some are born spies, some achieve spyhood, some have spyhood thrust upon them. I guess a normal life will never be an option for me. The others here needed safe communication, a way to get past the eyes and ears of the Computer. That was something I could offer.

(Suavity has joined the conversation. 3 of 5 users are online.)

Stargazer: Hello Raj.

Suavity: Hi Nadia. I see our numbers are up. That you, Charles?

Prof: Guess I'm not too surprised that you're in on this.

Suavity: Boris and I go way back. He taught me the cipher years ago when I was working for the Foundation on the Outside. I'm glad you figured out how to get in here. We have a tough job ahead of us.

Prof: You mean Aeternum?

Suavity: Not quite. I mean destroying the Magnus Foundation.

Prof: Are you serious?

Suavity: We know it's dangerous. We've lost a few people over the years. The latest was Tom Murrow. We think he may have panicked and talked to the wrong person. We heard he was transferred, and now we're wondering if he ratted us out before he left.

Prof: He wasn't transferred. He was murdered. I saw it happen.

Suavity: You were there? Do you know if he told them anything about us? He was just starting to find out what we're up to. We're usually very cautious about inviting new members, but Tom seemed to be changing for the better.

Prof: He didn't tell them anything. Magnus thought he was working alone, trying to be a hero.

Suavity: He was a hero, always will be. But if that's what it means to be transferred—and we had our suspicions—then the others, the ones we lost earlier, they're dead, too.

Prof: Magnus said something strange to Tom before killing him. They were going to put Tom's body in some kind of cryogenic state, and Magnus promised that he would bring him back to life someday.

Suavity: Interesting. Anna guessed something along those lines. She used to work in cryogenics, and one day she overheard some talk from the guards and connected the dots. Security are the only ones over here who know what's going on in Control. They're tight-lipped, though. If they aren't, they die. She never saw those guards again.

Prof: Magnus killed Tom with some kind of mechanical insect. He called it a Harvester.

Stargazer: It was operational?

Prof: Definitely. He was dead within seconds.

Suavity: This is bad, Charles. A working Harvester means they're way ahead of schedule in Control. I assume Magnus told you his plan?

Prof: He's a monster. Crazy one, too.

Suavity: Probably, but he's convinced that everything he thinks and believes is logical. Maybe that's a good definition of insanity. I don't need to tell you how dangerous he is. Our odds aren't good. If you'd like to back out now, this is your chance.

Prof: Thanks, Raj, but I'm sticking with Nadia. I assume you have a plan? That video of Boris from my funeral meant something else, didn't it?

Suavity: Yes and yes. I'm going to ask you one question. Your answer will determine whether we have a plan or a pipe dream.

Prof: I'm listening.

Chapter Fourteen

Harvesters

COULD FAZAL BE trusted?

Anna and Raj weren't happy that Charles had thrown a human wrench into their plan. In his defense, he had been in the dark himself when he asked Magnus to put Fazal on the team. And Fazal would be an incredible asset if they could convince him to help.

Nadia came up with a plan to bring the young mathematician into the loop without tipping off Security. The question was when to execute it without raising any flags.

An answer arrived unexpectedly on a Monday morning six weeks into Project Aeternum. Charles and Nadia were finishing breakfast in her quarters. Nadia had ordered tamales catered from the restaurant. He went with the usual. One orange, two pieces of toast, one egg sunny-side up, dark coffee, one glass of water.

Same breakfast, same clothes. At least something in his life was predictable.

There was a knock on the door.

"I'll get it," he said.

It was Thompson.

"Miss me yet?" Thompson edged past him into the room. "Hey, Nadia. How are things?"

"As well as could be expected," she replied in an even tone. "You?"

"Never better." Thompson fretted with the zipper on his jacket. "Listen, Charles, I'm here to haul you off to a meeting. Won't take more than an hour or two. And don't worry, Nadia, I'll bring him back safe and sound."

"You'd better." Nadia gave Charles a kiss on the cheek. "I'm working from here this morning, love, so come back as soon as you're done."

He nodded and followed Thompson into the hallway.

"Where have you been?" he asked as soon as the door was closed. "I thought you'd at least check in on me once in a while."

"Relax, Charles. With Nadia around, you don't actually need another babysitter, do you?"

"Very funny, Thompson. Hilarious. So what's this meeting about?"

"It's not exactly a meeting. More like a demonstration." Thompson's voice was shrill, and he seemed jittery. Not a good sign. "I told them you wouldn't like it, but he insisted on you being there. Fazal, too. I bet he'll like it even less."

Charles took a deep breath. Magnus had warned him this was coming.

"How are things at the college?" he asked.

"Haven't the slightest. I've been reassigned."

"What about your classes?"

"I imagine our dearly beloved biology department will survive." Thompson snickered. "I heard old Schaeffer threw a staff party the day I resigned. Got himself sloshed and tried to dance with one of the interns. Epic fail, of course. I don't need them, and they don't need me. Besides, you were my main assignment at the college. I still travel Outside from time to time, but I'm stationed here now."

"Here? So you're in the—" He lowered his voice and looked around to make sure they were alone. "The other department?"

"The less said, the better."

They rode the elevator down and over until it opened to the familiar hallway leading to Magnus's office. The doors with the golden lions slid open as they approached.

One of the side walls in the office was now filled with digital screens, the largest of which displayed a fleet of satellites floating in geosynchronous orbit. A dozen plush leather chairs formed a semicircle in front of the displays.

Researchers in white lab coats huddled together by a side table and munched on hors d'oeuvres. A few glanced at Thompson and Charles, then looked away again without the slightest acknowledgment. He'd never seen any of them, which meant they were probably from Control.

Fazal sat alone at the far end of the row of chairs with his eyes lowered and his hands in his lap. He wore jeans and a light gray sweatshirt, and his hair was in its usual state of post-electrocution chaos. He looked more like a teenager than ever around the wrinkled faces and silver and white heads of the Control scientists.

The door behind Magnus's desk slid open. Magnus entered with brisk steps, Heimler shadowing him as usual. Charles felt his legs going weak when another figure entered the room, a woman shrouded in black from head to toe.

It was *her*.

"Come here, Ferguson." Magnus waved them over. "I'm sure Aryana would love to have a chat with you."

He tried to stifle his panic, but it was overwhelming. His heart was pounding, the room spinning. He wanted to scream. As he approached Aryana, he heard a strange, whirring noise. It was coming from somewhere within her veil.

"Good morning, Charles."

Was it really her? It had to be, but her voice was different than he remembered. Youthful, soft, a little breathless. Almost seductive.

The head turned a little to one side, and as it did so, the whirring noise behind the veil intensified.

"Your nightmares," the voice said, "tell me about them."

He struggled to breathe as a visceral terror seized him. He could hear the whining of the drill in his mind, feel the sensation as the tip touched the side of his skull.

What had she done to him?

"I…don't have nightmares."

"Do you ever dream of an island?"

"I don't know," he panted. "I don't remember."

"We weren't sure how it would work with dreams," the seductive voice replied, "but you would certainly remember the nightmares. You look pale, Charles. You must not overexert him, Lord Magnus."

"We're all burning the midnight oil around here, aren't we, Ferguson?" Magnus replied cheerily. "Don't worry, Aryana. A few more months of honest work and I'll give him an overdue vacation. You have my word."

The veiled head tilted forward in acknowledgement. Once more, the whirring sound increased.

"I was just telling Aryana that she's a cornerstone of this Foundation," Magnus went on. "She's earned her place as first among all who serve me. You already know all my plans, Aryana. Now promise me you'll follow them to the letter should the need arise."

"I am your servant," she replied. "I will obey."

Magnus handed her a small black lacquer box etched with the same heraldic symbol of the golden lions that adorned the doors of his office. She pressed the box to her chest.

"You honor me beyond my merit, Lord Magnus."

Magnus reached over and gently brushed his hand against her veil.

"Go, my faithful one. You have a country to run."

She bowed her head, then turned and slipped through the door behind the desk.

"On to the main event." Magnus rubbed his hands together. "I've invited some of our friends from Control to join us. Find a place to sit, gentlemen. I'll be over in a moment."

Thompson and Charles took the chairs next to Fazal.

"What do you think that means?" Fazal whispered to Charles. He gestured toward a screen on the wall that depicted a map of the Middle East. The map was filled with thousands of tiny, glowing red dots.

"No idea," Charles whispered back.

"Quinten," Magnus called out, "are we ready for launch?"

"Yes, sir." The clipped reply came from a different screen, which showed a young man in headphones typing on a computer.

"Gentlemen, behold the future of warfare." Magnus strode in front of them and faced the largest of the screens. "These fanatics have shown us the wrath of their god. Now we will show them the wrath of ours. It's like that delightful old story they teach the little innocents in Sunday school, the one where the tribal deity slaughters every firstborn child in a single night. Only we are the gods in our story, and we're widening the net. How many targets, Quinten?"

"The total number of active targets in the war zone is 82,316, sir."

"Women and children?"

"14,329 women over the age of eighteen. 16,291 targets under the age of eighteen, mainly teenage boys. Some younger. They train their children from a very early age, sir."

"My father did the same for me, Quentin," Magnus replied, "and it gave me a distinct advantage over my peers. Prepare to deploy the Harvesters. Launch the electromagnetic pulses when they are in position."

"Yes, sir."

"Close your hearts to pity!" Magnus shouted suddenly, waving his fist in the air. "Act brutally! Whoever has pondered over this world order knows that its meaning lies in the success of the best by means of force. A fitting quote for today's work. Let's have music. Computer, give us something worthy of the occasion."

"Wagner?" the gentle voice asked. "Siegfried's Funeral March, perhaps?"

"You know me well."

❦

Far above the clear, star-laden skies of the Middle East, a group of fifty-six teardrop-shaped satellites activated thrusters as they arranged themselves over the most densely populated regions in the war zone. Once they completed their formation, small bays on the earthward tips of the satellites slid open to reveal narrow black cylinders, like miniature cannons. The satellites hovered for a few moments, holding orbit with the vast sphere below. Their sensors took measurements until they determined that every target had been successfully pinpointed.

A sudden eruption emanated from the tip of each cannon. NASA equipment picked up on the massive burst of electromagnetic activity. It was officially ruled a mechanical glitch.

Seconds later, the bustling streets of fifty-six cities and towns went dark. Every cell phone, every television, every radio—anything that relied on the mysteries of the electron was rendered dormant. Many thought it was a power outage.

Forty thousand feet above the darkened cities, the cargo doors of a small fleet of military-grade transport aircraft opened in unison. At that altitude, the aircraft were well beyond range of the known weapons capabilities of the terrorists. What emerged from their cargo bays appeared first as a thick haze darker than the darkness. The unnatural, obsidian clouds quickly dispersed into undulating swarms that resembled the mysterious murmurations of starlings.

The Computer began distributing targets among the drones. Within seconds, 82,316 human beings had been assigned to specific Harvesters. Some Harvesters would be lost before reaching their intended targets, but this was irrelevant. Research on Reaps had shown that a single Harvester could kill up to sixteen of them without needing to refill the poison it bore.

Improvements in their velocity and the quality of the tiny blade projecting from their mandibles had led to another discovery. A latest-generation Harvester could kill a Reap without using poison at all, though this was exponentially more painful for the target.

Humane slaughter, Magnus ordered, so they were programmed to use the poison.

The members of the Hand of God terrorist group realized at once that the foreigners were up to something. It wasn't a power outage. How could that kill cell phones and radios? They readied assault rifles and rocket launchers and took up defensive positions behind walls and barriers, tanks and armored jeeps.

The Harvester swarms descended at over two hundred miles per hour. Within moments, a distinct and ominous sound, the buzzing of thousands of tiny mechanical wings, drifted with the wind into landscapes now steeped in darkness.

The terrorists fired guns and rockets. Flares were launched, but what they illuminated made the blood of every man, woman, and child run cold.

This was something unheard-of, something so far beyond every known enemy that there was no logical path of resistance. Conventional weapons were useless against mechanized locusts. As it controlled the advancing swarms, the Computer evaluated threats and made individual adjustments within microseconds. When the Harvesters reached the cities, towns, and villages, their numbers were almost completely intact.

Charles and the other scientists watched the scene unfold in bursts. The Computer combined night vision video feeds from a number of Harvesters to create a single, unified view. Dark forms clothed in green and black collapsed as the machines mowed them down, one after another, thousands upon thousands. They watched as the tiny red dots on the map disappeared with impossible speed.

Within five minutes it was over. No more dots. No more victims. No more Hand of God.

Fazal lowered his head into his hands, his breath coming in ragged gasps.

"Computer, turn off the music," Magnus said as soon as the video feed switched off. "Get me General Anderson at the Pentagon."

"Confirmed."

The various screens vanished, replaced by a single image in which a fit, balding man sat behind a desk, his epaulette lined with stars and his chest bristling with ribbons.

"Hello, Anderson."

The general nearly jumped out of his chair. "Magnus? Good God! How'd you get into our comm system?"

"Come now, General, don't be absurd. It is finished. I have destroyed the Hand of God."

"So it *was* you." The general ran his fingers through his thinning hair. "What was that, anyway? Whole place went pitch black."

"That doesn't concern you, Anderson. What does concern you is the fact that there are now fifteen other countries placing bids on my Harvesters. I've told them that they aren't for sale unless their original buyer backs out. The price, as you might have guessed, has just gone up."

Anderson grumbled a curse. "I'm not Congress! I can't spend that kind of money without approval."

"Don't worry, General. There are many noble congressmen—and congresswomen—who will do anything for the right price. What I need is for you to go before them tomorrow and testify that the Foundation can be trusted without reservation, that our technology can put an end to any war on any front. You will go into detail about how today's exercise had zero collateral damage, that the only victims were terrorists.

"Don't forget to bring up Flight 109, the death of so many innocents at the hands of these monsters. You might even throw in Truman's infamous statement that 'having found the bomb we have used it…in order to shorten the agony of war, in order to save the lives of thousands and thousands of young Americans.' You can do that, can't you, General?"

"Yes, of course."

"Yes, what?" Magnus crossed his arms over his chest.

"Yes…" General Anderson looked around and lowered his voice. "*Lord* Magnus. But if the news—"

"We'll handle the news outlets. By the way, the Computer has informed me that you've just scrambled some jets near the target zone. You aren't trying to intercept our cargo planes before they return to Headquarters, are you, Anderson? I'd hate to have to bring you back here for another round of re-education."

Anderson swore fiercely and grabbed his phone. "It wasn't me! Don't worry, Lord Magnus. I'll handle it."

"I'm sure you will. I look forward to hearing your testimony to Congress tomorrow. You'll see me again soon."

The screen went blank.

"A complete success!" Magnus clapped his hands. "Every one of you contributed in your own way. Especially you, Mr. Al-Najjar. Your algorithms were flawless. As you may have noticed, we expanded your parameters a bit. You had excluded women and children, which was against my directive and, I might add, far too lenient.

"And I'm sorry we couldn't spare your illustrious cousin. There was a sort of genius behind his rugged brutality, a refreshing disregard for the sanctity of life. The world always needs talented butchers, eh, Heimler?"

Heimler grunted and made a guttural noise that might have been laughter.

"As for you, Ferguson, the goal is now six months. Control is ahead of pace, and I'm sure you'll be eager to match their efforts. To make things easier, I'll allow your project to narrow its range. I've heard about the bizarre testing you've been doing on the lab animals. Focus on biological immortality. We'll figure out the rest later."

Heimler stood and whispered something to Magnus.

"Yes, thank you, Heimler! I had forgotten about our guest of honor. Roll him over and we'll have a word with him."

Half-concealed behind a cluster of bamboo palms sat a business-man in a designer suit and tie. His head was shrouded by a black hood, his hands and feet bound to his chair with black cords. Heimler wheeled the office chair and its occupant across the room.

"Remove the hood," Magnus ordered.

It was a younger man with hair impeccably styled, skin lightly tanned, and a thin, close-shaven beard.

"Hello there, Turner, how are you today?" Magnus asked in a pleasant voice. "In case you didn't hear, the Hand of God has been destroyed. Every man, woman, and child. I told you I would do it, and I've kept my word."

Turner's face was suffused with terror. He whimpered through the black cloth that gagged him. His gaze roved frantically between Fazal and Charles and the other scientists, eyes pleading for help they couldn't possibly give.

"Did you know, Ferguson, that there are people in our country who deliberately prolong these wars instead of ending them? There's good money to be had in a perpetual conflict. Friends and foes alike need weapons. Modern, expensive ones. Turner here could tell you stories that would make your blood sizzle.

"His father, sadly deceased as of yesterday, owned a company called Tessara. They were our rivals in the arms industry. There's another war that's ending. Today, Tessara's board has decided to sell the company. They've found a buyer who can offer them a gift beyond any other. Survival."

"Don't misunderstand me." Magnus stepped behind Turner and rested his hands on the back of the chair. "This isn't about morality. It's never really about morality, is it, Turner? It's always power. In the old world, Turner here would have dined at Martha's Vineyard and rubbed shoulders with plutocrats and oligarchs. In the new world, I am the Power, and I will have no rivals.

"Don't worry, Turner, we'll put Daddy's toys to good use. Speaking of which, Heimler, you carry a Tessara handgun, don't you? Let Turner here see it."

Heimler withdrew a narrow black pistol from his jacket.

"What's the body count on that one?"

"Eight hundred sixty-one, sir."

"Good Lord! You've been going at the Reaps again, haven't you?"

"Reaps are the best entertainment, Master."

"Well, the great event is almost here, so I'll expect you to trim back on your little bloodbaths. But today's an exception. Make it eight sixty-two, then pour us some champagne."

Chapter Fifteen

Second Strike

"Slow down, will you?"

Charles had to jog to keep up with Fazal, who was working the wheels of his chair with fury.

Fazal stopped at once. He looked up at Charles with a frenzied gleam in his eyes. "I'm a murderer," he said. "I killed them. Do you understand? I killed every one of them. It's no different than if I'd done it with my bare hands."

"You know that's not true, Fazal. Besides, they were terrorists."

"Terrorists?" Fazal cried. "Were the five-year-old children terrorists? Or the women who themselves lived in terror of their husbands and their brothers? My work empowered Magnus, my calculations made this possible. I could have lied to them. I could have pretended it was beyond me."

"You could have," Charles said slowly, "and Magnus would have killed you for it."

Fazal lowered his eyes. "Death shouldn't frighten us. Like Rumi said, 'What strikes the oyster shell does not damage the pearl.'"

Charles looked around to make sure they were alone. He wasn't worried about the Computer's surveillance at that point. Surely Magnus would expect them to talk to each other about what they'd just been through. "So what was your project over there? Did you know what they were planning?"

"Surveillance." Fazal's shoulders drooped. "They told me they were working on a new technology that was going to help prevent terrorist attacks before they happened. I was supposed to save lives, not take them! They wanted to use my algorithm to sift through all the data they had from the region. It was exhaustive—spy plane transmissions, satellite feeds, mobile devices, agents on the ground. They even had these tracking chips they had secretly implanted into some of the terrorists.

"They wanted probabilities for everyone in the region. How closely were they associated with the Hand of God? How deep was their allegiance? We came up with factors, made an algorithm, and ran it against the data. All the current members in the region, along with those most likely to one day become members, were identified. I made a separate category for women and children and tried to remove them from the main query, but they must have merged it all together again. Now every one of them is dead."

Charles exhaled through pursed lips. "I'm sorry, Fazal. We can't change what happened in there today, but we may be able to do something about what happens in the future."

"How?" The young man's eyes mirrored the desperation in his voice. "What could someone like me possibly do?"

"Don't you realize? You're already working on a project that could save countless lives."

"Oh, that." Fazal met his gaze. "Anywhere else, and I'd agree with you. But here, in this place, in the hands of these animals, what good can come of Project Aeternum? Even if we somehow give them the key to everlasting life, they'll find a way to kill people with it. Besides, we both know that I'm not much help to you. I'm only good at algorithms and equations. Not exactly the science of life."

"Don't be so sure of that," Charles said. "Nadia came across some sort of mathematical conundrum last night in her research. She thought you might be able to make something out of it."

"Mathematical conundrum?" Fazal leaned closer. "Tell me more."

Charles held up his hands. "Hey, I'm just a biologist, remember? Why don't you come over to her quarters and see for yourself? She's probably working on it as we speak. We'll head back to the lab after you've had a chance to look it over."

⁊

Charles and Nadia sat on the couch in her quarters while Fazal scribbled away on a notepad at the kitchen table.

"How bad was it?" She leaned her head on his shoulder.

"I'll be all right."

Digital flames danced and crackled in the fireplace. At least they offered the illusion of the changing seasons. As he watched them, he could almost feel summer's warm winds yielding to the invigorating coldness of an autumn breeze.

"What will we do when we leave this place?" she asked.

"Leave?" He felt his pulse quicken. Did she just let her guard slip? "What do you mean?"

"You know, after we finish Aeternum. Remember what Raj told us? Once it's over, Headquarters goes public and we get to go home. Will you go back to the university?"

Right, that. He rubbed his lower lip. What would he do if he were free, if this nightmare suddenly ended? "As long as you were there, I—"

"I've got it!" Fazal wheeled into the living room and tossed the notebook on a chair. His face glowed with youthful energy.

"That was fast," Nadia replied. "We'll just have to find something harder for you."

"I'm up for anything."

Nadia graced Fazal with one of her irresistible smiles. "You keep telling us how you feel out of place because you're not a biologist, but

206

you know something? You may turn out to be the most important team member on this project."

October 29th, 9:21 p.m.
Welcome to Chameleon

(Prof has joined the conversation. 5 of 6 users are online.)

Suavity: Hi Charles. I hear you and Fazal were called in this morning. That attack in the Middle East was Magnus, wasn't it?

Prof: Harvesters. It was unreal. All those people dead within minutes. Magnus said our timeline is now six months.

Unequivocal: There's no way we'll be done by then.

Suavity: Any progress today, Charles?

Prof: Not much. We're hitting a wall.

Suavity: We'll keep on with the rest then. Anna and Miguel are getting closer with their side of it. Try not to worry too much. It'll come together.

Gol: That lab work on subject five looks promising. Once you and Nadia have worked it out, all we'll have to do is put the pieces together.

(Prodigy has joined the conversation. 6 of 6 users are online.)

Stargazer: Welcome to the team, Fazal.

Prodigy: Thank you for trusting me. I swear that you won't regret this. I'll do anything to help.

Suavity: Music to my ears. Raj here. We already have a job lined up for you, Fazal. What do you know about the Reaping?

❧

"How does Miguel do it? He's been eating this stuff for a dozen years!" Nadia glared at her spaghetti noodles and twirled them around her fork. "We've had this same spaghetti thirteen times now. You know what's crazy?"

"What?"

"The machines always put exactly six meatballs on it. Never five, never seven. Six. And the way they crush the meat into those smooth little spheres. No bumps, no ridges, nothing. I don't even think it's meat at all."

"It, um…" Charles glanced with suspicion at the thin pink slices on his sandwich, each the exact same width and shape as the others. "It has to be meat, right? Tastes okay."

When it came to the room service meals, there were five options for the freeloaders, all comparable to a school cafeteria lunch. Cough up some credits and you gained access to a dozen more options, including spaghetti, though the quality wasn't much improved.

"Ugh, Charles! You could eat this stuff for a thousand years without batting an eye, couldn't you?"

"A thousand? No way. Bet I could swing five hundred, though."

Her half-smile turned into soft laughter. "I'm so glad you're not like me. Could you imagine if both of us went teetering from the depths of despair to the celestial heights with every shift in the breeze?"

"Are you, um, teetering?" He took a large bite of mystery meat sandwich.

"I'm definitely on the lower end of the spectrum. There's no sunlight here, no wind dancing in the trees, no rain trickling down the windowsill, nothing to seep into your soul and remind you that you're a human being, a living, breathing part of this vast and mysterious universe with all its wonder and beauty, pain and suffering."

"Hey, it's not all bad around here." He took a swig of tea. "For one thing, nobody on the Outside can hold a candle to the woman I'm looking at right now."

"If you're going put it that way, I suppose I won't argue with you."

He checked his watch. "Let's call it a night. Tomorrow should be loads of fun. Work, work, and when we're done working, we'll mix things up with some more work."

"Sounds about right."

She started to speak again, then paused.

"What is it?"

"Something's been on my mind for a while now," she said, "but I never feel comfortable bringing it up. I want you to be perfectly honest. Don't worry about hurting my feelings."

Danger, Will Robinson.

He cleared his throat. "Yeah, okay. Shoot."

"Would you be willing to, you know, pray with me? The morning and evening prayers, I mean. I feel lonely sometimes."

He exhaled. At least this was something he could handle.

"Sure thing."

"Really?"

"Really."

⤙

January 7th, better known as Christmas Day for many Eastern Orthodox. The whole team took an evening off to hang out at Nadia's, chatting and doing their best to relax while they sipped on cups of steaming hot *vzvar*. The flavor was excellent. Apples, pears, raisins, and apricots mixed with just the right amount of cinnamon and honey. After finishing their drinks, Nadia and Anna treated them to a piano and cello duet.

Raj fell asleep in a recliner. He'd apparently pulled too many all-nighters that week.

Fazal and Miguel were chatting about soccer. The two had hit it off from the start, which was surprising considering that Fazal could never share in Miguel's two great passions, gambling on soccer matches and consuming anything and everything made by the Bogota Beer Company.

Charles leaned back in a recliner, his second cup of *vzvar* in hand. He closed his eyes and soaked in their rendition of Tchaikovsky's *Seasons*. His mind, calm for a change, drifted into the realm of memory, painting photorealistic scenes from things he'd seen and experienced years ago.

A realization came to him suddenly, hurtling through his consciousness at lightning speed.

He and Nadia had wrestled with the problem for weeks now. They'd wasted sleepless nights poring over the research, testing theories using computer simulations and even scrapping together something to test on a literal lab rat.

All to no avail.

Now, with work and its demands pushed to the farthest corner of his mind, everything fell into place.

It wasn't a single fact or idea but rather an entire system of concepts, thought-spheres floating in seeming independence until they inexplicably glided into alignment. A motley array involving studies on the Methuselah generation of monarch butterflies, venom resistance in honey badgers, and Control stem cell research on outlawed humanoid chimeras.

Beyond these, like a desert mirage shimmering on the horizon, loomed a possibility that took his breath away. Transdifferentiation in the cells of *Turritopsis dohrnii*, the immortal jellyfish.

Could the mirage become reality?

His mind raced through the implications as the musicians brought the piece to a close.

Thompson joked that procrastination was the real mother of invention. Maybe he was onto something.

❧

Month four. No strolls through the Garden, no splurges at the mall, no workouts at the gym or laps at the pool. They ate, drank, slept, and breathed the work. The pieces were coming together. They could glimpse the finish line.

Would they live long enough to cross it?

⁕

January 31st, 9:28 p.m.
Welcome to Chameleon

(Prof has joined the conversation. 2 of 6 users are online.)

Suavity: Hey Charles. They've done another test. I just got confirmation from our source. Some news outlets are starting to cover it, too, but no fingers pointing to Magnus.

Prof: Where did it happen?

Suavity: They hit a couple of small towns in Colombia just outside cartel territory. Harvesters swept through the area first. Our contact said he and some Control scientists saw a remote feed of a small farm getting hit. A father and some workers out in the field, the mother and five kids at home. Genetic targeting based on Project Alpha worked as planned. Harvesters skipped the mom and two of the kids since they weren't tagged as Reaps. The Foundation couldn't have any survivors talking, so they sent in Tessara drones afterward. Firebombed everything. There's nothing left. Over seven thousand casualties.

Prof: Miguel grew up in a Colombian village, right?

Suavity: Jeez, didn't think of that. Hope there's no connection. News is reporting that drug lords used black market military drones to pull off the attack. They say it was a warning to the government that the cartels mean business.

Prof: I wish people could know the real story.

Suavity: It's getting dicey out there. First the massacre in the Middle East, now an entire village of civilians.

Prof: Magnus is moving too fast. We have to end this.

❧

Charles found Miguel sitting in an empty hallway by Elevator Five with his head in his hands and his back against the wall.

"Miguel?"

No reply.

"Are you okay?"

"They murdered her." Miguel's voice was hollow. He looked up at Charles with swollen, bloodshot eyes. "They murdered all of them. My sister, her husband, her children."

He felt a chill come over him. "You're talking about what happened in Colombia last night?"

"They're saying the narcos did it." Miguel ran a hand through his hair. "Drug lords firebombing villages. Do you believe that?"

Two Progress researchers rounded the corner. They were arguing over their production quota.

"Come on." He reached down and lifted Miguel to his feet. "We'll talk about it in your quarters."

"I'm fine," Miguel said. "We've got work to do."

"Work can wait."

Clearly, the man hadn't slept last night. He looked exhausted, trembling, barely able to put one foot in front of the other. When they entered his living room, Miguel stumbled away from him and grabbed the back of a chair with both hands. "I think…I'm going to get sick."

"It's okay."

He helped Miguel get to the bathroom. Miguel leaned over the toilet and threw up vociferously.

"Go," he said. "I can clean myself up."

Charles went back to the living room and sat on the couch. No way he was going to leave Miguel alone after what he'd just been through. How was anybody supposed to cope with trauma on that level?

He looked around at Miguel's quarters for the first time. The place was tidy, the minimalist decor a stylish juxtaposition of black, white, and stainless steel with splashes of color from pillows and artwork. Stacked next to the front door were three cases of the Bogota Brewing Company's finest beer. The cases were untouched.

A few minutes later, Miguel emerged from the bathroom with his hair combed and his face washed and shaven. He took a chair across from Charles.

"Are you certain?" Charles asked. "About your sister, I mean."

Miguel nodded. "I read about it on a news site last night. They mentioned her village. I found a forum where people were uploading pictures and videos of the destruction. They had images of the farm, or what used to be the farm. All that was left was the foundation. My sister, my brother-in-law, all five of their children…"

"I'm so sorry, Miguel." His words felt futile and impotent.

Miguel bit his lip. "My little brother…it was his birthday today. He always visits my sister's farm on his birthday, which means he's gone, too. I've lost everything."

"Dear God." What could he possibly say that would help? What could he do?

"I have a feeling the Foundation's going to transfer me soon," Miguel went on. "I think I'm ready to be transferred."

"What?" Charles cried. "Why would they do that?"

"They know. They've always known. They don't like my kind in the Foundation. There's nothing official, but it's an unwritten rule. There used to be more of us when I got here. Now I think I'm the only one left. It doesn't matter. Listen, I'm going to sleep. If I'm not here tomorrow, if they transfer me, will you do me a favor?"

"They're not going to transfer you, Miguel. You're too important to the project."

Miguel shook his head. "This has nothing to do with the project. It has to do with me. I'm…different. I thought you already knew. I thought all of you knew."

"Knew what?"

Miguel met his gaze. "Look, just tell the others that I'm sorry. Sorry I wasn't more helpful." He stood and walked towards his bedroom.

"Miguel, wait!" Charles hurried after him.

"Please," Miguel waved him off. "Just let me sleep. I won't kill myself, I promise. I have a feeling I won't have to."

He went into the bedroom and closed the door.

Charles walked back to the couch and sat. He had an idea of what Miguel might have meant but couldn't be sure. The silence became unnerving. He went to Miguel's bedroom door and quietly opened it, terrified of what he might find.

Miguel lay in bed under the covers, his head turned to the wall. Breathing, alive. Charles exhaled and closed the door.

He began to realize how much he cared about his new teammates. He'd always had Thompson around in the old days, but this was different. Raj, Anna, Fazal, Miguel—they already felt more like family than colleagues.

"Computer," he said.

"May I help you?"

"Could you contact the Aeternum team and have them meet me here? Tell them it's urgent."

"Confirmed."

If the team had become a family, then Miguel's suffering was a family crisis. He needed all the help he could get.

Ten minutes later, the rest of the team had gathered in Miguel's living room.

"Is it true? A drug cartel really bombed those villages?" Fazal asked.

"Stranger things have happened before," Raj replied with a significant glance. Fazal hadn't checked in on Chameleon last night, so all he had to go on were the news reports. He apparently caught the hint.

"And Miguel's sure about his sister?" he asked in a more subdued tone.

"I'm afraid so," Charles replied.

"He and his siblings are close," Fazal said. "He talks about them all the time. His sister had a family, lots of kids."

Anna got up and walked with rapid steps to the other side of the room. Nadia hurried to her. A few moments later, Anna's muffled weeping accentuated the heavy silence.

"It's too cruel," she said. "How could those animals do this? How could they?"

She didn't mean the drug lords. She meant Control.

Raj and Charles exchanged glances. One of them would have to find out what was really going on. Why would they target Miguel's family when Project Aeternum was finally coming together?

Charles rose from his chair. "I need to step out for a few minutes. Keep an eye on him."

⁂

"I'm sorry, but Lord Magnus is still unavailable," the Computer repeated with indefatigable patience. "You'll have to try again later."

"Not happening," Charles shot back. "This isn't optional. You're going to get Alexander Magnus on a video call, and you're going to do it now."

"I'm afraid that's not possible."

"Fine, just send him a message. Tell him that it's over. He can get somebody else to finish Aeternum. I'm done with it."

"I have recorded your message and will pass it on to Lord Magnus as soon as he is available."

"You do that."

He stormed down the hallway toward the nearest elevator.

"Take me to the Garden," he commanded as he stepped through the half-opened doors.

"Confirmed."

Seconds later, the elevator came to an abrupt halt.

"Ferguson!" roared the voice of Alexander Magnus.

Charles jumped back and stumbled onto the cushioned bench on the side of the elevator. A four-foot-tall image of Magnus's face had appeared on the wall panel across from him. It was so vivid that he could trace the dark, mottled splotches on Magnus's skin and watch the dilation of his nostrils as he breathed.

"What's wrong with you, Ferguson?" Magnus snapped. "I'm trying to do a teleconference with a half-dozen global leaders, and the next thing I know the Computer tells me you're throwing in the towel."

"Can we talk in person?"

"Certainly not," Magnus replied. "This is personal enough. I only have a few minutes, so out with it."

"Fine. How about you tell me why you're trying to sabotage our project?"

He apparently caught Magnus off guard.

"What do you mean by that, Ferguson?"

"You just murdered Miguel's sister. Killed her, her husband, all their children. You probably killed his brother while you were at it. Are you insane? You do realize Miguel's the best biogerontologist in the world, don't you? He knows more about aging and cellular decay than any of us. He's not just important to Aeternum, he's critical. How are we supposed to finish without him?"

The enormous eyes blinked. "I don't know what you're talking about."

"Really?" Charles folded his arms over his chest. "You're telling me you don't know anything about those towns in Colombia that got incinerated last night? Or that one of them just happened the be the very village where Miguel grew up?"

"I heard about the incident on the news. Drug lords, wasn't it?"

"Drug lords with a fleet of top-notch military drones? You just took over Tessara. You bragged to us about all your new high-powered toys, remember? This has your fingerprints all over it."

Magnus's eyes narrowed.

"You're finally learning your lessons." His voice was soft. "Too well, perhaps. Have you told anyone else your suspicions?"

"No."

"I'm glad to hear it. Since you were clever enough to connect the dots and wise enough to keep that knowledge to yourself, I'll bring you in on the whole story. There was a slip-up in Control yesterday. The Harvesters were scheduled to take out a remote town in Colombia as a proof-of-concept. I knew the place was a few miles from Miguel's hometown. I also knew his sister lived in the region, but she was just outside of the target zone. That was part of my plan.

"Do you know he still wastes hours watching those soccer matches of his? That's time we can't afford to lose. We warned him. Wiping out a village near his closest relatives would have been the perfect reminder of how tenuous the strands of existence can become when we fall behind in our duties."

"You're sick."

Magnus chuckled. "I'm in perfect health, Ferguson, mind and body. I assumed that Control would treat my direct order as law. Instead, they took it upon themselves to broaden the range of the attack. They apparently thought I would be impressed with a higher body count."

"So you're not to blame, is that it?"

"Blame whomever you'd like, Ferguson. They disobeyed my direct orders, and believe me, they have paid the price for it. Despite his flaws, Miguel's expertise is valuable to your project. At the same time, being what he is, he'll always be something of a liability."

He felt his anger rising. "What are you saying?"

"It's a social question," Magnus replied, "but it's also a biological one. A male who will not mate with a female is the epitome of genetic undesirability. These things occur in nature, but that doesn't mean we have to select for it now that we are in command of our own bio-logical destiny. If, as research suggests, such tendencies are primarily determined by genetics, then that would mean they can be genetically purged."

Charles pressed his hands against his forehead.

Would the nightmare never end? Would it always have more layers, more hellish depths to plumb? Always so pragmatic, so precise with diabolical rationalizations. "He's our friend, Magnus. He's part of the team."

"Don't get too emotionally attached," Magnus replied. "Miguel can remain until you've finished Aeternum. Perhaps I'll even make an exception for him afterward, though you shouldn't count on it. He is a Reap, after all. For now, we face a predicament. How do we get him back in working order as quickly as possible?"

"In working order?" he cried. "Miguel's not some machine you can just reboot and send on its way. You'll have to give him time off. And counselling. This is going to slow everything down. Weeks, maybe."

"Out of the question," Magnus snapped. "He *is* a machine, Ferguson, just like the rest of us. The mechanics of our psyche may be more complicated, but we're quite capable of being reprogrammed. But how to go about it? An apology would be absurd. If he knew that the Foundation he's worked for tirelessly all these years had murdered his family, he'd never forgive us. It would render him useless to our purposes."

Charles glared at the monstrously proportioned face. The frigid indifference, the absolute detachment from the suffering of others—never had he so despised another human being. He'd always thought himself above this kind of physical rage. Scientists were supposed to be rational, detached. They weren't supposed to let emotion get in the way of objectivity.

All the same, if Alexander Magnus stood in the elevator with him right now, he'd beat the living daylights out of him.

"Our best solution," Magnus continued, "is for Miguel to believe that his family was murdered by a cartel. His own uncle worked for one of them, and it's a narrative people are accustomed to in his part of the world. Beyond that, along with the usual condolences, I've sent him some cases of his favorite Colombian beer to soften the blow. He'll drink and bawl and vomit for a few days, and then he'll go back to work. Humans are highly adaptable creatures. That's why we're still here."

Charles shook his head. "This is your fault. You need to help him."

"The greatest gift I can give him right now, Ferguson, is meaningful work, and that I have already done. I may grant him more when the time comes. Now if you'll excuse me, I have another meeting to attend, and you have a project to finish."

The image vanished. The elevator continued its journey to the Garden.

❧

For the next forty-eight hours, at least one of them stayed with Miguel at all times. On the afternoon of the second day, he and Charles sat in front of a televised soccer match that neither of them was actually watching.

"I need to tell you something," Charles said. "You mentioned earlier that you were different, that you weren't like the rest of us. I don't want to pry, and you don't have to say anything, but if you need to talk, I'm listening."

Miguel turned down the volume on the soccer match.

"Do you know?" Miguel asked.

He nodded. "Magnus told me. I didn't ask him, he just started talking about it."

"Man." Miguel scratched his fingernails against his temple.

The Brazilians scored in the soccer game. The camera panned to hordes of screaming fans, some with their faces and bodies painted in glaring yellow and green.

"There they go again," Miguel muttered. He glanced at Charles. "You should know that there's nothing between me and Fazal. He reminds me of Paulo, my little brother. Besides, Fazal's in love with a Lebanese princess. That's what her name means, anyway. Sareena. It might help the poor guy out if he just told her. I don't know if they've even talked, but apparently things work a little differently over there."

"I bet they do." One of the Brazilians in the soccer game fell and then rolled around on the ground, clutching his shin. A referee ran up and flashed a yellow card in front of a player from the opposing team. "Look, Miguel, no matter what you're dealing with, talking's a good place to start."

Miguel cleared his throat. "This is harder than I thought it would be. Let's go to the beginning. Do you know why I love soccer?"

Charles grinned. "Maybe because you're not from the United States? I hear it's all the rage in the rest of the world. What's the real reason?"

"When I was a kid," Miguel said, "soccer was what made my dad happy. I didn't have any other way to connect to him. I didn't like farming, didn't like girls, didn't like guns. I decided to like soccer. It wasn't enough for him, so one day I got into a fight with Jorge Perez. That kid was a monster. Knocked me out cold, but my dad was so proud of me when I came home with those bruises on my face.

"I tried for him, I really did. It was just never enough. Soccer stayed with me, but I eventually gave up on the rest. It's hard to act like someone else."

What would it be like to have to hide yourself from those closest to you? To pretend to be something you weren't to win their approval and affection?

A nightmare, that's what. "I'm sorry you had to go through that."

"One day," Miguel said, "I confessed everything to our priest. He was all right, Father Zepeda, but he drank sometimes. That day he was drunk. Drunk and angry. He listened to my confession, and then he yelled at me and said I was a disgrace to my family. He said God didn't listen to sinners, and that my sin was the worst of all, worse than anyone else's in the whole village. I was twelve years old. It would have been a lot different, I think, if he'd been sober. He even tried to apologize a few days later, but the damage was done."

"I can't imagine what that would be like," Charles said quietly.

Miguel shrugged. "The part about God was the hardest for me to hear. By then, I was already letting go of my father. He couldn't forgive me for being such a disappointment. But God…was it true that even God had no place for me? When I went to university in the States, I stopped going to Mass. I guess it might be easier for me if I were an atheist, but I'm not. I can't be. I still call myself a Catholic. I don't know if that's true or not."

He leaned back on the couch and took a sip of water.

"Do you see the irony?" He shot Charles a melancholy grin. "I feel like I'm condemned because of how I was made, but then I'm asked to love the God who made me. And you know something? I do love God. I love him for all the beauty in the world. I try to do what's right. Maybe you don't believe me. I drink too much, I gamble. I despise myself for that. I don't want to do it, but I can't seem to stop.

"Those things they could forgive, and maybe I could get free of them. This…what can I do with it? How do I change it? And they cannot forgive it. Do I marry a woman to please them? Would that be fair to her? I'm trapped. I don't know how it could ever happen, but I've always hoped that I would find a way back to God."

"Before I came to Headquarters," Charles replied, "I met someone on the Outside, an elderly monk. I wish he were here. He might know the way you're looking for."

Miguel shrugged. "I doubt it. Still, I've always wanted to meet a monk. A real one, you know? That monk isn't here, but you are. Thank you, Charles. My sister—" His voice faltered. "My sister loved God, she followed all the teachings of the Church, and yet she never stopped loving me. Isn't that a beautiful thing?"

"It is."

Miguel straightened up in his chair, "I've made up my mind. Wherever my brother and sister are now, I'm going to make them proud of me. You'll see. From now on, I'm giving it everything I have."

As Charles walked back to his apartment, he wondered what Alexander Magnus would think of their conversation. The Computer would have flagged it as important. A Reap had just admitted his crime.

No doubt Magnus would congratulate himself on manipulating another human machine, pulling the right lever to get what he wanted.

If he only knew.

Chapter Sixteen

Imago Dei

"YOU HAVE AN emergency meeting with Alexander Magnus in fifteen minutes."

Charles sat up in bed and rubbed his eyes. The Computer had turned on all the lights in his quarters.

"What time is it?" he asked.

"It is currently 2:27 A.M."

Did Magnus know the truth? Had someone slipped up?

Heart pounding, he scrambled out of bed, took a few minutes to freshen up in the bathroom, and was out the door.

"Please take Elevator—"

"I know, I know!"

He walked into Magnus's office five minutes later. Magnus was pacing back and forth in front of the fireplace. Heimler leaned against the massive desk.

"Finally," Magnus snapped. "What took you so long?"

"The Computer said fifteen minutes," Charles shot back. "It's only been ten. Not bad for two-thirty in the morning."

He was angry, but he needed to be careful. One mistake could wreck everything.

"Was it only ten minutes?" Magnus's voice softened. "Fine, I'll get straight to the point. The project needs to be finished sooner."

"You woke me up in the middle of the night just to tell me that? I'm sorry, but you've already cut our time in half. We're doing the best we can."

"Sooner!" Magnus hammered the desk with his fist. "You *will* finish it within *one* month. Do you hear me? One month…that's February 10th. Do it by then, or Heimler puts a bullet through her skull."

He opened his mouth to protest, then stopped. That was no idle threat.

"It can't be done, Magnus."

"It can, and it will. You'll find the way. Now there's someone I want you to meet. Heimler, go and fetch Nadia."

Magnus led them out of his office and toward the elevator. The guards standing by the doorway of the office silently fell into step behind them.

They rode the elevator for a few minutes before it came to a halt. The doors slid open. Charles felt his stomach twist into a knot.

The holding cells. Was this why Magnus had sent for Nadia?

The hallway was silent except for a measured beeping sound. He followed Magnus until they reached the last cell on the right. Magnus placed his palm on the door to open it.

Instead of a prison cell, the room looked like a makeshift hospital room with an IV, a heart monitor, and a breathing machine that rumbled and gasped as it pumped out oxygen. A shriveled old man lay in the bed. His skin was yellowish and hung loosely about his frame. His breathing was labored despite the ventilator. His eyes flicked open for a moment and closed again.

"You've beheld the spectacle of death a few times since your arrival here," Magnus said. "I forget, sometimes, what it was like before my father's lessons, before my own hands had taken a human life. I'm giving you an opportunity to make a small difference. This man's heart is failing. The physicians tell me he can hold out for a month at the most, but no longer. We're going to put him in a room next to your laboratory. You'll hear his every heartbeat while you work. Finish Aeternum in time, and you can save his life."

Heimler and a handful of guards arrived with Nadia in tow.

"Save him, Ferguson." Magnus nodded to Heimler. "And not just him."

The guards grabbed Charles's arms from both sides. Heimler stepped up to Nadia. There was a sickening clap as his open hand connected with her face. She staggered and dropped to the ground.

"Stop it!" Charles screamed. He struggled in vain to free himself from the guards. "Leave her alone! I'll do it. Do you hear me, Magnus? I'll do it!"

"I know you will." Magnus patted him on the shoulder. "You're a cardinal, remember? You just needed the proper motivation. Guards, take them back to their quarters."

✧

Charles's escort deposited him at his front door. He waited until they were out of sight, then hurried to Nadia's quarters.

She opened the door at once. She was silent, her eyes downcast. Rage swept over him when he saw the imprint on the side of her face, Heimler's fingers etched upon her in glaring red. She took his hand and led him into the living room. He sat on the couch, and she curled up next to him. She trembled in his arms as she wept.

What could he say? How could he protect her?

"It's not your fault," she said as if reading his thoughts. "There's nothing you could have done."

"We can't go on like this." He wiped his eyes. "I have to keep you safe."

She placed her hand gently against his cheek. "I love you."

He held her through the watches of the night, held her and listened to her soft breathing after she drifted off to sleep. He began to formulate a new plan, one far simpler in its aims.

Nadia had to survive. He had to get her out of this dungeon. The world would have to find another way to deal with Alexander Magnus.

❧

They ate breakfast together that morning, then he went back to his quarters for a shower and some rest. The Computer informed the other team members that he and Nadia would be late. When he awoke after a couple hours of sleep, he sent Nadia a message through Chameleon.

We need to talk in person. Can you make a place safe for fifteen minutes? Same as what you're planning with the lab, but somewhere with more privacy.

❧

Raj, Fazal, and Miguel acted like they hadn't seen the dark, purplish-blue bruise on the side of Nadia's face. Anna took one look at it and dropped what she was doing.

"What happened? Tell me the truth."

"It's nothing," Nadia rested her fingertips on the bruise. "I just—well, I got into a fight. Sort of."

"A fight?" Raj raised an eyebrow. He and Fazal shot dark looks in Charles's direction.

"It wasn't him," Nadia said quickly. "It was a perfect stranger, some researcher from Agriculture. She bumped into me last night and started yelling nonsense about her boyfriend. I tried to get her to calm down, but she was frantic. She just kept getting angrier. Then she slapped me on the face. The Computer must have reported it to Security, because a guard showed up and hauled her off."

Charles was amazed at how artlessly she wove her tale.

"Geez." Raj shook his head. "That's nuts. You sure you're okay?"

"I'll be fine." Nadia managed a wan smile. "Let's get back to work."

The others looked like they weren't buying it, but neither would they reveal their disbelief. They knew how to follow cues. Even Fazal, who they had worried about the most, played the game as well as anyone.

On his own initiative, the young mathematician had struck up a friendship with Landry during a chance meeting at the cafeteria. It was no small feat. Landry was prone to boasting about the love of his life, the Magnus AI Computer, and had already let slip a few vague hints about its inner workings.

Anna scowled at Raj, who was sitting across from her. "You're doing it again."

"I am?" Raj shifted in his chair.

"Yes, you are," Anna replied with a tart smile. "It's why I've been reading the same paragraph for the last five minutes while trying, and failing, to ignore the fact that you're over there scratching your chair like a feral cat."

"Oh, is that a fact?" Raj cried. "Feral cat, huh? Ironic coming from you. Tell me, Anna, have you ever wondered why you can't get a date?"

The silence became deafening. Raj plunged on like a madman.

"I'll tell you why. Some guys prefer feisty, but nobody wants a hellcat. You need to pull your claws in once in a while."

Anna shot to her feet, her face dark as a thunderstorm. She walked across the room with stiff steps and plopped down next to Nadia with a grunt.

"I hate him." Her lowered voice was still loud enough for everyone to hear. "I don't care what you say. We'd all be better off without him."

A few seconds later, she stood again.

"And how in God's name are we supposed to get anything done with that infernal beeping? Who's in that hospital bed, anyway? Does he have to sleep in our laboratory? Those idiots from Security just wheeled him in here and said he wasn't to be disturbed, as if *we* were going to disturb *him*."

"It was Magnus's idea," Charles said. "I don't know who he is, but Magnus wants us to save him."

"Save him?" Miguel asked. "From what?"

"Well, you know…death. His heart's failing. I think Magnus wants us to test things out on him."

"Revolting." Anna muttered. "If he has to stay, can we at least disconnect his heart monitor?"

"Anna!" Nadia gasped.

"Okay, fine. Never mind." Anna slammed her notebook down on the table. "I'm getting out of here. I'll be back in a few minutes. Or not."

Charles let out a deep breath. Was this part of the act? Or was the team just exhausted?

They'd been working like maniacs, stuck together in the same area without any break. Nerves were fraying. He and Nadia had managed not to blow up on each other, but he had a feeling that was about to change.

He also had a feeling he would be the cause of it.

✦

He read her reply to the message he'd sent her on Chameleon that morning.

I can do it. Give me a little time.

✦

February 4th, 9:02 p.m.
Welcome to Chameleon

(Tacitus has joined the conversation. 3 of 7 users are online.)

Prof: Is that you?

Tacitus: Like my pseudonym? I can't stay for long. Amazing work setting this up, Nadia.

Stargazer: Thanks. How's my father?

Tacitus: He's made the preparations. Did you get my sample?

Prof: We sequenced it this morning. The injection should be ready within a day. Two at the most.

Tacitus: Does that mean you've finished?

Prof: It's too early to tell. We need to do more testing. We have to be certain before we move.

Tacitus: We're running out of time. Control is going to wrap things up any day now. I'm heading to the Outside for a short trip. I'll try to warn you before Control initiates, but I can't make any guarantees.

Stargazer: We'll get you into the lab for the injection as soon as you're back. Be careful out there.

Tacitus: Same to you.

(Tacitus is now offline. 2 of 7 users are online.)

Prof: Did you find a way to get past the cameras?

Stargazer: It should work. Meet me over here in fifteen minutes. I can fool the Computer for a little while, but it would be dangerous to do much more. It's a good practice run for the real thing.

Prof: I'll be over soon.

Charles chewed on the skin beside his fingernail as he hurried along the carpeted hallway toward her apartment. She wouldn't like this. It was an act of cowardice.

It was also an act of survival.

She led him to the kitchen. They sat next to each other on a pair of stools in front of her counter height breakfast table. St. Dorothy, a 3rd-century martyr, watched them from a gilded icon on the kitchen wall, her red apples and wild roses in hand.

He let Nadia take the lead, and for a few minutes their conversation was mundane. The chemical reaction she'd tested that afternoon, the fact that neither of them had exercised in weeks, the endless griping about machine-prepared meals.

At 9:36 p.m., she held up her hand.

"We're clear," she said. "Twenty minutes max. Keep your voice down just in case."

"I can say anything?"

"It's not recording. The exploit is triggering random surveillance glitches all over Headquarters. Odds are good that Landry won't be getting much sleep tonight. Now what is it? What's so important that you can't even say it over Chameleon?"

His eyes lingered over the bruise on her face, which had turned a sickly purplish green.

"We need to scrap the plan."

"What?" she cried.

"The plan, the revolution—whatever you want to call it. We have to let it go."

She looked stunned. "Just like that? After all we've been through?"

He rose from his chair, walked across the kitchen, and rested his hands on the edge of the sink. He kept his back to her. "It's too ambitious. We're talking about bringing down the whole Foundation. We'll focus on a smaller goal instead. Let's just stop the Harvesters. That's the main thing, right?"

"We've been through this already, love," she said patiently. "It wouldn't be enough."

He turned to face her. "I heard Raj's explanation, but I don't get it."

"Blocking the Harvesters would delay things," she said. "But we'd still be stuck here, and they'd know that someone in Headquarters had interfered."

He sat again and rubbed his forehead. "At least it would slow them down. That would buy us time to finish our work."

"Did you hear me, Charles? We'd get caught, and we'd be powerless to stop them when they repaired the Harvesters." She rested her hand on his arm. "We have to deal with him. If he escapes, he'll just start over again."

He drummed his fingers on the tabletop. "Okay, but isn't there an easier way? Maybe we could just hunker down and wait for the others to show up. Why stick our own necks out if we don't have to?"

"You're not making sense, Charles," she said. "You should just ask the others about this on Chameleon."

He took her hand in his, relishing the coolness of her fingertips as they brushed against his palm. "If we move forward, he's going to kill you. Do you understand? No matter what happens, I have to keep you safe."

She lifted his hand and placed it against the bruise on her face. "It scared me. Okay? It terrified me. But I refuse to let them win. We are at war. Yes, it's dangerous, but you know what? When Heimler hit me, something changed. I can't explain it. All I know is that I'm not afraid of them anymore, not afraid to die for this if I need to."

Artificial sunlight slipped through the downward-slanted blinds over the kitchen window. He rose and twisted the rod to let in more light, then gazed upon a convincing field of digital wildflowers bowing beneath a summer breeze.

"You're braver than me, Nadia. I get what you're saying, but we should be smart here. You heard Thompson. Control will launch those Harvesters any day now. Maybe any *hour* now."

"Yes, but—"

"I know, I know!" He waved off her objection. "We're close, yes, but we haven't tested anything yet, not on humans. Listen to me. We need to start thinking about ourselves, about our own survival. I can get you out of here. I have…leverage. With Magnus. It may sound strange, but it's true."

Her face revealed her disbelief. "Wait, you want me to leave Headquarters?"

"Yes."

"Alone? Without you?"

"At first, but not for long. Thompson and I can find a way out if we work on it."

"Thompson and you?" she cried. "What about the others?"

"I don't know. I guess they'll have to fend for themselves."

"I don't believe this." She threw her hands in the air. "It's ridiculous, Charles! You're just going to abandon them? Run away and pretend we had nothing to do with this? What about Peter? What about the other five billion Reaps? We may be the only people in the world who can stop this massacre."

"And what if we can't?" he shot back. "What if it's impossible? Have you even considered that? We're talking about Alexander Magnus here. The man's insane, yes, but he's also brilliant. He gets what he wants, every time. If we fail, Nadia, he'll kill you. But you know what? He won't kill me. I'll be left here, alone, without you, without anyone."

"Oh, so that's what you're really afraid of, is it?" Her hands clenched into fists. "Being left alone? You said you wanted to protect me, but maybe this is all about you?"

And why did you choose me in the first place?

He barely bit back the words. What if Magnus was right? What if Nadia had started dating him because of his scanner, because of the wealth and fame it would bring?

"Is self-preservation a crime?" He'd almost shouted the words. He lowered his voice. "We should all be worrying about our own skin instead of trying to save the world. Playing it safe is what sane people do. If you and I are smart about this, we might survive."

She pressed her hands on the table, palms downward. "Let me get this straight. After all we've accomplished, you're throwing in the towel?"

"We're too late, Nadia." He ran his fingers through his hair. "We gave it our best shot, but we won't finish in time. What if our calculations are off? What if it doesn't work? What if their defenses are stronger than we realize? Without testing, the odds are a million to one that we'd be throwing our lives away for nothing."

He took a breath. "Listen, I promise that we'll find a way to get the others out too, okay? Maybe Thompson can talk to your dad, get some ideas. I know Boris would want to get you out no matter what happens. Does that help?"

She didn't reply, and she wouldn't look at him. She just kept shaking her head.

"You know something, Charles? You sound just like *him*."

"Who, your father?"

"My father isn't a coward. You sound like Magnus."

Her words pierced him like a knife. For the last two days, he had given every spare moment to planning their escape. First, he'd tell Magnus that he demanded Nadia leave Headquarters immediately. Magnus would resist, but Charles would lead him along, tell him that they were on the verge of completing Aeternum but that he refused to take another step until he was sure of Nadia's safety. That meant she needed to be out of Headquarters, back on the Outside where—though he wouldn't tell Magnus this part—her father and his team of machine-gun-toting angels could keep an eye on her.

Once she was safe, he and Thompson would find some way to escape. Thompson had access now that he was a higher-up in Control. He could make it happen.

That was the general idea, and to his exhausted and near-feverish brain it had seemed like a workable plan. He refused to acknowledge the gaping holes in it, to consider the obvious fact that a handful of Harvesters could hunt them down anywhere in the world.

He'd told her the truth. Magnus was going to kill her. He had seen it in the man's eyes, heard it in his voice. Magnus wouldn't hesitate when the time came.

That must never happen. Even if it cost him the world, he couldn't lose her.

Or so he had thought.

Truth be told, he was already losing her. He felt it now in the awkward silence between them. She wasn't entirely *his*, some inalienable possession that would follow him around no matter what he did. Right now, they were on the journey together, but that assumed they kept moving in the same direction.

She wouldn't tolerate cowardice. The truth was written on her face as plainly as if she had spoken the words aloud.

After all, she was Boris Petrov's daughter.

"There's nothing for it, then." He slumped into the chair beside her. "We don't have the sanity to get out of harm's way instead of stepping on a land mine."

"You think I don't want to give up, too?" Her voice rose in exasperation. "Yes, Charles, I'd rather stroll right out of here and go back to our cozy little life at the university. But I can't do that, not even if the doors were wide open. We have a responsibility, a sacrifice we can't avoid. I'm no saint, but I try to live by my beliefs."

He closed his eyes and forced down the bitter words that crept to the tip of his tongue.

This wasn't her fault. She didn't know all the facts, and he couldn't possibly tell her. "Just promise me this. If we're too late, if they launch before we even get a chance to move, will you at least think about it?"

She shrugged. "Honestly, I don't know what to think anymore." She rose and pushed her chair back under the table. "Good night, Charles. Make sure you leave in the next five minutes or the Computer might start asking questions."

Without another word, without even a glance in his direction, she walked into her bedroom and slammed the door.

◈

The next morning, for the first time since Project Aeternum began, he and Nadia started off the workday on opposite sides of the lab.

"Ah, the lover's quarrel," Raj said with a melodramatic sigh.

"What would you know about it?" Charles snapped. Anna snickered and gave him a thumbs-up.

"Touché." Raj leaned in closer and lowered his voice. "Seriously, are you two all right?"

"We'll be fine. Thanks, Raj."

"Listen, why don't you and I go check on our patient? Miguel's in there, I think."

"Lead the way." Any distraction was a welcome event.

Miguel stood by the bedside. The old man looked even sallower and frailer than he had at first.

"I think he might be related to Magnus," Miguel said. "Look at those facial features. I've only seen Magnus a few times, but there's a startling resemblance."

Raj peered down at the old man's face. "Anybody know what happened to Magnus's father?"

Miguel shrugged.

"Well, whoever he is," Raj said, "he's not long for this world. He was breathing on his own when they brought him in yesterday, wasn't he?"

"Seemed like it."

"That respirator's doing all the work now. What do you think, Charles?"

Their eyes met. Raj's question had a deeper meaning.

⌁

February 7th. Three days without Nadia.

Charles sat on the edge of his bed and gazed at the portrait on the wall. His Christmas present from her, the worn and battered icon of Christ.

She would be saying the evening prayers right now. Alone in her quarters, without him. He had proven himself a coward, so here he was, separated from her during this time between times that had become a part of their common life.

They still spoke, but a wall remained between them. The pain of that separation was killing him.

The questions he had once asked Father Anatoly were no longer academic. The road had split in two, and he had to make a choice. Could he really die for this? Did he believe in what they were doing? Did he believe in God?

Was there anything beyond survival?

He had wrestled for months with the scandal of particularity. According to her faith, it wasn't divinity in the abstract, but God in the concrete.

This Someone.

His eyes moved from the tranquil, silent expression of the face to the gashes torn from the top and bottom of the icon. It was all represented here, everything contained in this image. The mindless entropy gnawing at the heart of the cosmos and, right in the midst of it, the eternally conscious Being.

Either there is Nothing, or there is Someone.

Which would prevail?

Was he a temporary arrangement of chemicals? A biological machine duped into believing in his own consciousness? A miniscule gear in a system tumbling blindly towards annihilation?

He couldn't believe that. He couldn't believe that light and beauty and consciousness were illusions and darkest reductionism the only truth.

Humans weren't machines. They were icons, windows on the outermost walls of the universe. Living, breathing manifestations of deeper reality.

He remembered the path the man depicted before him had travelled. He held it up against his own cowardice. The two images, his own and that of the man, were so alike, yet so different.

Could he ever resemble someone like that, someone who stood his ground to the death, who forgave his own murderers? Whose words and deeds redirected the flow of human history?

This Someone.

He slipped his hand into his pocket, withdrew the prayer rope Father Anatoly had given him, and began the evening prayers.

When he finished, he sat on the floor, leaned back against the foot of the bed, and gazed at the icon. Calmness drifted over him. Inner silence. After all these days of darkness and fear and anxiety, he had found it again. He had returned to the monastery.

His eyes closed. He fell asleep.

～

It wasn't a nightmare, but it was vivid as a memory. Before him were two pale and grimy prisoners half-buried in a trench. Their clothing—tattered, striped rags—hung loosely around skeleton frames.

"This is where you've got to find your happiness," the first prisoner said as he drove the narrow blade of his shovel into the dirt. He was in his late thirties, but the grayness of his skin made him ageless.

The other prisoner turned his face upward to a leaden sky. "You have filled all things with joy," he proclaimed in a resonant voice. He turned and looked at Charles. "You're late, friend. Come, help us."

Charles climbed down into the ditch and discovered that he, too, now wore the tattered rags with the white and black stripes. The first prisoner handed him a shovel. As Charles dug into the rocky soil, the prisoner began to sing in a rich, deep-throated voice.

Wake up, call the voices

of the watchmen high on the ramparts,

Wake up, city of Jerusalem!

This hour is midnight.

They call us with a clear voice.

It was just after midnight when he woke from the dream. His mind felt clear and relaxed. He had no idea what the words of the song had meant, but their spirit remained with him.

He had made his choice. The time had come. He felt the pent-up fear and tension flowing out of him as he drifted back to sleep.

Chapter Seventeen
Level Nine

"CHARLES, WAKE UP. Get up!"

"Thompson?" Charles looked around in a daze. He checked his watch. 4:17 A.M. "What's going on?"

"It's time you knew the truth. They're going to kill me anyway."

"Kill you?" He was wide awake now. "Thompson, calm down. Why would they kill you?"

"You're so naïve." Thompson's laughter was tinged with bitterness. "I tried to talk to someone while I was on the Outside. Magnus will know soon if he doesn't already, and then he'll flip the switch."

"What switch?" Charles went to his closet and pulled out a set of clothes.

Thompson cupped his hands over his mouth and took a few breaths. When he spoke, his words tumbled on top of each other. "I didn't think it would be this terrifying. When Magnus needed a handful of researchers to work on the Outside, he took precautions. We were given a kill switch, a device they planted in our chests. Wherever we are, anywhere in the world, he can get to us within seconds.

"I saw him use it once on a woman, Merideth Gardiner. About my age, gratingly polite, computer scientist. Landry had her monitoring some tech leaders on the Outside. She tried to get around his tracking systems, so they brought her in. Magnus wanted me to see it, to know exactly what would happen to me if I ever betrayed him."

"But you haven't betrayed him, right?"

"Let's go," Thompson said. "They'll come for me soon."

He put on his shoes and joined Thompson in the hallway.

"Level Nine," Thompson ordered as they stepped into an elevator. "Top speed."

"Dr. Charles Ferguson has not been given Level Nine access," the Computer replied.

"Then grant him Tier One Control access, now. My orders!"

There was a pause.

"Confirmed. Tier One Control access granted."

The elevator lurched sideways with the speed of a roller coaster. Charles grabbed one of the hand rings just in time to keep himself from getting slammed against the wall. The elevator came to a halt and then descended.

"Do you know why she got that job at our college?" Thompson asked.

"You're talking about Nadia?" A dull dread crept over him. Was Magnus right? Had Nadia only pursued him for the fame and wealth the scanner would bring?

"It's my fault, you know," Thompson went on. "I'm the reason she got mixed up in all of this."

"What?"

Thompson sat on one of the benches and rested his head in his hands.

"I met her at a conference last year. We talked after one of the sessions, and I was attracted to her. Smitten. I must have mentioned it to someone in the Foundation. A few months later, I got a phone call from Magnus. He said that I'd been doing excellent work. Instead of a bonus, they would be sending another gift my way. He said I was a lonely man, that I'd given a lot to the cause, and that my sacrifice was about to pay off.

"The next week I found out that she would be joining our department. It's sickening, but she was supposed to be a sort of…present. For me. It's how these people think. They keep harems, you know."

"They keep *what*?"

Thompson's revelation disgusted him, but he also felt relieved. How could he have doubted Nadia's intentions? How could he have believed Magnus's lies about her?

"Magnus, Heimler, the top members of Security, the higher-ups from Control—they all have harems," Thompson went on. "Slaves, Reaps, women they've bought or captured. A few months ago, Magnus apologized to me about Nadia. He said they'd had no idea she would be attracted to you, but that when the two of you came together, they couldn't lose the opportunity to gain access to you. He's always looking for leverage, new ways to bend your will to his. After that, he offered me one. A harem, Charles, like it was some kind of blasted Christmas gift."

"His pride." Charles shivered. "Like he led a pack of lions. When he told me that, I didn't imagine—"

The doors opened. His words were drowned out by an ocean of noise. He swallowed the rush of fear that swept over him as he followed Thompson into the half-darkness of Level Nine.

They entered a vast warehouse floor filled with rows upon rows of cages, each one a cube eight feet in all dimensions. The cages were stacked on top of each other all the way to the cavernous ceiling. Every cage had a toilet and steel sink bolted to the back and a single bed toward the front.

Prisoners were packed into the cages, humans of every variety. Male and female, young and old, five or six to a cage. Most were awake. Some were dead. The squall of hungry infants, the wailing of children, weeping and cursing, dull thumps as fists and feet struck human flesh, heart-rending screams, the wild laughter and shrieks of the mentally insane. He had walked into a nightmare.

A young woman with jet black hair and olive skin stared at them with soft, dark eyes. Her cage was at ground level, right in front of them. An emaciated little girl was snuggled up against her, asleep despite the savagery around them. The mother ran a hand through her daughter's long, raven hair. As she did so, the girl awoke. She glanced at Charles and their eyes met. She smiled, raised her thin hand in greeting, then drifted off to sleep again.

The prisoners were clothed in the drab gray colors Tom Murrow had once worn. The child's mother also had the same expression Charles had seen on Tom. Hollow, sickly. The face of a living ghost. A deranged woman paced back and forth on the other side of the same cell, giving off an endless stream of dark mutterings in some foreign language and shaking her fist in the air.

"What is this place?" He raised his voice so Thompson could hear him above the din.

"Hell," Thompson said. "It's where people go when nobody wants them."

"But who are they? Where did they come from?"

"From everywhere. Refugees, slaves, beggars, political prisoners, spies, traitors, terrorists, witnesses, whistleblowers, lunatics, poets, prophets. Others, so many others. If they can be bought, Magnus takes them."

There was a piercing shriek from somewhere over them, a cage so high up that it was invisible in the darkness above. The cry cut off suddenly.

"They load them on ships in storage containers," Thompson went on. "Machines drag the containers from the docks, machines pack the prisoners into cages, machines haul them to Level Nine, machines toss them scraps of food, machines hose them down every three days, machines drag them off to Control for experimentation, machines devour their corpses, machines fertilize the Garden with their remains."

Thompson's trembling hand fumbled with the top button of his shirt. There was a wildness in his eyes and voice. "It's all so organized and precise. But they're human beings, Charles. They're just like you and me!"

It was too much.

How could this have happened? How could such a thing take place on this scale? How could thousands of people vanish off the face of the earth, disappear into this vast abyss of darkness, cages, and blood?

Had no one noticed?

"I swear to you that when I joined the Foundation, I didn't know." Thompson grabbed his arm. "You believe me, don't you, Charles? It was just a high-paying job. All I had to do was keep an eye on you. I heard their rhetoric about overpopulation. God help me, I thought they were just words. By the time I discovered the truth, it was too late."

"How many are there, Thompson?"

"I don't know. It's always changing. *She'll* know. Computer, what's the number?"

"We are currently holding 92,216 live Reaps."

"Dear God," Charles whispered.

"I had to show you. You had to understand. You can't—"

The door to the elevator slid open.

In the same moment, Charles heard a hissing sound that came from somewhere inside of Thompson's chest. Thompson groaned and collapsed like a puppet whose strings had been cut. Blood poured from his mouth and nostrils.

"Hello there, Ferguson!" Magnus's voice was cheerful as he stepped out of the elevator. His gaze shifted from Thompson's prone body to the endless cages of the Reaps. The grin never left his face. "Not a pleasant place, is it? We need it, though. If it weren't for us, they'd be building these all over the world before long. I'll make a deal with you, Ferguson. Finish Aeternum and I'll set them free, every last one of them."

"What about Thompson's corpse?" Heimler edged forward. "Shall we incinerate it?"

Magnus pondered for a moment. "That won't be necessary. Take him to a cryo-chamber. He was one of us, after all, even if he betrayed us."

"As you command, my lord," Heimler replied.

"Are you all right, Ferguson?" Magnus rested a hand on Charles's shoulder, inches from where Thompson's hand had been moments before.

He looked at Magnus, but for some reason he couldn't understand the man's words. He turned and stared at what was left of Thompson, watched the thick, crimson pool forming at his friend's mouth. At those glassy, unblinking eyes.

Then he looked with a vague curiosity at Level Nine.

Why are there so many cages? What are they keeping inside them? Are those animals?

His legs buckled beneath him.

"Get him to the infirmary, Heimler. Hurry!"

That was the last thing Charles heard before he lost consciousness.

Father Anatoly and Charles stood on the peak of a barren hill overlooking the monastic garden, which now sprawled out as far as the eye could see in every direction. An army of people, thousands strong, worked in the fields, bringing in the harvest. The woman with the long black hair and the olive skin threshed wheat at the base of the hill. Her little girl, three or four, perhaps, clung to her skirts until she spotted a butterfly and went chasing after it.

"A human being is a glorious thing," Father Anatoly said. "No matter how much it is distorted, the icon is there. A window into another realm, a mirror made to reflect Absolute Beauty. One of these icons you will recognize. That's her, isn't it?"

Charles followed the monk's gaze and saw his own mother. Young and vibrant, joyful. She was just like she had been before the cancer destroyed her, with one striking difference. She bore no traces of the grief that had pierced her when Charles's father abandoned them.

He heard her words drifting up with the breeze, but he couldn't distinguish them. His legs refused to take him to her.

"Tell me," Father Anatoly said, "does your mother only live in your mind, or does a greater Mind now sustain her?"

The people vanished. In their place were dozens of enormous, robotic combines that began to reap the fields. When they finished, they turned as one and climbed up the hill from every direction. Roaring, razor-sharp blades whirled and glimmered in the sunlight. They would rip him and Father Anatoly to pieces. There was nowhere to run, no way to escape.

"Death has been swallowed up in victory." Father Anatoly's words were serene as he watched the approaching machines. "All things shall be transfigured. Do not despair."

✥

He opened his eyes. Nadia sat in a chair beside the bed.

"You're awake!" She leaned over him and ran her fingertips along his cheek. "What happened?"

"My mind feels a little blurry." He sat up on the bed. "Where are we?"

"The infirmary. They said you passed out. Magnus called me through the Computer and told me you were here."

"Magnus?"

Something had happened. What was it?

Cages.

"Charles, what is it?"

He saw his own terror reflected in her eyes.

"They murdered Thompson. He said he'd made a mistake on the Outside."

She pressed her index finger over her lips. "Don't think about that now. Are you well enough to walk?"

"He showed me Level Nine. Have you heard of it? Did you know?" He swung his legs over the side of the bed.

"No."

He looked at her closely but couldn't decide if she was telling the truth. "Listen, Nadia, I'm sorry about everything. I was a coward, but that's all changed. I'm ready now."

"You were just trying to look out for me. You're a brave man, Charles Andrew Ferguson."

"Computer," he said, "what time is it?"

"It is currently seven eighteen in the morning."

"Tell the other members of the Aeternum team to meet us in the lab in fifteen minutes. Tell them it's critical. We need to talk about—" He looked at Nadia. She shook her head slightly. "About the status of the project."

"Confirmed."

He leaned over and whispered in her ear. "If something happens to me, I want you to know that I love you. I'll always love you."

"Nothing's going to happen to you." She kissed him lightly on the cheek. "Whatever Thompson did, he did on his own. Just try to relax."

As they rode the elevator to the laboratory, he could hear in his mind the growing roar of the combines.

Closer. Closer.

Chapter Eighteen
Death

Anna Mueller drew the horsehair bow across the open third string of her great-grandmother's Leonhardt cello. She then slid her left hand along the upper string and planted her index finger on the second note. Her right hand pushed the bow back and forth across the string as her fretting hand created a smooth vibrato.

So began the opening melody of Liszt's *Liebesträume*. When she played it, she could imagine, if only for a moment, that she was back home in Heidelberg. Her mother would be standing on the balcony, humming the tune to herself as she folded the laundry. Her father would be reading a spy novel with his feet propped up by the fireplace while her brother, Max, scribbled away at one of his portraits.

The music meant hope, and hope was how Anna had survived in Magnus Headquarters. Hope had drawn her away from the apathy and lethargy she had seen in others, from the inefficiency that caught the eyes of supervisors and led to an unplanned transfer—or rather, as she now knew, to an execution.

She had always believed that one day she would escape this place. She had believed she would see her family again, that she would hear their voices and drift along once more in the gentle rhythm of their laughter and sorrow.

She glanced at her reflection in the standing mirror, then quickly lowered her eyes as if she'd been caught staring at a stranger.

The pale face, the weary expression, the crow's feet that marched ahead with every passing hour of this never-ending project—she was no longer the same woman who had disappeared from the university three years ago.

She had grown colder here. She had been forced to harden her mind against horrific realities. She had lost something that was irretrievable. Her soul had diminished.

The music continued, the sound rising to fill every corner of the bedroom. A clump of trees outside the window stood guard along the banks of the gently flowing Neckar. The morning sun had pierced the horizon. Its reflection rippled on the water. A digital mirage, but it comforted her.

She would never see the river again. She would never hear her mother's voice in song, never feel her father's arms around her or hear her brother's laughter. She would die in this place. They were out of time. It had come to that.

She could still turn back. She could confess, she could repent on her knees before Magnus. He would, perhaps, forgive her. Reward her…with freedom?

That path had never tempted her. The moment Raj opened her eyes to the darkness of this place, to the monstrosity and barbarity of Control, her decision had been made. It was not for nothing that her great-grandfather had been hunted down and executed for his association with the White Rose, a band of courageous students and intellectuals who stood up against the Nazis. It was not for nothing that her family still honored her great-grandfather every year on the anniversary of his death.

The music stopped. She pressed the back of her hand against her eyes and blinked away tears. She looked at the mirror again and was surprised to discover a smile hovering on the corners of her lips.

"Silly girl," she scolded her reflection. "You're still hoping, aren't you?"

That was her great-grandfather's gift to her. The courage to hope. Her life, like his, would be an offering. Perhaps her family would learn the truth someday and remember her as well.

So be it.

She heard them as she was placing the cello in its case, heard the dull thumping of their black jackboots in the hallway. The clicking sounds as they prepared their assault rifles.

She sat up in her chair, took a deep breath, and folded her hands on her lap.

They could take her life. They would not take her dignity.

The door slid open. Four members of Security charged into the room. Their guns were levelled on her, though they must have known she would be unarmed.

She rose from her chair and looked their leader in the eye.

"I'm ready," she said. "Do what you will."

❧

Charles and Nadia walked into an empty laboratory. No equipment, no monitors, no cages for the research animals, no books or journals, no tablets.

No colleagues.

The heart monitor emitted a single, steady tone from the patient's room. They both ran to the doorway and looked in. The hospital bed was empty, its sheets tossed to one side.

Nadia stared at him with wide eyes. "Do you think—"

"Good morning."

Franz Heimler stood behind them, flanked by a half-dozen guards.

"Where are the others?" Charles asked. "Where's our equipment?"

"Take her first."

One of the guards stepped forward and grabbed Nadia's arm. Without thinking, Charles did something he had never done before in his life. He punched a man in the face.

A moment later, he was thrown to the ground by the other guards. He heard Nadia scream and struggle as they hauled her away.

"Where are you taking her?" he cried.

Heimler knelt in front of him, his face only inches away. "You can't make mistakes in a place like this. Didn't you understand who you were dealing with?" He nodded to the guards. "Bring him."

The guards handcuffed him. They marched him to the elevator, then rode with him in silence to the sixth floor. They stepped into the frigid, pale-lit hallway that led to Magnus's office. They approached the golden doors with the engraved lions and halted in front of them.

Heimler checked his watch. "Any moment now. We're to wait here until he's ready."

Seconds ticked by. The guards grew restless and began shifting on their feet. Heimler leaned against the wall and crossed his arms.

The sudden blast of a gunshot made Charles's heart leap into his throat. Two more followed it in rapid succession, and then silence descended.

"Shall we enter now?" one of the guards asked Heimler.

"No," Heimler replied. "That was only three."

Several minutes passed before a fourth gunshot rang out.

"You two go in," Heimler said. "Help the machines clean up."

The doors slid open for the two guards and closed again before Charles could see what was happening within.

Four gunshots. Five team members.

A few minutes later, the doors opened again. Medical robots pushed four hospital gurneys into the hallway, one after the other. On every bed was a bloodstained sheet, and beneath every sheet was a corpse. One of the sheets revealed the contours of a woman's body.

"All right," Heimler said after the last medical robot had passed. "Your turn."

Charles rushed into Magnus's office.

Nadia was alive. She was tied to a chair behind Magnus's desk. They had gagged her with black cloth. Magnus sat next to her, polishing a silver handgun with a handkerchief. As Charles drew near, he noticed six syringes on the desk, each filled with a cloudy, slate-blue liquid.

The guards grabbed him by the elbows and shoved him into a metal chair in front of Magnus's desk. He breathed in the pungent odor of disinfectants. A medical robot was scrubbing the stains. Blood was everywhere—spatters on the Victorian rug, crimson droplets running down the front of the desk. Fazal's empty wheelchair sat a few feet away. Blood glistened on the back cushion.

On a side wall, a map of the world illuminated an enormous digital display. A galaxy of tiny red dots populated every inhabited inch of the map.

"Go, Heimler," Magnus intoned. "Free our Harvesters. Let the world be reaped. When your task is complete, return to me. You, too, shall partake of the mysteries."

Heimler cast a longing glance at the syringes, then turned and strode away with brisk steps. Three guards fell in behind him, and only one remained. The guard turned to face Charles, and at once he recognized the burn marks on the man's face. The guard gave him a slight nod of acknowledgement, and his lips curved into an ironic grin.

"Computer," Magnus called when the door had closed, "grant Franz Heimler permission to leave Headquarters and enter the storage facility. You are to await my command before allowing him to re-enter Headquarters."

"Confirmed."

Magnus slid a desk drawer open, withdrew a clip of bullets, and loaded them into the handgun. "I just met with your other team members. It was, as I'm sure you have gathered, an unpleasant discussion. They're on their way to the cryo-chambers now. The last one to die—the weak one, Miguel—broke down and told me everything after the others had been killed. Is there anything you'd like to add before we go on?"

Charles remained silent. He kept his gaze fixed on Nadia.

"I warned you what would happen if you betrayed me," Magnus continued. "Random blackouts of the surveillance system, only they weren't random, were they? Very clever, Ferguson, but you were out of your league."

The only question now was whether Miguel had kept his wits about him. It was too late to worry. All any of them could do was buy time.

"That old man—he's your father, isn't he?" he asked.

"Father?" Magnus grinned. "Oh no, I dealt with my father the day I seized control of his empire. My mother may have been a traitor, but she was also the only person who truly cared for me. He shed her blood, so I repaid him in kind, and I did it with my own hands. Someday you'll understand the riddle of the old man in your laboratory, but not today. Today you will pay for your rebellion.

"It was a daring scheme, I'll grant you that. Complete Aeternum in secret, test it on the old man, inject yourselves with the final doses once you're certain it will work, then destroy all the research. Of course, you'd have to murder me to get out of here, wouldn't you? Your plan sounded a little vague on that minor point."

"We had to try." Charles lowered his head. "You win, Magnus. You always win. Raj and I were behind all of this, start to finish. She had nothing to do with it."

"Oh, I know you're the center of the wheel," Magnus replied. "The problem is that I can't lose you. I can't afford to wait for you to come back from cryo-sleep in some distant era. Your mind holds the keys to our collective future. The Reaping is just the beginning. One day you'll realize that this was for your own good."

Magnus turned to face Nadia. "She truly is a beautiful woman, isn't she?" He reached over and brushed the hair from her face with his hand. Nadia jerked back, trying in vain to escape from his fingertips. "Who knows what she could have become? Forgive me, Ferguson. We'll find you another cardinal."

He pressed the gun against Nadia's chest and pulled the trigger twice. The gunshots echoed through the room.

"No!" Charles scrambled out of his chair and crouched in front of Nadia. She had slumped forward against the ropes that bound her. He rested his cuffed hands against her neck, holding her head up for her. She coughed up blood.

Her breathing stopped.

He staggered back. Strands of raven hair had drifted over her face. Her eyes were open wide, her mouth clenched against the cloth they'd used to gag her. He looked in horror at his own hands, stained red with the blood that had fallen from her lips.

"Why?" he rasped. "Why would you do that?"

An amused smirk hovered on Magnus's lips. "Why would you betray me?"

A feral energy surged through Charles. He lunged forward, screaming at Magnus, straining with his shackled hands to reach him, to tear the grinning lips off the murderer's face and crush every ounce of life from his body.

The guard grabbed him from behind, dragged him back, and slammed him into his chair on the other side of the desk. A damp and hideous bloodstain had appeared on Nadia's shirt.

"Stop whimpering, Ferguson." Magnus rose from his chair. "She was one of us, after all. You'll get her back someday, but now you're in Purgatory. Punishment for your sins, isn't that how it works? And it wasn't all in vain. Rebellion or not, you've finished Aeternum. When we bring them back, the rest of your team will reap the benefits of their labor. But for now..."

Magnus picked up one of the syringes and jabbed it into Charles's arm. An icy tingling flowed through his body as the fluid entered his bloodstream.

"How does it feel?" Magnus asked.

Charles kept his gaze on the ground and remained silent.

"It doesn't appear to have caused you any negative side effects."

Magnus waited another minute, then picked up a second syringe and injected himself. He took a deep breath, grabbed the handgun, and walked to the displays.

"Immortality! The longing of a thousand ages, earned now by our own sweat and blood. You and I are the first gods of this new world. All will be forgiven, Ferguson, and all that is worth saving shall be restored. Now for the second act. The cleansing of our species."

Franz Heimler tossed the rusted iron padlock to one side and yanked free the chain that had held it. The time for secrecy was over. He swung open the creaking gate, climbed onto his supercharged Vyrus 987, the finest motorcycle ever made, and sped off into the vast storage complex.

The complex had no security, no cameras, no watchtowers. Nothing but row upon row of windowless storage buildings. Only three miles from Headquarters, the place had been deserted for years with the recent exception of Unit Thirty-Nine.

On the surface, Thirty-Nine looked like every other building in the complex, but underneath it lay a hidden facility over a hundred feet deep and a half-mile wide. Here the Foundation's greatest treasure was kept. Laying in neat and orderly rows on a mile of shelving, millions of dormant Harvesters awaited activation. With them, lined up on the concrete floors of the facility, lay a fleet of high-altitude drones that would soon bear the Harvesters to every corner of the globe.

A casual thief would have found that the door to Unit Thirty-Nine had a mysterious ability to resist the usual lockpicking techniques. A more determined invader would discover something far worse. Unless Alexander Magnus had given his express permission, any attempt to enter the building would trigger an all-out war with the Foundation's mechanized arsenal.

Heimler released the kickstand on his motorcycle and climbed off. He'd taken three steps toward Unit Thirty-Nine when he heard a voice behind him.

"Target acquired. Delta Two requesting permission to fire."

By the word *Delta,* Heimler had whirled around and buried three bullets in the speaker's head.

But the speaker didn't die.

Have A Nice Trip!

The message was emblazoned in bold white letters on Little Boris's shirt. The two-foot-tall doll had been strapped with duct tape to the wall of an adjoining building. As Heimler read the words, the razor-sharp tip of a tranquilizer dart burrowed into his neck. His sidearm slipped through his fingers and clattered to the ground. After a few seconds of hazy euphoria, he tumbled to the ground in a heap.

A silence followed.

"What do you think?" Boris emerged from behind the adjacent building, flicked a half-spent cigar to the pavement, and crushed it with the toe of his boot.

"Give me a moment." The Chemist tossed her lone black braid over her shoulder. She knelt beside Heimler's inert body and wrapped her slender hand around the man's wrist.

"It should get us through the doors." She let Heimler's hand drop to the ground. "I'll keep his levels stable until you're done with him. Let's hope we have good intel on that detection system."

"If their Computer hasn't seen us yet, it's not going to," Boris replied. "The intel's good, and so is the hack. Let's get this door open. Think they can fit some bunker busters in here?"

"That's not our department," the Chemist said, "and I'm not sticking around to find out."

∽

"Franz Heimler has opened the main door to Unit Thirty-Nine," the Computer announced. "Do you wish to launch the Harvesters now?"

Magnus rubbed his hands together. "You have my permission."

"Confirmed."

"And grant Heimler permission to re-enter Headquarters. He has fulfilled his mission."

"Confirmed."

Magnus walked over to the world map that bristled with red dots. "Computer, focus the map on our vicinity. I'd like to watch as the first ones disappear."

The map zoomed in until it displayed the northern portion of South America. It zeroed in further and finally stopped over a region of shoreline southeast of the Panama Canal, just past the border into Colombia. Within minutes, clusters of red began to vanish, first a few, then dozens all at once. The screen panned out to a wider area. The onslaught continued, dot after dot snuffed out as the Harvester attack progressed.

"So it begins," Magnus said. "Five billion Reaps under the crosshairs. Soon enough, there won't be a single one left to burden us. You see, Ferguson? I always get what I want."

Charles leaned back in his chair. "Is that a fact?"

Magnus sniffed. "You know better than anyone. It seems to be a universal law."

"Some laws are made to be broken." Charles was surprised at the evenness of his own voice. But the matter was settled. Everything was in play now. Nadia and the team, Boris, all of it.

"What are you—"

There was a distant boom, like a massive thunderclap or an explosion of heavy artillery. The room shook with the force of an earthquake, toppling busts of Roman emperors and throwing the portrait behind the desk askew. Bits of plaster dropped from the vaulted ceiling and peppered Magnus's hair.

"Computer, what was that?" Magnus shrieked.

Silence.

"Computer?"

"Processing. Please wait."

"What?" he roared.

"Processing. Please wait."

Charles broke into wild laughter.

Magnus whirled on him, eyes blazing.

"Have you gone mad, Ferguson?"

Charles shrugged. "Don't worry, it's just a little math problem. A tiny, Half-Remarkable Question."

Magnus levelled the handgun on him. "You will tell me exactly what you're talking about, or I'll end you."

"Too late for that, Magnus," he replied. "I'm already dead. But if you really want to know, the Half-Remarkable Question is a song by her brother Peter's favorite band. Hippies, I'm sure you'd hate them. You'd hate Peter, too, because Peter has Down Syndrome, which means Peter is a Reap."

Magnus glanced at the guard and nodded. A ring of light exploded on the right side of Charles's vision as the man's fist crashed into his face.

"I grow impatient," Magnus said softly. "Tell me what I want to know, or this man will crack your skull like a walnut."

"Okay, fine." He wiped the blood from his lips with the back of his hand. "The Half-Remarkable Question. It's what Nadia and Fazal called the math problem they dished up for your AI Computer. Envy-free cake-cutting. One whole cake, eleven partners, connected pieces, everybody wants the good frosting—the whole thing's a logistical nightmare. They had alternatives lined up just in case. The halting problem, Rice's theorem, busy beaver champions. But I'm guessing the cake did the trick."

Magnus stared at him. "Cake-cutting, busy beaver? What are you raving about?"

"Champions. As in winners. In the end, the whole thing came down to Nadia and Fazal. I bet those two never factored into your calculations, did they? A disabled pacifist and a woman. What's there to worry about? We all know you don't think much of women. You and your *pride*."

"Computer!" Magnus screamed.

"Processing. Please wait."

"Nadia inherited brilliance from both her parents," Charles went on. "Her mother's blend of musical virtuosity and scientific genius. From her father—"

"Yes, what of him?" Magnus waved the gun distractedly. "Boris the drunk? Boris the madman? We all know he was CIA once, but he washed out long ago. We checked everything. Landry and the Computer spent a whole week charting out the life and times of the ridiculous Boris Petrov."

"Then Landry and the Computer failed." Charles glanced at the antique grandfather clock by the fireplace. Just a few minutes more.

"Nadia once wrote a paper on artificial intelligence," he said. "Never published it, thankfully. If she had, you'd never have let her within a hundred miles of your precious Computer. From now on, your AI is following her orders. See for yourself."

He pointed to the map. The red dots that had vanished began to reappear.

"Looks like those Reaps are tougher than you thought." He grinned at the stupefied expression on Magnus's face. "Your death machines won't be reaping anything today, which means they also won't be protecting Headquarters, doesn't it?"

A flicker of alarm passed over Magnus's features before he slipped back into his usual composure. "You've been misinformed, Ferguson. I assume that you're counting on an attack from the Outside to liberate you. Whoever Thompson managed to contact—Boris Petrov and his old associates, it would seem—they will never step foot within this building, nor shall they lay a finger on a single Harvester.

"Drop all the bombs you want. We've built the real Alpine Fortress. As long as it remains sealed, this place can withstand anything they throw at it. Heimler alone could open these doors, but he'd have to be alive and well to do it. I'm afraid your friends will be locked out forever."

A siren erupted in the hallway outside Magnus's office.

Charles snickered. "Glad you have everything under control."

"You, there," Magnus yelled. "Jennings. What's that siren?"

"It may be a perimeter breach," Derrick Jennings stammered. "It's the manual alarm."

Magnus's hands began to shake violently. "That's not possible." His whole body trembled as if he were having a seizure. "You have no idea what you've unleashed, Ferguson," he shouted. "Jennings, implement the Final Orders at once. Send the message yourself. Move!"

"Yes, my lord." The guard snapped a salute and sprinted out of the room.

Magnus turned his back to Charles and faced the map. "I thought you were a rational man. Avoidance gets us nowhere. Now everything will have to wait, for years perhaps, while billions of useless people lap up the world's lifeblood. Have it your way, Ferguson. Let it burn. Alexander Magnus will survive."

Magnus made it as far as the desk. He braced himself against it with both hands, swayed from side to side, then toppled to his knees.

Charles watched as Magnus's body was jolted by spasms. A rivulet of saliva slid out of the corner of the man's mouth.

"I'm sorry, Magnus," he said. "You left us no choice."

Magnus's eyes were wide with terror. "Poison? But you…" His words began to slur. "You…took it…yourself."

"I know." Charles looked at his hands, which had begun to shake. Only a little, as if he had an early stage of palsy. "We finished our project. It just wasn't the one you thought."

Magnus groaned as a violent tremor wracked his body. He gasped and fell silent, his unseeing gaze locked on the portrait behind the desk.

Charles's extremities tingled and became cold as the nerves went dormant. He staggered over to Nadia and knelt on the floor beside her. The two bullets that had lodged in her chest now lay on the ground in front of her.

The Phoenix would slow the poison's advance but couldn't stop it. The decision to use a high-powered neurotoxin on Magnus instead of anesthesia had come at the eleventh hour and had been known only to Raj, Charles, and Miguel. Miguel had done everything he could to adapt the Phoenix to the poison, but there hadn't been enough time to finish the modification.

He felt a strange and unearthly sensation as one region of his body after another collapsed under the irresistible weight of the neurotoxin. He closed his eyes. Each breath became fainter than the last.

He laid his head on her lap. The warm stickiness of the blood on her pants leg pressed against his cheek, a sharp contrast to her ice-cold body. It was the same coldness that now crept over him. The Phoenix was active. The colder he became, the better.

His heart skipped a beat. Her legs quivered beneath him.

All became darkness. All became Light.

Chapter Nineteen
Renewal

CHARLES OPENED HIS eyes. He felt his abdomen rising and falling with his breath. He heard the rhythmic beeping of a heart monitor.

"Charles? Can you hear me? Charles!"

A cool pressure on his arm, a delicate brush of lips against his cheek. There was something about that voice.

Something...

He drifted off.

❧

He awoke in a hospital bed. Thompson sat on a green, stiff-looking armchair a few feet away with his nose buried in a fantasy novel.

"Thompson?" He was surprised by the dry rasp of his own voice.

"Charles? Good God!" Thompson tossed the book to the ground and rushed to his bedside.

"It...worked?"

Thompson grinned from ear to ear. "Well, I'm here, aren't I? That means you definitely aren't in paradise, though that monk friend of yours might disagree. We've been chatting in the cafeteria over bowls of canned green beans and cherry gelatin cubes. He seems to think heaven is right in front of us, like we could just reach out and grab it. Crazy, right? But what am I doing, prattling like a magpie. She'd kill me! Wait a minute, Charles."

Thompson pulled out his phone, typed on it for a minute, and slipped it back into his pocket.

"Nadia?" Charles asked.

"Just texted her. She's fully recovered, but we still have to make her sleep once in a while."

"The others?"

"Everyone from Project Aeternum made it," Thompson said after a pause. "Magnus fell for the trap, every step. Boris and company managed to rescue most of the Reaps. The prisoners, I mean. It took them days to empty out Level Nine."

"What is it?"

Thompson looked away and stuck his hands in his pockets. "There's no easy way to say this. Our plans were good, Charles, but they weren't perfect. Security had a secret protocol from Magnus in case things ever went south. We'd assumed they'd put all their efforts into defense or, worse, go after the Reaps. But they didn't. As soon as that manual alarm went off, Security broke into two teams. One went to Control, the other to Progress. The researchers and their families—they never had a chance. They burned all the documents, detonated explosives in the Computer's server room and in every laboratory. Blew everything to bits. It's amazing the whole place didn't collapse. They were so busy with the destruction that Boris's team had an easy job of it. Magnus's office was unscathed, and they didn't bother with the cryo-chambers. Not too worried about us zombies, I guess."

"The Final Orders," Charles said. "He really was a monster, wasn't he?"

"Final Orders?" Thompson's eyes narrowed. "Where did you hear that?"

"From Magnus. He told one of the guards to implement the Final Orders when the manual alarm went off. You think there's something else to it?"

"I heard something in Control once about the Twilight of the Gods." Thompson shook his head. "It doesn't matter now. As far as we know, the only survivors from Headquarters were those of us lucky enough to have a Phoenix. Oh, and that old man you saved, he's still around here somewhere. They found him in Magnus's personal quarters. The boost from the Phoenix may keep that heart of his ticking for a few more months."

"What was it like?" Charles asked. "Coming back, I mean."

"Creepy. Boris's team pulled our bodies out of the cryo-chambers, and ten minutes later I was awake. Awake and incredibly hungry. The others were still dead when I came around. Then they started moving. Twitching, you know? I have no idea how you did it, Charles. I don't believe in miracles, but I'll make an exception for this."

"The others did most of the work," he replied. "I added in a few pieces here and there, but my real job was recordkeeping."

"Recordkeeping?"

"They didn't tell you?" He took a sip of water and cleared his throat. "We were afraid to hold on to the Phoenix research. We input the sensitive data into Chameleon. But Nadia was worried Landry—or even the Computer itself—would hack into it, so everything got wiped out daily after I'd had a chance to read it over. Even if they did hack it, all they'd see was one day's worth of test results, statistics, and so on. It would never be enough to connect the dots."

"You memorized the research? All of it?" Thompson's eyes widened.

"Most, not all. There was enough of an overlap between Phoenix and Aeternum that much of what we worked on wouldn't raise any suspicions. But there were exceptions, and they put those into Chameleon for me to read over. They wiped the program every day at midnight. I ended up becoming a sort of human search engine. If they needed to go back to something, all they had to do was ask."

Thompson grinned. "I knew that parlor trick of yours would come in handy someday. I didn't know just how powerful it was. But what about Aeternum? Do you think we'll ever get there?"

Their eyes met for a moment, then Charles looked away.

"You solved it, didn't you?" Thompson almost shouted the words.

"It doesn't matter," he said. "We'll never know without their technology."

Thompson folded his arms over his chest. "Incredible. Well, it's all over now, and I'm glad you made it. We thought we'd lost you."

"I wasn't supposed to make it."

"I know." Thompson reached over and rested his hand on Charles's shoulder. "It's February 27th. You've been out of it for almost three weeks. They said your Phoenix gave out on the second day. It brought you into a coma, but that was it. You did the rest on your own."

"On my own?"

It didn't make sense. He wasn't supposed to come back at all, Miguel had been clear on that. Could it have been what they'd done to him as a child? His alterations?

A nurse and doctor burst into the room. The nurse made a fuss about Thompson not notifying them that the patient was awake. Thompson shrugged and went back to his fantasy novel while they checked Charles's vitals, made notes, asked him a dozen questions and, last but not least, promised to send food. Canned green beans and cherry gelatin cubes, no doubt.

"Tell me, Thompson," Charles said as soon as the door closed. "Magnus—is he really gone?"

Thompson came back to his bedside. "He was dead when they broke into his office. I imagine some from Security were taken prisoner, but Boris has been tight-lipped about it. He and his team swept through what was left of Headquarters a few times. They took what could be salvaged, though I doubt there was much left. Once they were certain everything—and everyone—was cleared out, they sealed it off and left some guards around to frighten any visitors."

"What about the Foundation?"

"That's a trickier question." Thompson folded his arms. "You remember that Trapper fellow?"

"Alpha Financial's lawyer?"

"He knows what he's doing. Turns out the Foundation only had a few hundred million dollars in assets. What's worse, there's no legal connection between the Foundation and any of the companies it controlled. The companies made donations to the Foundation, but the deals going the other way were all under the table. Boris said they're looking into Alpha Financial, which is officially headed by Rius Ludovic, but they haven't done anything illegal that can be proven. The feds did seize Magnus's personal funds, around eighty billion dollars. If there's any justice, some of that will go toward the prisoners."

Charles closed his eyes. "I wonder if she survived."

"Who?"

"That woman in Level Nine, the mother with the little girl. Do you remember her? She was in that cage right in front of us."

"Yeah, I remember her now. We can look through the prisoner database if you want, see if we can find her."

"Thanks, Thompson." He opened his eyes again, held up his hand, and flexed the fingers one by one. It felt like a miracle. His nerves had been subjected to the deadliest neurotoxin imaginable, and here they were, zipping along signals as if nothing had happened. "What's the next step?"

"Boris will want to meet with everybody once you're back on your feet. He's kept us under lock and key around here. Not very kind considering what we've been through. If they ever let us go, I'm planning on beaches, sunsets, and, if fate has any kindness at all, a beautiful woman. Raj has convinced me to try my hand at sailing. We're hoping to hit the Florida Coasts once we're free."

"I don't know, Thompson. Raj's last sailboat ride turned into a disaster."

"That's all a matter of perspective, Charles."

Thompson went to his chair, leaned back, and gazed at him thoughtfully for a few moments.

"Listen, I know it's none of my business, but are you like Nadia now? You know, God and all?"

"I've started the journey," Charles replied. "At this point, I'm little more than a child when it comes to that."

"That's what I figured. I'm not quite ready for a second childhood myself, but I won't laugh at you, either. Not anymore. I used to think that there were only two kinds of people, the starry-eyed fools who thought the universe had a plot and the snake-eyed cynics who knew it was all absurd. I'm not so sure anymore. The devil of it, though, is that some of the things Magnus said make a lot of sense."

"Most of it could make sense if—"

Thompson held up a hand. "I know what you're going to say. I have no idea what a human being is, but after all this, I'm pretty sure I know what we aren't. The world is never as simple as we would like it to be, is it?"

Charles thought of his mother, remembered her broken, pain-seared body stretched out on a deathbed, and then the carefree version of her from his dream. "Reminds me of a song by Boris's hippies that I heard on the way to the monastery."

"Boris has hippies?"

"Turns out you can learn a lot from the Incredible String Band."

Nadia showed up a little after eleven. Dark rings hung beneath her eyes. Weary but radiant, she strode across the room, her gaze lit with the joyous flame that had drawn him to her when they had first met. She looked too magnificent for this world, like something approaching the divine. Perhaps she was.

Thompson lowered his eyes and quietly left the room.

She leaned over Charles, wrapped him in her arms, and pressed her lips against his.

"I knew you would come back to me."

⚘

"So how did you find out about the others?" Charles asked. "I never thought to ask before."

Nadia swirled her spoon in a bowl of bran flakes. It was ten in the morning on February 28th, and they were sharing a late breakfast in his hospital room. For the first time in months, she had slept through the night. "Anna introduced herself to me in the cafeteria. I noticed that she started tapping her fingers on the table while we talked. I do that myself sometimes, playing the piano in my head. Her rhythm was unusual, so I started paying attention."

"Your grandfather's cipher?"

"Exactly. *Friends of Boris. Need safe communication. Can you hack Computer?*"

"How did she know the cipher?"

"It turns out Dad was doing some recruiting of his own these past few years. He's with some newer organization, I think, but I don't know the details yet. He met with both Raj and Anna before the Foundation grabbed them. They had attended ivy league schools, and they were singled out for their abilities. He and his friends had started tracking that sort of thing."

"Did she know about your hidden talent?"

"Dad must have told Raj. I can't believe how much he was doing right under our noses all those years."

He nearly told her about the true contents of Boris's infamous bottle but decided to let Boris deal with that one himself.

"You know something strange?" she said. "The Computer wasn't as sophisticated as it could have been. They added limitations, safeguards to keep it from going too far in its own self-improvement. I was surprised it never caught on to what we were doing. All the same, it was a masterpiece, decades of work from some of the most brilliant computer scientists the world has never heard of."

"And you hacked it in six days." he said.

Nadia lowered her eyes. "Only because of human weakness. Like I said, the Computer's hands—or circuits—were tied. And do you have any idea how many people at Headquarters were playing Crimson Reaper 3? It was getting updates constantly. New maps, new addons, program patches, user mods. The Computer's code was foreign, but they'd written an API to let the game run within the Computer. It's the kind of code I'm used to. I started small, injecting some routines into a game mod to see if it would set off any alarms. It didn't, so I added more. Then I used the game process itself to monitor other systems within the Computer. The network was what I expected. Tons of security on the perimeter, very little on the inside. Landry had some tripwires for standard intrusions and hacks, but they weren't monitoring the game at all."

"And then you built Chameleon," he said. "Total concealment, impossibly encrypted—it was just like you described it in that paper, wasn't it?"

"I guess so." She blushed a little. "Nothing too special."

"I can think of a few billion people who would beg to differ."

Father Anatoly visited Charles on the third night after he regained consciousness. They greeted one another, which included, on Anatoly's part, a priestly benediction. The monk took a seat beside the bed and sipped a cup of aromatic tea.

"I'm surprised you left the monastery," Charles said.

"We monks occasionally travel when the need arises." Father Anatoly set down his teacup and rested his hands on his lap. "I hear you've had quite the adventure since we last saw one another."

"I hardly know where to start."

"There's no hurry. How about the day you left the monastery?"

Charles hesitated, wondering if it would break some rule of confidentiality. On the other hand, Boris had apparently asked for the monk to be there. Who better to trust with a secret?

So he told him everything. The Foundation, Progress and Control, Aeternum and Phoenix, Level Nine, the Reaping, the final encounter in Magnus's office—all that they had seen and suffered. Then he told him the one thing that no one else knew, not even Nadia.

"I don't know what they did to me, Father. I was just a child. Magnus said they altered me, turned me into something they call a Paragon. It was more than just the enhanced memory. Maybe it doesn't matter now, but I can't stop thinking that in some way, maybe in a very crucial way, I'm something other than human."

"You have nothing to fear," Father Anatoly replied at once. "Our mental capabilities are important, but they are only a piece of a larger whole. Our ability to love and be loved, our consciousness, our ultimate calling to divine union—these are what make us human. They are what make us like God. These things you certainly do not lack. If anything, you have journeyed deeper into your own humanity through all that you have suffered."

There was a gentle knock on his door the next morning. He was sleeping much more than usual, which, the doctors assured him, was perfectly normal. Well, maybe normal. The medical staff had top-level security clearance, which meant they had seen a lot of strange things, but they'd never dealt with anything like this. How many people had been killed off by a neurotoxin and then brought back to life by a classified biomechanical organism?

"Come in." Charles pushed a bright red switch, and there was a purring sound as the hospital bed moved up into a reclining position.

Nadia sidled through the door and kept it nearly shut behind her. "Fazal's here. Are you up for a visit?"

"Sure." He ran his hands through his belligerent hair, took a sip of water, and sat on the edge of his bed.

Nadia opened the door, and Fazal wheeled himself into the room. "Good morning, Charles. How are you feeling?"

"Better. The doctor's expecting me to break out of here later this week."

Fazal grinned. "That's good news for the rest of us. We're all stuck here until you leave, you know."

"So I've heard."

"I'll leave you two to it," Nadia said.

"I have some news for you, Charles," Fazal said as she closed the door. "Thompson told me that you were looking for some of the prisoners. A little girl and her mother."

"Did you find them?" Charles leaned forward.

Fazal cleared his throat and rubbed his earlobe with his forefinger. "In a way. The mother—she was dying when the rescuers found her. They tried to bring her back around, but it was impossible. They must have done something to her in Control. Miguel and Anna think it may have been long-term poisoning. The little girl survived. She's a bit underweight but seems to be stable."

"Do we know who she is?" Charles asked. "Where she's from?"

Fazal shrugged. "She speaks Arabic, but we don't know much more than that. The counselor working with her said that she seems relatively happy. She's only four years old, and I suppose we are very resilient at that age. Whatever she thought of Level Nine, her mother must have done a good job of shielding her mind from it. She told them her mother's name, but she couldn't tell them where she came from. She doesn't seem to remember much of anything before Level Nine."

"What will happen to her?"

"It's likely her mother was a refugee from the war, which means her daughter will be sent to one of the refugee camps. She didn't seem to know of any other family members, so I imagine she'll end up in a children's home somewhere."

"Thank you, Fazal," he said. "It must have taken some work to find her among all those prisoners."

Fazal drummed his fingers against the armrest on his wheelchair. "I wish we could do more for her. For all of them. They've suffered so much. I've asked Boris about it, but he says it's out of his hands. There are laws and governments and committees who will determine their fate."

"Maybe we can do something," Charles said. "Or one thing, if nothing else. Could you ask Nadia to come in? If it's okay with you, I'd like to talk to her in private for a few minutes."

"Of course. Care to join me for lunch at the cafeteria? I hear we're getting mashed potatoes today."

"Sounds exciting. I'll see you there."

Fazal turned and wheeled himself to the door. He rapped it with his knuckles, and Nadia opened it from outside. After a few words with Fazal, she came into the room, sat next to Charles on the bed, and took his hand in hers.

Two hours later, a little wisp of a girl with long black hair and olive skin slipped through the doorway, her hand tightly clasped in Nadia's. Charles was seated in the dingy green chair. He had dressed himself with care and done the best he could with his hair, which, truth be told, wasn't much. The girl watched him with artless curiosity.

"Hi." He held out his hand. "My name is Charles. I saw you once. Do you remember?"

Nadia translated, Arabic being one of the languages she had learned in her youth. The girl listened with an attentive face and looked at his hand. Then she suddenly burst out in a prolific torrent of words.

"Okay, I'll do my best to translate," Nadia said hurriedly. "She says she does remember you and that you were the kindest man she'd ever seen and she thought you were just a dream and that her name is Safiya and she's four years old and she's hungry right now but she ate

French fries for the first time yesterday. Oh, and she drew a picture of a butterfly but forgot to bring it."

He looked into those dark little eyes, alive with all the mystery of the universe. "I'm sure it's a beautiful picture, Safiya. You'll have to show it to me." His gaze met Nadia's for a moment. "Listen, we were wondering if you might like to spend the day with us? We could go for a walk, maybe find some more of those French fries to eat."

The girl looked at Nadia to hear the translation. Her face turned radiant when she heard about the French fries. She reached up a diminutive hand and placed it in his.

⁓

He was back on his feet again and getting stronger by the hour. He and Miguel strolled along the hospital corridors, reminiscing about those final days in Headquarters. The doctors planned to release him in the morning.

"I can't find the words to thank you," he said. "You saved my life, Miguel."

Miguel gave a self-deprecating shrug. "We all did our best. We saved each other if you get down to it."

They rounded a corner and nearly collided with Boris. He grunted and gave Charles a set of keys.

"What are these?"

"Your car keys," Boris replied.

"Um, no they're not."

"They are! Not for that piece of rust-eaten manure you used to drive. We bought you something new, transportation that won't bring shame to a father's heart when he sees his daughter riding around in it. A token of appreciation for what you've done."

"Boris, please tell me you didn't buy a racecar. I don't even know how to drive a stick-shift."

"Of course we didn't buy you a racecar. Happy? It's just a boring sedan like your last one. Well, maybe not exactly like your last one. There are one or two minor differences. Custom armoring and bulletproofing, six hundred horsepower, V12 engine—"

"V12 engine? Is that a good thing?"

"Is that a good thing?" Boris echoed in disbelief. "Can you even change a tire, Mr. Charles?"

"Well…"

Great. Now he knew firsthand what emasculation felt like.

"I pay for roadside assistance," he finally mumbled.

"Roadside assistance?" Boris thundered. "Sweet Saint Maria Skobtsova! And this from the man who's going to marry my Nadia?" He started muttering a perfect storm of what had to be Russian imprecations.

They wandered out to the parking lot.

"Where is it?" Charles asked.

"Just click the button, Mr. Charles."

They heard a pair of shrill mechanical beeps. The lights flicked on and off on a nearby vehicle that looked like it had just arrived from an Italian car factory.

"How much did you pay for that thing, Boris?"

Boris barked a laugh. "Not a dime, Mr. Charles. I spent a tiny fraction of your money from the OneScan device, money you were kind enough to hand over to me in your will."

"My *what?*"

"Your will! Remember our little walk in the park? You were worried about what would happen if you died, and I told you I'd taken care of it."

"I thought you were kidding," he cried. "And I never signed anything."

"Oh, but you did! In spirit, at least. It's freezing out here, Mr. Charles. Are you going to start that car, or should I?"

Charles eased into the yawning leather cocoon of the driver's seat and closed the door, utterly shutting out every sound but his own breath. Boris hopped into the passenger seat, and Miguel climbed in the back.

"Where do you put the key?" Charles asked.

Boris leaned over and pushed a button beside the steering wheel to start the car. Sixteen speakers sucked up fourteen hundred watts to pour forth, in all their crystalline clarity, the unforgettable strains of the *The Hangman's Beautiful Daughter*.

The hippies never sounded so good.

He slipped the car into drive and tapped the accelerator. They went for a little spin around the parking lot, which was shielded from the public view by towering concrete walls.

"You know, Boris," he said, "I still have no clue what a V12 engine is, but I think I could get used to it."

Miguel pointed at the empty seat next to him. "Look, Charles, there's already a car seat for Safiya."

As they walked back to the facility, Boris slipped a piece of paper into Charles's hand.

"What's this?"

"A bridge to the past, if you choose to cross it."

He unfolded the note and read the six words written on it.

John Flying Hawk

Cherokee, North Carolina

"Who's John Flying Hawk?"

"An enigma," Boris replied. "A man who shouldn't exist. He was presumably killed by the Foundation but was spotted outside Cherokee last week. I saw him at your funeral."

"What was he doing there?"

"I wasn't sure at first, but I think I've worked it out. If anyone knows where your father is, it's John Flying Hawk."

"My father?"

Boris clapped him on the back. "You don't have to cross the bridge. Think it over, Mr. Charles."

Boris walked ahead, but Charles stood rooted in place, his eyes fixed blankly on the note in his hand. After a few moments, he shook his head, wadded up the piece of paper, and stuffed it in his pocket.

&

The voting was fierce over where they would eat on their first escape from the facility. In the end, the Thompson Consortium—Thompson, Raj, and Anna—carried the day. Boris and his team made detailed arrangements to ensure the place would be secure and their conversation unmonitored. Charles, Nadia, and Safiya climbed into the V12 beast and headed off to the Thai Paradise restaurant. A pair of SUVs escorted them, one in front and one behind.

It was a short drive, and the town felt almost as if it had been evacuated. The only cars in the parking lot were the now-familiar SUVs used by Boris and his friends.

"They sure plan ahead, don't they?" he said.

"That's my dad," Nadia replied.

Rich, spice-laden air drifted out when he opened the door to the restaurant. They entered the dimly lit lobby. There were no workers in sight, so they made their way to the only occupied table. Most of the others had already arrived. He pulled back a bright red chair for Nadia and plopped down next to her.

She reached over and squeezed his hand. "Adventure eating today?"

"No, thank you very much, ma'am. Those days are far behind me. No more adventures, no more excitement, no more wild-eyed fascist maniacs. Nothing but boring, mundane, Ferguson-style living. I'll find myself a safe-looking soup and be thankful."

She arched an eyebrow. "Not exactly a Ferguson-style car you were driving."

"Hey, I had nothing to do with that. Blame your dad."

Boris glared at his menu, then at Thompson, then at the menu again. No matter how hard he looked, no matter which way he turned it, there wasn't a single Russian or Chinese favorite to be had. He threw the menu down in disgust. Their waiter, whom Charles recognized as one of the cafeteria workers from the facility, came up to take their orders.

Safiya sat next to Nadia and colored on some paper. Another butterfly. It was amazing how much this pint-sized little being had changed their lives in the space of only a few days.

"Rice with meat," Boris snapped at the waiter. "And don't try any nonsense."

"Yes sir, Mr. Boris."

Charles looked across the table and caught Thompson ogling Anna. Again. He'd mentioned it the day before, and Thompson had insisted that it was nothing more than an academic, psychological interest in a fellow scientist.

In other words, Thompson was toast.

Charles's soup looked harmless enough when it arrived. He dug in with zest.

"How is it?" Nadia asked.

"Not bad. It's got some kind of brownish tofu in it. Tastes all right, though."

"Brownish tofu?" Boris leaned over for a glance, then smacked the table and roared with laughter. "You call that tofu, Mr. Charles? You're eating blood! Congealed pig blood. They cooked with it when I was in South China."

Charles pressed a hand against his mouth to stifle the sudden pressure in his throat. He scrambled out of his chair and sprinted to the bathroom.

After they'd have enough time to eat—or, in his case, to examine in minute detail a porcelain toilet bowl from a distance of about two inches—Boris cleared his throat. "You are wondering, perhaps, why we haven't let you return to your homes? I'm sure you're all itching to get back to your starched lab coats and your filamentous algae, but I have some bad news for you. You're not going back."

"What?" Thompson exploded. "You're kidding! We just—" he lowered his voice to a terse whisper. "We just saved five billion people, remember?"

"It's true." Boris said. "And in the process, you became the most dangerous people in the world. You're the only surviving researchers from Headquarters. Your minds may be the last records of what lay hidden there."

His eyes met Charles's.

"Once we have more information," he went on, "we'll decide on the next step. Whenever you venture outside the facility, you must keep absolute silence about everything you saw and heard in Headquarters. If the Foundation really is wiped out as we hope, these measures will only be temporary."

"Then they won't be temporary."

Every eye turned to Thompson, who was staring down at his plate.

Thompson looked up at him.

"You remember her, Charles."

Epilogue

Shadows cast by the torchlight flickered on the stained concrete floor of a fortress deep in the mountains of Khatizan. Rius Ludovic strode briskly down the corridor, the heels of his polished dress shoes clicking with every step. He entered the throne room, bowed deeply, and approached with his eyes lowered. When he reached the throne, he threw himself flat on the ground before it.

"You may rise," a voice said.

As he stood, Rius glanced at the silent Youth Corps cadets on either side of the throne. Poised, taut, ready to strike.

"Any word from Headquarters?"

"Yes, my lady. A message arrived only moments ago."

"Give it to me."

Aryana Voss sat upon the throne, her back straight as a ramrod. She was clothed in her perpetual black with her face concealed behind a veil. A small lacquer box rested on her lap.

She extended a sable-gloved hand and took the note from Rius.

"My fears are proven true," the voice said. "Our lord has died, but he has left us a commandment. Does our scientist know of this?"

"She's heard nothing of the attack, my lady. The American press is reporting that they raided the headquarters of an international human trafficking ring and freed thousands of slaves. No mention of Lord Magnus or the Foundation."

"Their secrecy makes our task far simpler. You have the candidates?"

"As you commanded, I have narrowed the list." Rius reached into the pocket of his suit jacket, withdrew three photographs, and handed them to Voss.

First, a foreign woman with jade eyes and flaming red hair whose family had been killed by an airstrike. Next, a statuesque supermodel who had played a minor role in some of the latest Central Party propaganda films.

She held the third picture up to the flickering light.

"Who is this one, Rius?"

"Her name is Darya Alexandrovna. She's a Youth Corps lieutenant. Her mother died recently in Prison Factory Six. Darya distinguished herself at a Youth Camp. You may remember the story. An officer at the camp attempted to assault her while she was on patrol. She killed him in self-defense, then went straight to the Camp Office and reported her actions. They immediately promoted her to lieutenant."

Voss lifted her gaze upward as if in thought. "She may be the one. Test her blood in case it is a match. Bring her to me either way."

He bowed. "Yes, my lady."

"There is one other matter of a sensitive nature."

Rius listened to the low crackling of the torches, the deep, mellow humming from the throne and, faint as a whisper, the whirring sound from within Aryana's veil.

"Tell me, Rius, did Lord Magnus ever speak to you about the Twilight of the Gods?"

Acknowledgements

*"If there's a book that you want to read, but it hasn't
been written yet, then you must write it."*

- Toni Morrison

During an evening walk on our university campus, my wife, Carol, listened to an outlandish idea about a villain who planned to save the world by one horrific act of violence. From that moment of inception to the final draft of *The Reaping*, Carol has helped me build and shape the storyline by dreaming with me, painting out characters and relationships, and tinkering with plot elements. Without her constant support, this book would never have existed.

Several years ago, I attended an ACFW (American Chistian Fiction Writers) conference in Dallas, Texas. I had interviews with two agents, and one of them, Jim Hart, decided to sign me with Hartline Literary Agency. Sadly, the agency has since closed due to hostile winds in the publishing world, but that doesn't change the massive impact Jim had on this story and on my self-confidence as a writer. Without him, *The Reaping* would have never gone beyond the confines of my own computer.

I'd also like to thank ACFW for the amazing contests and support they provide to new and upcoming authors. Anyone who wants to dip their toes into the Christian writing scene should join ACFW. Special thanks also to the judges who critiqued and edited the early sections of *The Reaping* for ACFW's Genesis competition.

Many thanks to the friends and family who have read various drafts of this story and provided feedback and edits. I would like to especially thank Trisha Wells, Dan Long, Chris Long, Dan Cutchens, James Burgess, Dan Boerger, Nathan Southern, and Cati Goyer.

Special thanks to the creative team at Damonza (*https://damonza. com/*) for their amazing cover design and formatting.

I came across the quote from Victor Frankl in the concentration camp while reading *In The Spirit of Happiness*, a wonderful book by the Monks of New Skete.

As for Boris's favorite band, I grew up listening to the hippie groups my parents enjoyed in their long-haired days. The Incredible String Band has always been one of my favorites from that era.

Finally, my deepest thanks belong to you, the reader. You bring every story to life.

About the Author

Matt began writing stories when he was seven and loves reading classics both old and new. He and his wife lived in Southeast Asia for two years, where they worked with a minority language group on a dictionary project and helped develop a multilingual education program. They now live in Texas with their three children, mother-in-law, and an indomitable cat who deigned to move into their garage. Matt's debut novel, *The Reaping*, won an ACFW (American Christian Fiction Writers) Genesis award.

Visit Matt online at mattaynes.com

Facebook: *https://www.facebook.com/mattaynesauthor*